ALL OR NOTHING

Yes, they were the two musketeers, wiring stuff to blow and taking names, both on an express route to Hell with a connection in Atlanta, as they liked to say. That's the way they rolled. And if you didn't like it, then you'd best clear the area, because the fire was most definitely in the hole.

And now, barely able to see through his sand-filled goggles, it was up to Sullivan to save his best friend's life.

All he could do was open fire, empty his entire damned magazine if he had to, so long as Figueroa had time to get out of the guy's bead.

Yet something else quite unexpected happened that sent Sullivan diving face-first into the dirt: A grenade exploded at the bad guy's feet, shredding him with exquisite efficiency before he could fire again.

Just as the smoke began billowing hard and fast from all the wind, Hojo appeared, a silhouette in goggles and *shemagh*, running past the torn, wet remains of the fighter and dropping down beside Figueroa.

Sullivan burst to his feet and joined Hojo. He didn't realize he'd stopped breathing until he arrived beside his friend. "Jon? Jon, you all right?"

Titles by Peter Telep

Special Forces Afghanistan

DIRECT ACTION
CRITICAL ACTION

CRITICAL ACTION

SPECIAL FORCES AFGHANISTAN

Peter Telep

BERKLEY BOOKS, NEW YORK

THE BERKLEY PUBLISHING GROUP
Published by the Penguin Group
Penguin Group (USA) Inc.
375 Hudson Street, New York, New York 10014, USA
Penguin Group (Canada), 90 Eglinton Avenue East, Suite 700, Toronto, Ontario M4P 2Y3, Canada
(a division of Pearson Penguin Canada Inc.)
Penguin Books Ltd., 80 Strand, London WC2R 0RL, England
Penguin Group Ireland, 25 St. Stephen's Green, Dublin 2, Ireland (a division of Penguin Books Ltd.)
Penguin Group (Australia), 250 Camberwell Road, Camberwell, Victoria 3124, Australia
(a division of Pearson Australia Group Pty. Ltd.)
Penguin Books India Pvt. Ltd., 11 Community Centre, Panchsheel Park, New Delhi—110 017, India
Penguin Group (NZ), 67 Apollo Drive, Rosedale, North Shore 0632, New Zealand
(a division of Pearson New Zealand Ltd.)
Penguin Books (South Africa) (Pty.) Ltd., 24 Sturdee Avenue, Rosebank, Johannesburg 2196,
South Africa

Penguin Books Ltd., Registered Offices: 80 Strand, London WC2R 0RL, England

This is a work of fiction. Names, characters, places, and incidents either are the product of the author's
imagination or are used fictitiously, and any resemblance to actual persons, living or dead, business
establishments, events, or locales is entirely coincidental. The publisher does not have any control
over and does not assume any responsibility for author or third-party websites or their content.

SPECIAL FORCES AFGHANISTAN: CRITICAL ACTION

A Berkley Book / published by arrangement with the author

PRINTING HISTORY
Berkley edition / July 2009

Copyright © 2009 by Penguin Group (USA) Inc.
Cover illustration by 3DI Studio.
Cover design by Edwin Tse.
Interior text design by Kristin del Rosario.

ISBN: 978-0-425-22416-8

BERKLEY®
Berkley Books are published by The Berkley Publishing Group,
a division of Penguin Group (USA) Inc.,
375 Hudson Street, New York, New York 10014.
BERKLEY® is a registered trademark of Penguin Group (USA) Inc.
The "B" design is a trademark of Penguin Group (USA) Inc.

PRINTED IN THE UNITED STATES OF AMERICA

10 9 8 7 6 5 4 3 2 1

In memory of
William David Telep

ACKNOWLEDGMENTS

I owe a special thank-you to my editor, Mr. Tom Colgan, for his trust, insights, and encouragement during the years we've worked together on various projects.

Randy McElwee is a retired master sergeant, U.S. Army, and decorated Special Forces combat veteran with eighteen years special operations experience, including service in Afghanistan. Randy is the person who suggested focusing on the tri-border area for this book, and I'm indebted to him for a great idea.

Vietnam veteran and Chief Warrant Officer James Ide, a fellow Floridian with twenty-one years of active naval service, once again brought his considerable experience to this book, helping me create the story from the ground up and reading every page of the manuscript. I can only repeat here, as I did in the first book, that he is a great collaborator and a true friend who never stops inspiring me.

Troy L. Wagner, TMC(SS), EOD, USN, is a retired chief torpedoman, a submariner, and a specialist in explosive ordnance disposal who helped with the EFPs.

Major William R. Reeves, U.S. Army, has served as a technical advisor on many of my novels, and his research and advice served me well with this manuscript.

Mike Noell is the president and CEO of Blackhawk Products Group, recognized as the world's leading supplier of military and law enforcement equipment. Once again, Mike gave me complete access to any and all equipment I was writing about.

Tom O'Sullivan, director, Government and Military Programs at Blackhawk, has been a great technical advisor and friend over the years. Tom helped clarify many of my equipment questions, drawing upon his long and distinguished career as a lieutenant colonel in the U.S. Army.

Michael Janich, a brand manager at Blackhawk, is one of the world's leading edged-weapon experts, the creator of the Jani-song, and author of numerous books and instructional videos on self-defense. He has more than fifteen years of distinguished military service and has studied and taught martial arts and defensive tactics for more than twenty-five years. Mike answered my many questions and helped me choreograph many of my combat scenes to keep them technically accurate. I deeply appreciate his assistance and am truly honored to know him.

Steve "Mato" Matulewicz, command master chief (SEAL), retired, is director of Special Operations at Blackhawk and was kind enough to answer questions on both equipment and the "character" of Special Forces operators. Mato is a true operator in every sense of the word.

Laura Burgess, public relations agent for Blackhawk, and Robin Hart, also of Blackhawk, were again exceedingly helpful in regard to much of the equipment described here.

Michael Rigg, manager of Sales and Marketing at Paladin Press (paladin-press.com) provided me with many nonfiction resources as part of the extensive research process involved in writing this book.

Carole McDaniel created a very nice map to better orient you to the locations. I thank her and her husband, my teaching partner Dr. Rudy McDaniel, for their help and support.

The listing of these individuals is a humble way to express my gratitude. None of them were paid for their services. The fact that their names appear here does not constitute an "official" endorsement of this book by them or any branch of the U.S. military.

Special Forces Creed

I am an American Special Forces soldier. A professional!

I will do all that my nation requires of me. I am a volunteer, knowing well the hazards of my profession.

I serve with the memory of those who have gone before me: Roger's Rangers, Francis Marion, Mosby's Rangers, the first Special Service Forces, the Jedbrughs, Detachment 101, and the Special Forces soldiers of the Vietnam War, who earned seventeen Medals of Honor, and ninety Distinguished Service Crosses. I pledge to uphold the honor and integrity of all I am—in all I do.

I am a professional soldier. I will teach and fight wherever my nation requires, to liberate the oppressed. I will strive always, to excel in every art and artifice of war.

I know that I will be called upon to perform tasks in isolation, far from familiar faces and voices. With the help and guidance of my God, I will conquer my fears and succeed.

I will keep my mind and body clean, alert, and strong, for this is my debt to those who depend on me.

I will not fail those with whom I serve. I will not bring shame upon myself or the forces.

I will maintain myself, my arms, and my equipment in an immaculate state as befits a Special Forces soldier. My goal is to succeed in any mission and to live to succeed again.

I am a member of my nation's chosen soldiery. God grant that I may not be found wanting, that I will not fail this sacred trust.

Special Forces Motto

DE OPPRESSO LIBER

To Liberate the Oppressed
or
From Oppression We Will Liberate Them

A Special Forces guy has to be a lethal killer one moment and a humanitarian the next. He has to know how to get strangers, who speak a different language, to do things for him. He has to go from knowing enough Russian to knowing enough Arabic in a few weeks, depending on the deployment. We need people who are cultural quick studies.

—Major General (Ret.) Sidney Shachnow,
U.S. Army Special Forces

We ain't making no goddamn cornflakes here.

—Colonel Charlie Beckwith,
founder of Delta Force

CAST OF CHARACTERS

ODA-555 "Triple Nickel"

Captain James Pharaoh—detachment commander, call sign *Titan 06*

Chief Warrant Officer 3 Reginald Church—assistant detachment commander, call sign *Track Star*

Master Sergeant Robert "Zulu" Burrows—operations sergeant, call sign *Zulu*

Sergeant First Class Michael "Hojo" Johnson—assistant operations sergeant, call sign *Thunder*

Sergeant First Class Jason "Mr. O" Ondejko—weapons sergeant, call sign *T-Rex*

Staff Sergeant Gregory "Gator" Gatterson—assistant weapons sergeant, call sign *Tombstone*

Sergeant First Class Jonathan Figueroa—engineer sergeant, call sign *Tarzan*

Staff Sergeant Larry Sullivan—assistant engineer sergeant, call sign *Tomahawk*

Sergeant First Class Steven Borokovsky—medical sergeant, call sign *Triage*

Staff Sergeant Anthony Grimm—assistant medical sergeant, call sign *Trauma*

Sergeant First Class Jerry Weathers—communications sergeant, call sign *Talk Radio*

Staff Sergeant Rudy McDaniel—assistant communications sergeant, call sign *Typhoon*

OTHERS

Chief Warrant Officer 3 Karl "Walrus" Kowalski—assistant
   detachment commander, call sign *Tacoma*

"Rock"—CIA operative

Major Barry Nurenfeld—Operational Detachment Bravo
   (ODB) commander

Sheikh Abu Hassan—new al-Qaeda leader in Afghanistan

Saeed Hanjour—senior al-Qaeda operative

Marwan Ali—aka "Libra," former CIA operative turned
   mercenary

Junaid Qureshi—aka "Jersey," Libra's partner

Fatima—prostitute

Ezzat—madam and Fatima's boss

Jafar—Fatima's brother

Jack Andropolis—Rock's contact at Langley

Nasser, Kourosh, Yousef—Iranian contacts working for
   Rock

President James Gallagher

Secretary of Defense Dennis MacIntyre

ODA 555 Rendezvous POINT
AFGHANISTAN
IRAN
PAKISTAN
Zahedan
Test Site

1. STYX AND STONES

Captain James Pharaoh raced along an old wooden fence separating one row of mud huts from the other. He stole a glance over his shoulder, where Master Sergeant Robert "Zulu" Burrows was all moonlit eyes behind the *shemagh* wrapped tightly around his head and face. Although Zulu was in his forties, a decade older than Pharaoh, he easily kept up and put to shame most guys half his age.

Soon the six-foot-high fence leaned sharply, some of its pickets and supporting posts broken off like rotting teeth, as they reached a gaping hole that Zulu had found during their first recon two hours earlier.

After a deep breath, Pharaoh let his assault rifle hang freely by its V-Tac sling. He dropped to his hands and knees and crawled through the opening. Back on his feet, he charged ten more meters, past a power-line pole to reach the largest hut, its domed roof rising above the others with their thatched or corrugated metal roofs.

Out beyond the rows of huts, about a hundred yards south of the town, sat a shimmering strip of oily black water: the Helmand River, snaking its way through southwestern

Afghanistan, then turning northwest toward the much larger town of Chahar Borjak. From there the river ran north toward the Iranian border. The river was used by terrorists and smugglers alike as a highway into Iran and was a much more hospitable route than driving through the desert. Dozens of little towns were strung along the river, and although Londo was one of the more insignificant places on the map, it had suddenly become famous among those in the intelligence community.

Pharaoh crouched down and surveyed the area. To his right lay two guards, both dead and shoved up against the wall.

Off to his left, near the front corner, lay another pair. All of them had been knifed or shot with silenced pistols by several others from Pharaoh's twelve-man Special Forces team.

Riding a surge of adrenaline, Pharaoh shifted along the wall, then huddled beneath the rear window, which was just a square hole sans framework or glass. Although thermal images and portable radar devices could tell them exactly how many people were inside the hut, Pharaoh opted for one of Zulu's low-tech, lighter, and highly reliable intelligence gathering devices: a small mirror. He held it up near the opening, adjusted the angle, then studied the reflection.

Dim light shone from a bulb dangling from the ceiling, and beneath that bulb sat five men around a small table, drinking and smoking, their voices low and burred.

Zulu joined Pharaoh beneath the window. He raised his brows: What do we got?

Pharaoh held up five fingers.

According to the CIA and the army's own intelligence assets, at least three high-level al-Qaeda leaders were stopping in Londo, where they would meet, stay the night, and depart in the early morning hours, bound for Iran. A new rash of roadside bombings and attacks on convoys throughout Afghanistan had been orchestrated by these thugs.

Consequently, Pharaoh's Operational Detachment Alpha team, ODA-555, nicknamed "Triple Nickel," had been tasked with capturing these men, high-value targets of the ever-growing terrorist network in Afghanistan. The team had no authorization to engage in any hot pursuit border crossings into Iran, so it was imperative these men be captured before they left Londo.

Pharaoh reached into his pocket and produced a set of intelligence photographs to see if he could positively identify any of the men inside the hut. He used a small penlight with red bulb to study the pictures.

He swore inwardly. Every guy in Afghanistan had dark hair and a long beard. You had to study eyes, shapes of noses, round versus long faces, and at two in the morning and in dim red light, they all blurred into one big target.

And worse, they'd run out of time. Higher had been getting restless, and the CO had ordered them to move in.

The hut had at least two more rooms up front. Pharaoh watched as Zulu reached into his pack and produced another of his low-tech surprises: his telescoping blowgun. He inserted a small lead fishing weight into the tube's business end. Then he worked his way forward, to the next window on the east side of the hut, where he chanced a peek inside. Satisfied that he was clear, he raised the blowgun to his mouth and faced the opening.

A faint crack sounded, and the light in that room went out, drawing the attention of one man at the table. He mumbled something about another damned bulb going out and rose.

Pharaoh lowered his mirror as Zulu returned, reloaded his blowgun with another weight, then suddenly shot the second bulb over the table.

They had considered simply cutting the power lines, but the engineers had reported that the spaghetti of wires was a nightmare and that they might accidentally cut power to other huts, drawing too much attention. Electrical wiring in Afghanistan was anything but sophisticated and safe.

Consequently, Zulu had offered his remedy via his ancient warrior's weapon.

Now with the lights out and the men inside shouting, Pharaoh got to work. He lobbed his first M84 flashbang grenade through the window, the boom and brilliant light already behind him as he took off running for the second window, reached it, and lobbed in a second grenade.

Then, as he backed away, he tugged down his *shemagh* to get better air. Zulu did likewise, and the two of them charged to the front of the hut, where the team's new assistant detachment commander, Chief Warrant Officer 3 Reginald Church, was using a Blackhawk Thunderbolt on the front door. The fifty-year-old Special Forces veteran drove the battering ram into the wood, shattering it quickly, smoke from the grenades steaming through the opening.

The team's assistant operations sergeant, Michael "Hojo" Johnson, was first through the door, wearing his small helmet and attached night vision goggles (NVGs).

Staff Sergeant Gregory "Gator" Gatterson, the assistant weapons sergeant, was next in.

Meanwhile, the team's two engineers, Sergeants Jonathan Figueroa and his assistant Larry Sullivan, had moved to cover the rear windows.

The rest of Pharaoh's team had taken up outer cordon positions in and around the other mud huts, with the team's two communications sergeants, Jerry Weathers and Rudy McDaniel, posted near the southernmost huts, near the river.

Weathers's voice sounded in Pharaoh's earpiece: "Titan 06, this is Talk Radio, over."

"Talk Radio, this is Titan 06, go ahead."

"We have five, maybe six guys on the move down here, running toward the river. Not sure who they are. You didn't lose your guys, did you?"

"Negative."

Suddenly, Zulu grabbed Pharaoh by the shoulder. "Could be the wrong hut!"

Hojo came running outside to report that all five guys were down for the count.

Church jogged over and said, "I'll get down to the river and see what's—"

Automatic weapons fire suddenly raked across the hut, originating from somewhere behind them. They all hit the deck—everyone but Church. The old-timer cursed and hustled off toward the river, barking orders over the radio at Weathers and McDaniel.

Pharaoh looked to Zulu, who pointed off to the right, where muzzles flashed atop a hut: Two guys were up there, targeting them. The team sergeant tipped his head, and they burst to their feet, returning fire and running toward the next hut a dozen meters away.

As soon as they reached the wall, a pair of small boys appeared in the window of the opposite hut. Pharaoh hollered for them to get down, but they started throwing rocks and yelling for Pharaoh and Zulu to go home. One stone hit Zulu in the back, and he groaned, while another caught Pharaoh in the leg.

Ducking and turning their heads away, they rushed along the wall and rounded a corner, out of the incoming, but suddenly Zulu raised his rifle and fired once, twice.

And just as Pharaoh turned his head, the men who'd been up on the roof collapsed, their AK-47s now silent.

"Damn . . ."

The team sergeant ignored Pharaoh and got on the radio. "Rock, this is Zulu, over."

"Go ahead, Zulu," said the CIA agent, who was back with one of the team's Nissan Pathfinders parked beneath a large stand of trees a quarter kilometer away.

"The domed hut is secure. We have five detainees in there, over."

"Roger that. On my way."

Rock was a middle-aged, cigar-smoking wheeler-dealer with multiple agendas that often got him in serious trouble. To say that he and Triple Nickel had a love-hate relationship was just scratching the surface. But they both needed each other, and so it was that Pharaoh and his men danced with the devil whose gray ponytail fell over his shoulder like a snake.

Zulu looked at Pharaoh, was about to say something, when a powerful explosion sounded from somewhere south, near the riverbank.

The boom sent both of them running in that direction, with Pharaoh already crying over the radio for Church to report.

But it was Assistant Communications Sergeant Rudy McDaniel who responded, "Titan 06, this is Typhoon. The riverbank is mined. Track Star is down. Legs gone, bleeding out bad, over."

Track Star was Church's call sign, and Pharaoh's heart sank as he realized one of his own had been hurt.

"Typhoon, treat him immediately."

"But we got at least another five guys getting in boats, over."

Zulu got on the radio. "This is Zulu. Trauma, Triage, and T-Rex rally on the riverbank. We'll meet you there, out."

That was a good call, and Pharaoh appreciated Zulu's help. As team sergeant, Zulu "fought the men," which in effect meant he made most of the battlefield decisions. But for the past six months, he had been allowing Pharaoh to do more and more, turning him into a more seasoned combatant who intimately understood boots-on-the-ground operations.

And at the moment, their particular boots were in very high gear, until they both ran past a hut where two gunmen were waiting for them, rifles at the ready.

"Sel-lah-heh-ta par-taw!" shouted the taller guy.

Before he even finished ordering them to drop their weapons in Dari, Zulu had his XSF-1 combat dagger drawn from its Kydex sheath. He deflected away the man's rifle with his left forearm and brought down the chisel-tipped dagger into the man's neck.

At the same time, Pharaoh reacted instinctively, firing point-blank into the second man. The guy fell back, triggering his weapon, and suddenly Pharaoh thought he'd been hit.

He dropped to the ground, shifted his arms and legs. No, he felt okay. At least for now.

With a groan and quick wrench, Zulu withdrew his dagger from the man, who wasn't dead yet, but he would be in a few minutes. "I don't think they were with the al-Qaeda group. This guy's Dari sounded pretty good. And they wanted to take us alive." He sheathed his dagger. "This is bad."

Pharaoh swore and got to his feet. "We'll come back for them and find out."

They hustled off, toward the river, where small boat engines gurgled and chugged to life.

Church was lying on the ground, with senior medic Steven Borokovsky, call sign Triage, and his assistant Anthony Grimm, call sign Trauma, working frantically to save the man's life.

Behind them, lights were on all over the village, with locals cautiously drifting out of their huts. Pharaoh sent Weapons Sergeants Ondejko and Gatterson, aka T-Rex and Tombstone, off to get those people back inside.

"There's another boat there," said Zulu, lifting his chin at a small dock. "Come on. I'll drive, you shoot."

"What about the mines?"

"We'll follow their tracks." Zulu thumbed on his Gladius light, the powerful beam illuminating a row of muddy footprints leading to the docks.

As they hustled off, Pharaoh called McDaniel and instructed the commo guy to contact the AC-130 gunship serving as their close air support asset. "Get Black Owl over the river and have them relay the position of those other boats. Think we got two."

"Roger that."

Zulu hopped in the aluminum boat and tugged the cord,

firing up the outboard. Pharaoh climbed in, and they roared off, heading upriver.

"Let's send a couple guys up in one of the SUVs," said Zulu.

Pharaoh nodded, got back on the radio, and ordered the engineers to take the other Pathfinder, keeping close to the bank.

"Titan 06, this is Typhoon," called McDaniel. "Black Owl says your two boats are about a half click northwest of you, over."

"Roger that," Pharaoh answered. "Keep those reports coming."

The river took a lazy turn to the left, and suddenly the water erupted with gunfire.

They had been gaining on the other boats, all right, and the fleeing bad guys had taken issue with that.

Pharaoh dropped down to his hands and knees, pulled himself up to the bow, and leveled his rifle. He opened fire on the rearmost boat, his bead going wide as the man at the engine jogged left.

With one hand on the throttle, Zulu raised a flare gun he'd fetched from his pack and fired off a glowing red rocket that arced over the river, illuminating a pair of foamy trails leading back to the targets.

Both motorboats now beat serpentine paths, making it hard to get a good shot unless Zulu could gain on them and tighten the angle.

Already seeing this, the team sergeant throttled up, and the little outboard screamed.

Pharaoh took aim once more, as the flare began to die. He fired just ahead of one boat, assuming its driver was about to make another turn, which would take him directly into Pharaoh's fire.

But the guy cut left instead of right, and Pharaoh cursed and aimed at the other boat.

Somewhere above came the thundering engines of the AC-130, its crew reading the infrared and thermal images and waiting for Pharaoh's request to open fire with guns that would totally obliterate these fools. But Pharaoh would only issue that request as a last resort. He hoped they could take at least a few of these guys alive and gather more intel.

Zulu cut hard to the left, crossing wakes, the spray kicking up into Pharaoh's eyes.

He blinked and fired at the second boat, and suddenly the man at the engine fell backward, and the boat swung hard right, heading straight for the bank.

"Follow them!" he shouted to Zulu.

An odd sensation began to creep up Pharaoh's legs.

He glanced back. "We're sinking!"

"I know," said Zulu.

"Why didn't you say anything?"

"I didn't want to alarm you." With one hand on the throttle, Zulu fished out his small helmet and began haphazardly bailing out the boat.

"Jesus, Zu, what now?"

"All hands, prepare to abandon ship."

The wiseass wasn't kidding. The boat slowed. The engine coughed, smoked, began to spit—and that was it. They were in the water, the deck dropping away beneath them.

2. PHARAOH'S CURSE

Sergeant First Class Jonathan Figueroa sat in the passenger's side window of the Pathfinder, clutching the roof rack with one hand, his SCAR-L rifle with the other.

His assistant engineer, Staff Sergeant Larry Sullivan, was at the wheel, taking them along the riverbank. The ruts, rocks, and mud played havoc with the SUV and violently tossed Figueroa as the wind tugged at his *shemagh* and whipped into his eyes.

Despite the engine's roar, he could still hear the remaining motorboat fleeing off to his right, its wake spreading across the glossy black surface.

"They're just ahead," he cried. "Pedal to the metal!"

Sullivan stomped on the gas, and Figueroa almost wished he hadn't. The sudden acceleration nearly blew him off the truck, but as he regained his seat, he caught a glimpse of the boat, beginning to turn.

"Get closer!" he ordered.

The Pathfinder burst into the water, keeping parallel with the river, as Figueroa balanced the rifle in one hand and opened fire.

A few rounds thumped into the boat, until Figueroa's bead strayed and a sudden splash knocked his aim even wider.

He swore, swung the rifle back, fired again.

Sullivan veered left, just as incoming fire from the boat shattered one of the back windows. Two men with AK-47s—easily identifiable by their popping sounds—now had a bead on them.

"Oh, they got me pissed!" Figueroa shouted. "Gun it again! We're moving in for the kill!"

"I keep telling you, the captain wants 'em alive."

"They messed up our truck!"

"You're looking for any excuse."

"Damn it, Sully, we're losing them."

The Pathfinder's engine roared once more, and suddenly the truck fishtailed in the mud. "We need to move up. We'll get stuck here," warned Sullivan.

"No, keep going. Another minute. Looks like he's slowing down."

Another salvo popped from the river. One round shattered the side mirror near Figueroa's legs, and the other punched a hole in the door beneath him.

Figueroa raged aloud and returned fire, though he could barely see the boat through all the spray kicked up by the tires, a spray that reeked like sewer water.

Sullivan was now on the radio, reporting their progress, and Figueroa was hoping to give him good news to report.

But when he ceased fire and blinked, he observed the boat moving on. One of the bad guys stood tall near the stern and waved good-bye.

The bastard!

Figueroa couldn't raise his middle finger, but in his imagination he had both fingers extended in utter defiance.

The SUV bounced hard, jarring him, forcing his gaze forward, and he gasped. "Where you going, Sully? Watch out for those trees!"

The engineer was on the radio, his attention split between his report and the path ahead. He wasn't changing course.

"Sully, turn!"

"What?"

Damned distracted drivers was all Figueroa could think as Sullivan realized why he'd called and cut the wheel so hard to the left that Figueroa lost his grip on the roof rack—and went flying out of the truck.

Every muscle in his body tensed as he realized what was happening. He took in a breath. Held it.

Then belly flopped into the mud, the air expelled from his lips. A wave of smelly brown muck rose and crashed over, covering him from head to toe. He groaned, rolled over, and looked up as Sullivan continued to drive away, oblivious that he had just lost his partner.

"I'd rather die here than in some hospital bed," said Assistant Detachment Commander Church, his legs blown off, blood still jetting from those wounds and several others on his neck and abdomen.

Senior medic Borokovsky and his assistant, Grimm, were doing everything they could to stop the bleeding. They had quickly started an IV to get some fluids on board, but their tourniquets and big trauma bandages would not be enough, Borokovsky knew. Even Church had told them to stop. "It's okay," he'd said.

"I'm going to hit you for the pain," said Borokovsky, a needle in his hand.

"Forget it. I want to feel it till the end."

"You don't have to," said Grimm, his voice cracking. "Let us take off the edge."

Church's mouth twisted in a grimace. "I got no regrets. I had a good run. I died doing what I loved."

"Don't talk like that," Grimm said. "You ain't dead."

"Guess you never talked to a dead man before, eh, son?

Thought as a medic you would have. Doesn't matter. Won't be any miracles here tonight."

The man was strangely relaxed, resigned to his fate, and that unnerved Borokovsky. He was used to guys screaming in agony, begging to be saved, scared that they were going to die. The screams forced him to detach himself and just problem-solve. That's what good medics did. Now all he could do was watch . . . and try to detach . . . but it was hard. So damned hard.

"First Bull, now me," said Church, his voice beginning to crack. "Pharaoh might think he's cursed."

Church was referring to Chief Warrant Officer 3 Dennis Bull, who in the mountains three months ago had sacrificed his life in order to save Mr. Abdul Abdali, the president of Afghanistan, and the rest of the team. Church had been the new replacement, even as the team still grieved over Bull's loss.

Now they'd all be attending another memorial service for a man who had spent nearly half his life in the military.

Losses like these were beginning to wear on Borokovsky. He was fiercely loyal to the team, to their mission in Afghanistan, but he couldn't help thinking about the tragic waste of life. He tucked those thoughts away as carefully as he could, but in the wee hours they always returned, whispered his ear, made him second-guess the path he had chosen. As he treated Church, he already knew the man would be waiting for him in his nightmares.

"Doc." Church groaned. "Maybe you oughta give me that—"

Borokovsky felt the man's body grow slack, and his eyes slowly turned vacant.

"Oh, man," whispered Grimm.

Borokovsky rose, tugged off his gloves, and drew in a long breath. After an awkward moment of silence, he finally cleared his throat. "Grimm, let's do what we need to do here."

"Roger that. I'll bag him up."

* * *

CIA field agent Rock hopped out of the Pathfinder and directed his Gladius light into the faces of the coughing and spitting men who sat in the dirt outside the domed hut.

He cursed exactly five times.

Because none of these five were the Taliban leaders they were after.

So those guys must be on the boats. He called Pharaoh, but the captain wasn't answering his radio. Neither was Zulu, so Rock tried to call the engineers. Sullivan said that Pharaoh and Zulu had stalled one boat but that he and Figueroa were losing theirs because Figueroa had fallen out of the truck and Sullivan was turning around to get him.

So Rock did what he had to do. He got ahold of the team's senior commo guy, Sergeant First Class Jerry Weathers, who patched him into the crew of the AC-130 still rumbling overhead. "Black Owl, this is Rock. Do you have that boat, over?"

"Rock, this is Black Owl, we have the target, over."

"Take it out."

"We have permission to fire on your authority, over?"

Rock sighed in resignation. "You have permission. Take it out."

"Roger that, moving in to fire. Stand by."

Rock lowered his mike and closed his eyes. It was better to kill them than let them get away.

And where the hell was Pharaoh?

At first Pharaoh thought Zulu would swim for the riverbank, but instead he aimed for the boat they had struck, the one now sinking as it barely reached the opposite bank. Two men jumped out and jogged off.

Pharaoh sloughed off his pack and swam up behind Zulu. His boots suddenly hit bottom, and within ten seconds the men were back on their feet, splashing out of the river, rifles slung over their shoulders.

"No rifles. We get in close, take them alive," said Zulu.

"I knew you'd say that." Pharaoh groaned. He was exhausted but wholeheartedly agreed with the plan.

"You hear that?" asked Zulu as they shifted away from the river. "That's spooky up there, laying down fire."

Pharaoh called Weathers on the radio and learned that Rock had ordered the strike. He grunted in disgust, signed off, and increased his pace.

Just ahead lay several clusters of trees and the more heavily wooded sections beyond. The two men appeared a moment before vanishing into the woods some fifty yards off. Pharaoh couldn't tell how well armed they were, but he planned to find out.

Zulu now had his dagger in one hand, his pistol in the other, for a little close-quarters work.

As he ran, Pharaoh reached into his side pocket and withdrew the Jani-Song that Zulu had given him after their mission in the mountains. Once he had engaged the thumb switch, Pharaoh flipped open the inner handle and blade and locked the blade into the open position. Then he touched a button on his SERPA holster and removed his own Special Forces sidearm, the reliable Heckler & Koch .45-caliber compact tactical pistol, which, thankfully, had passed the NATO mil-spec mud, rain, and water immersion tests with flying colors.

Abruptly, Zulu darted to the right, waving Pharaoh on. He'd seen something, and now so did Pharaoh:

Their two thugs had broken to the right and were ready to dart to another stand of trees to the east.

But one of them had tripped, fallen, twisted his ankle possibly, and the other had doubled back to help him. The injured guy was back on his feet, limping, and his buddy was now slinging his arm over his shoulder.

Zulu was a wet, mud-caked animal that had locked onto his prey, and Pharaoh could barely keep up with him.

They knifed through some low-lying scrub, bounded up a small hill and back down the other side, then fell in directly behind the two men.

While the air was still warm, nearly eighty degrees, running around in wet clothes chilled Pharaoh, and he shuddered against his nerves and the gooseflesh fanning across his shoulders—

Just as the two bad guys spotted their approach.

The uninjured guy abandoned his limping friend and darted off. No team players in this bunch.

"I got him," shouted Zulu.

With that, the team sergeant broke into a full-on sprint that left Pharaoh tired just watching him.

As Pharaoh approached the limping guy, he covered him with the pistol and shouted in Dari for him to halt, but the guy whirled, lifting his own pistol.

Pharaoh fired, even as he threw himself onto the ground.

Two more shots cracked loudly as Pharaoh rolled to the left, came back up on his hands and knees, and spotted the man, limping quickly toward the trees on his left.

Pharaoh didn't want to kill this guy, but his own life was worth a hell of a lot more than intel—in his humble opinion.

He sat up, took careful aim at the guy's legs, and fired two more rounds.

The guy screamed.

Then he dropped hard to the ground. Pharaoh burst to his feet and charged toward him.

Zulu clutched his XSF-1 dagger in a reverse grip, the blade resting tightly against his forearm. As he neared the still fleeing thug, the guy swung back, taking aim with his rifle.

Zulu fired.

But so did the guy.

And while Zulu had aimed for the guy's legs in an attempt to take him alive, the bad guy wasn't nearly as merciful.

Three shots struck Zulu squarely in the abdomen, knocking him onto his back, blasting the wind from his lungs as the star-filled sky seemed to descend and swallow him. He remembered his Dragon Skin flexible body armor and could only hope that the high-tech ceramic fish scales had stopped the rounds.

He wanted to sit up, but when his vision cleared, he saw a glowing white line above, along with two shimmering orbs.

The line was the guy's mouth. The orbs were his eyes. He leaned over, pointing his rifle at Zulu's head.

Pharaoh reached the thug and told him in Dari to hold his fire, that if he didn't resist he wouldn't be hurt.

"Okay, okay," the guy answered, then suddenly raised his pistol.

The movement sent Pharaoh's finger slamming down on his trigger. It was reflex. Muscle memory. No thought.

The thug wrenched back as the round burrowed into his head.

Pharaoh was already cursing before the man's body hit the ground. He lowered his pistol, flipped closed the Jani-Song, then hustled off after Zulu.

Time to pay for my sins, Zulu thought.

But, aw, hell, if he was going to die, it had better be while fighting. He rolled onto his side, slamming his own boots into the guy's shins and knocking him off balance.

That the guy pulled his trigger and the rifle jammed or clicked empty was the only reason why Zulu was still alive. His seemingly clever escape maneuver had nothing to do with it.

But that didn't fully register. He thought only of knocking

the guy down, which he did. Then he lunged forward and seized the thug's throat in one hand as he forced him down, onto his back, about to pin him.

The guy rattled off something in Dari so fast that Zulu only caught a few words: drugs, smuggling, who the hell are you guys? It was time to put an end to that hot, smelly breath wafting in Zulu's face. He reared back with his dagger.

"Hold it right there, Sergeant," said Pharaoh. "Got you covered. Let him go."

Zulu's arms were trembling. He wanted nothing more than to finish this guy, release the adrenaline, exact vengeance for every operator killed in A'stan. It was an evil desire, intoxicating, nearly uncontrollable.

He glanced over at Pharaoh. "Let me do him."

"We need him."

"We got others."

"Sergeant, I'm warning you . . ."

The wave of anger began to wash off, and Zulu swore and released the man. He confiscated the guy's rifle while Pharaoh searched him for other weapons. The guy just laid there, palms extended.

Once Pharaoh was certain the thug was clean, he stood, covering the man with his pistol. He turned and gave Zulu a hard look. "Let's go."

"Titan 06, this is Triage, over."

Senior medic Borokovsky was calling. Pharaoh found his microphone, keyed it, and appeared to brace himself for bad news. "Go ahead, Triage."

"I'm sorry, Titan 06, we did what we could, but we lost Track Star, over."

"Roger that. Rally back to the hut. We'll meet you there. Titan 06, out."

Zulu grabbed the thug by the shirt collar. "Did you mine that riverbank?"

The guy just looked at him, wide-eyed, scared.

"Did you mine that riverbank?"

"Zu, enough. Church is dead. We need to bail out that boat, get it across the river, or come up with another way to get back. Maybe Sullivan can get down to the bridge. We're not swimming. Come on."

"All right." Zulu shoved the thug, then sighed deeply. "What a night."

3. FRAGMENTS OF TRUTH

Pharaoh stood outside the domed roof hut, getting reports from his men. If the atmosphere hadn't been so grim, he might have laughed at Figueroa, who ambled up looking as though he'd mud wrestled with a bear.

"The one-thirty shredded those guys in the other boat," he said. "We think three guys were on board. We'll need to clean up that mess."

"Might need a team to clean you up, too," said Pharaoh.

Figueroa grinned crookedly.

Sullivan, who arrived at Figueroa's shoulder, shrugged and said, "Captain, we tried, but the terrain along the river is pretty rough."

"Yeah, I know you were on 'em. Best you could do."

Figueroa licked his lips, spat mud, then said, "Rock's over there now, trying to ID what's left of them. I don't think he'll have much luck, but he's not a happy camper, I'll tell you that."

Hojo and Gator moved up to Pharaoh's right, and Hojo gestured to the five men cuffed and seated on the dirt.

They were still rubbing their eyes and ears from the flash-bangs. "These guys are just local smugglers, sir. They were taking a little shipment down to Pakistan in the morning. We already seized the stuff, about ten bricks of opium paste and nearly ten thousand in greenbacks. Got it back in the truck."

"Good. Then it wasn't a total loss."

"Excuse me," said McDaniel, holding the mike to their Shadowfire radio. "I have the CO for you, sir."

Major Barry Nurenfeld, Pharaoh's company commander, was calling from Forward Operations Base (FOB) Cobra located two hundred miles northeast, on the outskirts of Lashkar Gah. The dry and arid city was the capital of the Helmand Province.

All right, Pharaoh thought, *time to sound optimistic.* Somehow.

Zulu paid a local cabdriver to give him a ride upriver to the location where the AC-130 had taken out the boat.

There, he found one of the team's SUVs parked nearby, and beyond it stood Rock, smoking his cigar as he sifted through body parts and debris. The damage caused to the men and the boat by the 130's guns was, in a word, devastating.

Zulu swallowed against his gag reflex, then took in a long breath. "What's the matter, Rock? You lose your wallet?"

"Yeah."

"Your al-Qaeda buddies aren't here, are they?"

"Go play with the other Boy Scouts."

Zulu shifted closer to the shattered boat, the mud coming up to his ankles. "We lost Church."

"I know."

"And for what? Ten bricks of opium and some cash?"

"I don't owe you any explanations."

"The hell you don't. It's the same old story. Every time

you pull higher's strings and get us on board, we lose time, equipment, operators."

Rock stood upright, crossed around the boat, took a long pull on his cigar, then blew smoke in Zulu's face. "I'm going to tell you something, not because I owe you, but because we've been working together for so long."

"You mean you've been using us for so long."

"Just shut up and listen. The intel I got didn't just come from a reliable source. It came from the best source I have in this entire country, which is why I don't have a clue why those guys weren't here."

"Embarrassing."

"More than that. Scary."

"Meaning—"

Rock snorted. "Everything—and I mean *everything*—about those reports was legit: sat images, news from informants, photos of the guys en route. I would've bet my life that they'd be here."

"Then what the hell happened?"

"Zu, if I was fed bad intel, then the Agency has an even bigger intelligence problem than we thought. But you didn't hear that from me. We never spoke."

"Well, you'd better figure it out. You keep taking us down dead ends, and look what happens. You know, I wish you guys would do the math on these missions. For every one where the intel is good and we capture the bad guys, we got like, what, twenty misses?"

Rock swore then reached into his breast pocket. "Cigar?"

"Hell, yeah." Zulu accepted the stogie, lit up, savored the taste. "I'll give you a lift back."

"I guess it's your truck I borrowed."

They crossed to the Pathfinder, got in, with Zulu at the wheel. "Aren't you getting tired of this?" he asked Rock.

"Nope."

"Why not?"

"Come on, Zu. This is what we were born for. Eat, sleep,

meet exotic people, and kill them. I had that bumper sticker on the back of my car once."

"Yeah, you're right. But first we take pictures before we blow them all up."

"Exactly. And what could be better than working with a well-respected and impeccably groomed field agent like myself? I'm a straight shooter, easy to read. My agenda always comes first. You come last. No secrets here."

"You never told me how you weaseled your way out of that weapons planting scheme the Agency was trying to pin on you and Scorpion."

"Funny you should ask. The guys who helped me get out of that are the same ones who provided the intel for this mission."

Zulu cocked a brow. "You sure they're still your friends?"

"Hard to believe they're not. We have a lot of history between us. But money always talks."

"Give 'em a call."

"Already have. Just waiting to hear back."

It was seven A.M. by the time the Black Hawk set down to pick up the prisoners and deploy a few explosive ordnance disposal (EOD) techs and cleanup crew for the boat. Pharaoh and his men had spent the last few hours speaking with and paying off the village tribal leaders, trying to keep them calm. As partial payment for the two men Zulu and Pharaoh had accidentally killed they gave the old men the ten thousand in greenbacks they had confiscated.

Pharaoh also had the unenviable task of calling back his CO to report that the intel was bad: No high-value targets captured. No high-value targets anywhere in the area.

The major was incensed, all right, and Pharaoh was sure Rock's superiors would hear about it.

As they packed up the SUVs, Borokovsky pulled Pharaoh aside. "Sir, thought you might like to know that Grimm

and I were talking to Church before he died. He was glad
he wasn't dying in some hospital bed. Said he died doing
what he loved. Thought you could put that in the letter to
his family."

"Thank you, Sergeant, I will."

"Sir?"

"Yes?"

"Ah, nothing." Borokovsky's lips twisted.

"What is it?"

"This." He closed his eyes.

"You all right."

"I don't know. Maybe when we get back I'll talk to
somebody."

"Hey, man. It's all right. Honestly, I'm glad I wasn't
there, watching him die. That's the second assistant I've
lost."

"Like a curse."

Pharaoh drew his head back in surprise. "What are
you? Superstitious?"

"Not really, sir. Maybe it's all of us."

"Oh, give me a break. There's no curse here. Only first
class operators—like you."

"Thank you, sir." The senior medic nodded and climbed
into the truck.

"Uh, Captain Pharaoh?" called one of the EOD techs
who had returned from the riverbank. He was a young corporal with the hard expression worn by most of the techs
Pharaoh had encountered. He had the long boom of a metal
detector in one hand and a two-foot-long mine probe that
resembled a skewer in the other. "Sir, I'm Corporal Mis-
tarz, sir."

Pharaoh went to shake the corporal's hand, then thought
better of it. "How many you find, Corporal?"

"None, sir. That area wasn't mined. We did pick up some
fragments from a grenade, though, same area where your
guy was hit. Just no evidence of antipersonnel mines."

"So they tossed a grenade at him before they took off. I thought for sure it was a mine."

"Sounds possible. But the fragments definitely come from an M67, so the bad guys acquired some of ours or—"

"Or what?"

The corporal shrugged. "I don't know, sir."

"How about the thumb-clip safety or the pin?"

"Figured we'd find those, but we didn't."

"That's weird."

"Yeah, I know."

"All right, do me a favor. Just write it up that you didn't find any mines."

"No problem, sir."

"Thanks."

Pharaoh jogged over to McDaniel, who was stowing his radio gear in the back of the Pathfinder. "Hey, Rudy."

The baby-faced operator perked up at hearing his first name. "What's up, sir?"

"You told me the riverbank was mined."

"Yeah. Church stepped on a mine."

"You're certain?"

"We were pretty far back, but he was running toward the river, then boom, he lit up. I saw the whole thing. What else could've happened?"

"Nothing else could've happened. Thanks."

"Captain, what are you thinking?"

Pharaoh shook his head. "Nothing. Don't worry about it. Almost ready to pull out?"

He nodded.

Pharaoh crossed in front of the truck and watched as Church's body was loaded onto the Black Hawk. Behind him, the other Pathfinder rolled up. Zulu and Rock climbed out, and Pharaoh waved them over as the chopper's rotors began whipping up the dust clouds. They shifted behind one of the smaller huts to talk in the alley.

"You ID your guys?" Pharaoh asked Rock.

"What do you think?" Zulu countered with a snicker.

"Oh, man. More bad intel?"

"I'll find out what happened. Trust me," said Rock.

"I need to talk to Zu," said Pharaoh, gesturing that Rock head back to the truck.

"Got a few calls to make myself," said the agent as he started off.

"What now?" asked Zulu. "You don't look so good."

"The riverbank wasn't mined."

"So what happened to Church?"

"Well, one of the EOD techs found M67 fragments where Church was hit."

"Really?"

"You don't want me to say what I'm thinking," said Pharaoh.

Zulu took a step forward, leveled his gaze, his eyes never more penetrating. "What are you thinking? That one of our guys—"

"I don't know, I—"

"Jesus, Captain! Other than you and McDaniel, I've worked with these guys for a long time. No way, no how. Not on my team. *No way!*"

"Look, this mission has already gone to hell. We don't need to add this to the mix."

"You don't need this on your record is what you're trying to say."

"The other possibility is that the grenade was his."

"Church killed himself?"

"You told me you were on an ODA team with him for three months, but how well did you really know him?"

"He was a cranky old fart, but he didn't want to die. And there are a hundred better ways to do yourself than drop a grenade. Damn, he was smarter than that."

"I'm going to say that we believe the enemy tossed a grenade at him before they fled."

"We could always question the guy we caught."

Pharaoh lowered his tone. "I almost don't want to—because he's going to tell us they didn't have any grenades."

"How do you know?"

"I just know."

"So you're thinking one of two things: suicide or murder."

Pharaoh averted his gaze and groped for a response.

"If anything, it was a suicide," Zulu continued. "There's no one here capable of that."

Pharaoh whirled around. "How do *you* really know?"

Zulu's lips rose in a crooked grin. "I just know."

"This is . . . I don't know, man. Isn't it the young, inexperienced captains that get killed by their own guys?"

"Look, the only operators down there were Weathers and McDaniel. Why the hell would they want to kill Church?"

"I don't know."

"And if Church did kill himself, you can't disgrace that man or punish his family by putting that in a report. I say we keep this between you and me. Higher won't pursue it, especially since all we're coming back with is some opium. No need to rub salt in the wound."

"I'm going to do some digging on my own. Who knows, maybe the guy was really unstable, personal problems—"

"We would've known. And now we're zero for two with assistants." Zulu frowned. "I wouldn't want to be the next guy to take the job."

Pharaoh released a snort. "Thanks a lot."

"No offense, Captain."

"Yeah, right." Pharaoh shuffled out of the alley, his paranoia growing, making him feel sick to his stomach.

4. ROADSIDE ASSISTANCE

As they drove back to FOB Cobra, Rock sat in the back-seat, chatting online via satellite with Jack Andropolis, an old buddy at Langley who sometimes served as a go-between for himself and Rock's two old friends, Libra and Jersey, the men who had provided him with a large portion of the intelligence about the al-Qaeda leaders' presence in Londo.

Half a lifetime ago, Rock and Libra had been in the Marine Corps together, and while Jersey was an army vet, he, too, was a former military man who had joined the CIA's Special Activities Division and shared their politics, sensibilities, and the paramilitary skills required of that group. They were all in their late forties now, hardcore intelligence gatherers who'd sacrificed families for what they did.

Their kinship was stronger than any conventional family, and it had been founded upon three crucial principles: hot women, cold beer, and good intel.

But the one thing that made Libra and Jersey different was their ancestry. Both were American-born, but Libra's parents were Iraqis, and Jersey's were Pakistanis. Both could pass for Afghans, Iranians, and Arabs, which made them very valuable in the region.

The bottom line was that they all made life-and-death decisions, relying entirely on one another's loyalty.

About two years ago, Libra and Jersey had retired from the Agency, founded a small company, and become independent contractors. They had tried to convince Rock to join them, but he still had a few years left with the Agency. While Rock missed their camaraderie, he had never stopped relying upon their assistance. As private contractors, they weren't dragging the shackles of the law like he was.

There were times when they preferred that he not contact them directly and insisted that he use the secure lines provided by the Agency. That usually meant they had a high-profile client closely monitoring them. Just last week they'd said they were working for a European group who required intelligence gathering in the tri-border area of Afghanistan, Iran, and Pakistan. They wouldn't even tell Rock the group's name.

But now what? Had Rock just taken a knife in the back from the two guys he trusted more than anyone else in the world?

How could they have been wrong? Had they deliberately fed him misinformation?

Andropolis said that he, too, had lost contact with the men, but he'd do what he could. While Libra and Jersey weren't officially on the CIA's payroll, Andropolis tapped them now and again for information and provided them with a lucrative and tax-free "stipend." Rock looked forward to a similar arrangement, once he finally made the big leap and retired.

"How's the weather back in Virginia?" Zulu asked from the driver's seat.

"They're getting some rain," Rock lied.

"When it rains, it pours," said Zulu.

"Ain't that the truth," Pharaoh said.

Rock slammed shut his laptop. "You look like you got food poisoning, Captain."

Pharaoh glanced over his shoulder. "I feel like it."

"Sorry again about Church. He was a good guy. Seemed easy to work with. I heard he was a real asset during the 9/11 invasion here."

"What else did you hear?" asked Pharaoh, in a suspiciously demanding tone.

"That's about it."

"You, uh, you were at the main hut when Church stepped on that mine."

Rock gave a half shrug. "Maybe. Or wait, yeah, I think so. I heard the explosion from over there. Why do you ask? Do I need to call my attorney?"

Zulu lifted his fist and punched Pharaoh in the arm. "Don't mind the young Jedi here, Rock. It's been a long night. We all need twenty hours of sleep. At least."

McDaniel, Ondejko, and Gatterson were also in the truck, the latter two in the backseat with Rock, the former jammed into the far backseat with the equipment. And it was Mc-Daniel who suddenly spoke up. "Captain, I have to ask. Do you think something didn't, I mean, when Church stepped on the mine, do you think—"

"Spit it out, Sergeant," called Rock, raising his voice.

"I mean to say, was Church's death, I don't know, suspicious, I guess?"

"Suspicious?" Pharaoh answered quickly. "Nah. Just need to be sure, you know. And I know the CO will want to talk to you guys when we get back."

"Yes, sir."

"You saw him die?" Rock asked McDaniel.

"Yeah, from a distance. So did Sergeant Weathers."

"And you saw him step on a mine."

McDaniel nodded. "That's what it looked like to us."

"Captain?" Rock called. "Is there a problem?"

"Absolutely. And it's your intel. Better shut up, get back on your little magic box, and figure out why."

Rock grinned darkly. "Once again, I have to compliment the Special Forces on their gratitude and hospitality." Rock opened his laptop, connected to the satellite once again, and saw that his e-mail box was still empty.

Ondejko and Gatterson leaned in to steal glimpses of his screen. He glowered at them and said, "Gentlemen, if you think I'm surfing for porn like you whores, think again."

About thirty minutes later, Zulu was honking his horn and waving at the driver of a truck just ahead of them on the narrow stretch of desert road. The truck's flatbed was covered with a tarpaulin, but pallets of concrete cinder blocks were visible from the back, as was the truck's buckling suspension. The beast crawled along at barely thirty miles per hour.

"I'm going to pass this knucklehead," Zulu said.

Suddenly, the truck pulled over to the side of the road, steam wafting from its engine.

"That's right, get off the road!" cried Zulu.

"Let's stop, too," said Pharaoh. "Maybe we can give them a hand."

"A hand? These idiots did it to themselves. That truck's overloaded."

"Just do it."

Swearing, Zulu pulled over, threw the Pathfinder in reverse, then backed up to the overheating vehicle.

The rest of the team, in the other Pathfinder, turned off the road just ahead and began to get out.

To their north, the more modern buildings and factories of Lashkar Gah rose on the distant horizon. Distant was the operative word. If you had to break down, this was not the place. Next repair station: thirty miles or more.

The morning sun beat down hard, and Zulu was already sweating by the time he shuffled up to the driver, a bony guy who appeared so uncomfortable that Zulu might as well have drawn his pistol.

"Uh, hello, hello!" said the man, spying their trousers, which were military issue and betrayed them as Americans.

Zulu gave a little wave and a weak smile while muttering several four-letter words through his teeth.

Three other guys hopped down from the cab, all in their twenties, with one guy wearing a Yankees cap.

Zulu addressed them in Dari: "Looks like you have a problem."

The scrawny guy rubbed his eyes, cocked a thumb over his shoulder, and cried, "It's all my brother's fault. We are carrying too much weight!"

"Where are you guys headed?" asked Pharaoh. "Lashkar Gah?"

The guy nodded.

"We'll see if we can help you," said Pharaoh. "If not, we can give you a ride to the city."

"Where the hell are we going to put them? On the roof?" asked Zulu.

"If we have to," said Pharaoh. Then he gave orders to a few of the other guys to search the truck and for Figueroa and Sullivan to inspect the engine. Pharaoh would check their IDs.

Zulu gestured with his head for the guy with the Yankees cap to come over. "You like the Yanks?"

The guy just looked at him.

"Baseball, dude. The Yankees." Zulu pointed at his cap.

"Oh, yes," the guy said. "Let's go Mets!"

Zulu couldn't help but grin. "Yankees."

"Yes!" The guy removed his cap, swung it around backward, and flashed some gang signs. "It's good to be a gangsta, yeah!"

"Hey, Captain, we got a comedian over here."

Pharaoh didn't answer. He was scrutinizing the others' papers while the men examining the back of the truck cried that the load looked clear—just cinder blocks. They had even broken a few apart to be sure they were just concrete.

Zulu drifted back there and pointed out that it was still possible these guys were smuggling drugs inside the cavities of each brick.

"You want us to unload them all?" asked Weathers. "That'll take hours."

"Nah, we'll call it in."

"Captain, looks like the radiator's cracked and leaking bad. She won't make it back," Figueroa told Pharaoh.

Pharaoh nodded, turned to Zulu. "All right, their IDs look okay. We'll leave two guys here and give them a lift. They can figure out what to do from there."

Zulu explained that to the men, who nodded and thanked them profusely.

Then two guys climbed up onto the roof of one Pathfinder, two onto the roof of the other.

Zulu sighed. "I got Weathers calling the CO to send out a team to search this truck more thoroughly. Hojo and Gator will stay here and ride back with them."

"Good deal. There's a lot of construction going on in the city, though. Probably just another delivery. There are three or four factories south of the river. And besides, if they were smuggling drugs, they'd be headed out of the country, not into it, you think?"

Zulu shrugged. "Depends on what they're smuggling."

The city of Lashkar Gah was located between the Helmand and Arghandab rivers. Major highways came in from Kandahar to the east, Zaranj to the west, and Herat to the northwest. There was a small airfield with only a gravel runway, so most army personnel arrived by helicopter. Despite the desert conditions, farming did take place near the rivers, where the ruins of the old fortress of Bost and the famous decorative arch depicted on some Afghan monetary notes drew tourists, both civilian and military alike.

Back in the 1950s, the city had been a headquarters for American engineers who'd established brick homes and wide, tree-lined streets. Then the Soviets had invaded, the trees were cut down, and the walls had gone up.

Since the Global War on Terror (GWOT) had begun, and more skirmishes occurred in the surrounding areas, Lashkar Gah had become a safe haven and its population had increased to over 45,000, which in turn had driven housing prices to over $400,000. Pharaoh and his men had marveled over the fact that a house in an ancient, third-world desert city where opium production was booming cost more than most places in the United States.

And while Lashkar Gah had come a long way from its darker days, like many cities, it still had a seedy underbelly, most notably its dump.

The men of ODA-555 were quite familiar with it.

Unfortunately, Forward Operations Base Cobra, an unremarkable rectangle of tents, sandbags, concertina wire, and dust-caked vehicles, mostly civilian, was located just a kilometer downwind of mountains of garbage.

On those more windy days, ODA-555, two other ODA teams, and their Operational Detachment Bravo or "B team" support group, headed by Major Nurenfeld, all wore their *shemaghs* against the rank odor that seemed to get into everything.

Nurenfeld had already put in his request to have the operations base moved, but city leaders would not have it. The land adjacent to the dump was specifically designated for the American military, which was why Pharaoh was deeply grateful when they had to saddle up and leave the FOB.

At the moment, he sat across from the major, who had just finished listening to Pharaoh issue his after action report and was rubbing his chin in thought.

Nurenfeld was a quirky officer who seemed hell-bent on showing off his education. Pharaoh found it a little off-putting when he'd use words like "arcana," "obsequious," and "posit" (among dozens of others) to demonstrate his "smarts" and intimidate others—because he'd never clarify the meaning of a word, even if his own context wasn't clear.

"Captain, according to the prisoner you captured, none of his cohorts possessed M67 grenades, nor did any of them throw a grenade at Chief Warrant Officer Church. Perhaps you'd like to elucidate further?"

Pharaoh thought a moment. Did elucidate mean speak? Sounded more like having the runs after a bad meal. "Sir, with all due respect, that guy doesn't know what he's talking about. Give him a drug test. They were all high. He doesn't remember what they had or didn't have. It's our assertion that before jumping in the boats, they tossed a grenade at Warrant Officer Church."

"Why not just shoot him?"

"I don't know, sir. Men on drugs make irrational decisions, sir."

"Maybe they weren't high. Maybe it was too dark to shoot accurately. Maybe they reacted out of instinct. Point is, they killed him, right?"

"Yes, sir."

"But I'm still tortured by the fact that Church was killed with one of our frags."

"Why, sir? That's become pretty common in the past five years. Bodies have been looted. Taliban, local smugglers, al-Qaeda . . . they've all gotten their hands on our weapons."

Nurenfeld shook his head.

"You disagree, sir?"

"Not with that. I'm just disconcerted. And we're going to get to the bottom of it."

Pharaoh frowned. "Sir, we received bad intelligence. We busted some smugglers, yes, but this was not a good outcome. I'm unsure we want to launch an internal investigation on top of all this."

"An internal investigation is exactly what we need, Captain. Just not an official one—because I agree with you on that point." The major leaned forward and lowered his voice. "This is your first command of an ODA team, my first command of Bravo. Neither of us needs this."

"Yes, sir."

Nurenfeld sat back, pursed his lips. "Tell you what. You take a couple of men, go back to Londo, poke around. See if anyone else saw anything. See if you can find that pin from the grenade."

"Sir, I appreciate your confidence, sir."

"I am warning you, Captain. If you discover anything that points to one of your own men, you're obligated to report it to me. Then we'll be forced to call for that official investigation. If we don't, we'll both be hanging out to dry."

For the first time, Pharaoh felt like the major was speaking to him as a peer, a friend . . . almost. He had even toned down his vocabulary. Interesting how his arrogance evaporated when his own butt was on the line.

"I've called higher to see if anyone can spare another warrant. I'll let you know how we make out."

"Thank you, sir."

"Why don't you catch a couple hours of sleep, then head back to Londo this afternoon."

Pharaoh rose and shook hands with the major. "I will, sir. Thanks." He left the tent, turned into the wind, and gagged. Flocks of birds wheeled over the trash hills.

After tugging his *shemagh* up over his mouth and nose, Pharaoh headed back toward his billet, while deciding who would accompany him to Londo.

5. MADE IN ZAHEDAN

Saeed Hanjour, thirty-four and a senior al-Qaeda operative, listened to his man Majed babbling about how they had overloaded the truck, that it had broken down, and that they had been picked up by American soldiers on their way back to Lashkar Gah. The truck would be thoroughly searched by the Americans.

Hanjour gnashed his teeth, quickly finished the call with that fool wearing his Yankees cap, then went outside the concrete-and-brick factory for a smoke.

Majed's team had been making a dry run, the first of three, before they began shipping in earnest.

Sheikh Abu Hassan, the top al-Qaeda leader in Afghanistan, would not be happy with this report. He had already called twice to complain about delays, and Hanjour had assured him that he would receive his shipments very soon.

Hanjour and his men were in the Iranian city of Zahedan, home to over half a million inhabitants and located in the southwest portion of the country, with the wedge-shaped borders of Afghanistan and Pakistan less than fifty kilometers to the north. In addition to highways, an international airport and a broad-gauge railway line linked the city to the rest of the Iranian rail network.

Because of Zahedan's key location, ground, air, or rail shipments from the factory could be moved quickly from Iran into Iraq, Pakistan, and Afghanistan. The city had become the main economic center of the region, having come a long way from the ancient days when it had been a meeting place for bandits in search of water. The Soviet invasion of Afghanistan in the eighties had helped triple its population, and now the city thrived, its people producing rugs, ceramics, milled rice, reed mats and baskets, and bricks. There were two other brick-making facilities besides theirs—all the better to conceal their operation.

Hanjour lit his cigarette than stared down the long street, past the colorful Rasouli Bazaar, toward the spiny rows of mountains that ringed the city. Winter was gone, and the peaks were bare, the long shoulders of rock draped in shadows.

He drifted toward the back of the building, where two teams of men stacked cinder blocks onto pallets while a pair of flatbed trucks sat idling at the docks. The men tensed as he shifted by, scrutinizing their every move. He was prone to great outbursts, and he could see in their eyes that they expected another. And yes, he felt like exploding, but he remembered his relaxation technique, taught to him by his grandfather. He pictured himself fishing, casting out all of his anger. He would make sure the men did not overload the next truck, scheduled to make the second dry run.

The men were preparing standard shipments bound for Pakistan. Nothing special about them, and the men worked without care as to how roughly they placed each brick. They were local Baluchi tribesmen, paid double what they would make at the other factories. Of course they knew that some of the "special" bricks, as they called them, were identical in appearance but slightly heavier than the others, and they should be handled much more carefully. As Hanjour had instructed them, they would conceal each group of special bricks in the center of the pallet, but mark them with three nail scratches on the top. He was paying them very well to work hard, look the other way, and keep their mouths shut. While the tribesmen had never seen the insides of any brick, their expressions revealed they knew what was there.

Hanjour moved inside the long, single-story factory, passing the rolling metal doors. Within an area completely cordoned off by his security team, his engineers were preparing the special bricks, whose inner foam padding contained parts that when assembled became the wrath of Allah.

The infidels referred to the weapons as EFPs—explosively formed penetrators (or projectiles). They were used to penetrate four-inch-thick armor at standoff distances. The EFPs were six- to nine-inch pipes filled with explosives. One end of the pipe was sealed, and a curved copper or steel plate was fitted to the other end, forming a weapon that was essentially a giant bullet.

EFPs had been pioneered by al-Qaeda's colleagues in Lebanon, the Hezbollah, who had trained many al-Qaeda operatives in bomb-making and disposal. The sheik's plan was to move hundreds of EFPs into Afghanistan within a month. They could take out American tanks and other armor. They could disrupt convoys.

Hanjour had seen it for himself.

It had been an extremely cold winter night in Kabul. He and his men were on foot, positioned along Kabul's airport road, Bibi Mahro, and their intelligence indicated that the American ambassador to Afghanistan, Mr. George Tanner, would be leaving the embassy to fly out for a meeting in the United States.

They had set up three EFPs with infrared triggers along the route.

Hanjour had crouched down with his men, waiting. The blood had escaped his legs and the pins were stabbing by the time headlights appeared. He groaned and shifted position, tightening his grip on the AK-47 in his gloved hands.

He got on the radio. Alerted his team. They were ready. His scout, who was lying in a ditch one hundred meters off, was first to report in.

Yes, it was the ambassador's convoy: American HMMWVs, two Strykers, and the armored limousine rolling down the highway, headed directly for the infrared beams.

As a boy Hanjour had watched his own mother detonate herself for the cause, and he relived that moment in the time it took for the convoy to near the triggers.

"Take care of your father," she had told him. "Never forget that God is great."

She had looked back over her shoulder, then she had stood, walked off into the crowd of American servicemen coming off the plane to poison and taint the holy land of Saudi Arabia.

The explosion had knocked him to his rump.

As did a similar explosion when the convoy's lead Hummer broke the beam—

Triggering the EFP. Molten lead blasted through the vehicle, killing the men inside.

At the same time, the second HMMWV veered off the road, triggering the second bomb, which blew it apart, leaving plumes of fire and smoke in its wake.

The limousine came to a screeching halt, and the Strykers moved up to flank it, one of them triggering the third and final bomb, which punched a gaping hole in the crew compartment, sending burning soldiers fleeing from the back.

Hanjour signaled his men to engage the remaining soldiers and attempt to destroy the ambassador's vehicle, while he and his two bodyguards ran off toward the nearest hill, behind which they had parked his truck.

He knew every man left behind would die, but that did not bother him. The Prophet Mohammed wanted to be a martyr, and that was a worthy goal for every Muslim. They should fight and be martyred, then enjoy the riches.

In his heart, Hanjour knew it was not yet his time. He should continue to lead mortal men. As his father had once told him, "You will know when the time comes. Your mother knew."

But Hanjour's father had never had a chance to do the same. He had been killed by an assassin, and Hanjour had gone to live with his uncle, remaining in Saudi Arabia until he was eighteen and received his student visa via falsified papers, to study engineering in Florida.

Now, twenty years later, with the blood of his family still on his hands, and with an American education that allowed him to better know his enemy, he was more than ready to continue the jihad. The Americans in Afghanistan would pay the price for their aggression. God was, indeed, great.

Allahu Akbar!

6. THE WALRUS

Chief Warrant Officer 3 Karl "Walrus" Kowalski shot the first guy in the back and caught the second guy in the face as the thug was turning.

Nearly in unison, the two al-Qaeda fighters dropped to the limestone cave's rocky floor as another pair, much farther up the long tunnel, returned fire, sending the burly Walrus to his gut, the dust fanning into his eyes.

He might be in his forties and might resemble that damned bewhiskered creature that had inspired his nickname, but as God was his witness, he was not finished yet.

Walrus and the rest of ODA-558 were directly west of Kandahar, less than a kilometer from the Pakistani border. They were pursuing at least twenty al-Qaeda fighters who were using the caves to slip back and forth across the border, into the tribal lands of Pakistan. There, they had established their training and recruitment camps and were left alone by the Pakistani Army, who wouldn't enforce the government's will in those areas. To some critics, especially those in the liberal media, Walrus and his boys were fighting a losing battle.

But this time Walrus thought they had a damned good chance of disrupting the group's operations. Intelligence had indicated that at least two men in this little band were lead instructors at the camps. You can't have a school of terror without expert maniacs to train more maniacs. Remove the teachers. Shut down recruitment. Destroy the camps. It was all part of the master plan in higher's collective brain.

Walrus blinked hard, and the second the enemy's weapons went silent he sprang up and jammed down his trigger, sparks and the crackle of chipping rock echoing as his rounds sliced and ricocheted through the tunnel.

Two of his men were coming up behind him as he ceased fire, his barrel smoking, the gunpowder heavy in the air. "Snake, I want you and Scarface to hold three meters behind me," he said into the radio. "Do not get any closer, over."

"Roger that," answered Snake, one of his weapons sergeants.

Walrus took off running, crouching a little as the tunnel's ceiling dropped a quarter meter. He had a Gladius duct-taped to his rifle, beside his grenade launcher, and the light's brilliant beam peeled back the shadows.

Up ahead, the tunnel divided into two, with arrows painted on the wall, along with Arabic characters that Walrus didn't waste time translating.

He dropped to his knees, directing his light along each path. The tunnel with more dust hanging in the beam's shaft was the one he'd take.

Left was clear. Right was dusty. Bingo. He charged off, telling Snake and Scarface where he was headed. He tugged down his *shemagh*, his face already covered in sweat, and breathed in the musty air.

Walrus's father had been a tunnel rat in Vietnam, and Walrus liked to say that weeding out bad guys from confined spaces was not only part of his family's history, it was in their blood. And they paid for their ambitions with blood. Back in 1971, on an August evening so humid that you could barely breathe, his father had entered a tunnel seventy-five kilometers northwest of Saigon to hunt down a squad of Viet Cong. Sergeant Raymond Kowalski had entered that tunnel courageously, bravely, with conviction and purpose.

He did not return.

Walrus was only two when his father died. He had never known the man. But his uncle had shared everything, even the most gruesome details of what they had done to his father before they killed him.

So maybe he did this for Dad. He felt certain that his father was up there watching. Walrus would make him proud. It was simple, clean, correct. No deep psychology involved.

And it made Walrus shift even faster through the tunnel, which began to jog left and grow even narrower, his right shoulder brushing here and there along the wall.

Believing he'd heard something, he froze, hunkered down, and pricked up his ears.

Yes, there it was. A voice. Muffled. Arabic. Straight ahead.

He rose, ready to spring off, just as a tremendous explosion resounded from behind him, the shock wave punching through the tunnel, air blasting over him, nearly knocking him onto his back.

"Snake, this is Walrus, over." Though his radio call sign was an S name like theirs, "Scarecrow," his nerves got the best of him and he just used his nickname. "Snake, this is Walrus, what the hell was that?"

"Walrus, this is Scarface! Snake's dead. They blew up the tunnel! I'm trapped in here, too, over."

"I'm going for you, buddy. Hang on."

The voices ahead grew a little louder, a little less muffled.

A chill woke at the base of Walrus's spine as the realization took hold. It was a trap. They'd baited his team, led them into the caves, which they'd rigged with explosives. They were willing to destroy some of their rat lines in order to strike a victory for their twisted cause.

The team's young captain—and weren't they always oh-so-young?—was on the radio, demanding a SITREP.

Walrus ordered the rest of the team to evac the caves immediately—then he told the captain he was heading back to Snake's position.

The captain would send in two more guys.

Walrus simply told him, "No."

"Are you disobeying my order?"

"This is a *trap!* Get 'em all out!" With that Walrus turned down the volume on his radio and continued rushing back through the cave.

His light swept onto a wall of shattered rock and dirt. The entire tunnel had caved in. First thought: *It'll take forever to get him out.*

Second thought: *Get to work!*

He shoved his rifle back, the sling sliding over his shoulder, and reached out with gloved hands to begin lifting stones and throwing them back.

The voice grew even louder. Those al-Qaeda fighters were coming back to inspect their handiwork.

Walrus began digging more furiously, tossing repeated glances over his shoulder, his breath growing labored, his pulse mounting.

He pulled away several more stones then glanced back at the tunnel. Footfalls began to echo.

Indeed, the approaching men were a grenade away from killing him.

A burred voice rattled in his earpiece: "Walrus, are you coming for me, man? My leg's hurt bad. I'm pinned. Can't see anything. The air's getting thinner, I think."

"I'm coming for you, Scarface," he whispered. "But they're coming for me. Got something I need to do first."

Walrus switched off his Gladius and tucked himself into a corner near several larger stones.

He pulled up his *shemagh*, then placed a pair of grenades on the ground beside him, ready for action.

After a long breath, he leveled his rifle on the tunnel and waited.

More footfalls. Several loose stones came down from the ceiling, clattering onto others and leaving a hiss as more dirt and pebbles sifted down.

Clipped, guttural voices became distinct. The Arabs were just ahead.

He took a deep breath, held it.

Two lights appeared and began to sweep up the floor, toward him.

He would need to fire before they spotted him, but he wanted them as close as possible.

One word blared in his mind: *Wait!*

A beam panned along the floor then rose, coming within a meter.

And that's when he jammed down the trigger, sending a hailstorm of fire as the men screamed and the lights tumbled to the ground.

Just then, Walrus broke off his fire, snatched up a grenade, pulled the pin, and let her fly.

Three, two, one . . . *boom!*

The explosion flashed, blinding him momentarily, as the sound of collapsing rock and its accompanying vibration struck the tunnel hard. Smaller pieces of limestone blasted over him as he buried his head in his chest.

Yes, this was exactly what he wanted: To bury himself alive. To give himself time to dig through and reach Scarface without being harassed by those thugs.

Once the dust was beginning to settle, he switched on his Gladius, rose, and inspected the damage to the tunnel. A nice wall of rock now blocked the entire passage.

And a leg jutted out from beneath two larger stones. The leg flinched involuntarily.

Walrus turned back, ripped off the *shemagh*, set down his rifle, and began to dig.

He spent the next ten minutes moving rock, but it seemed the more pieces he moved, the more the ceiling above wanted to cave back in around him.

Out of breath and soaked with sweat, he sat, dialed up the radio. Only static now. Scarface wasn't answering.

Congratulations, you idiot, you just did yourself in. He cursed, stood, and got back to work.

Four hours later, Walrus was having a hard time breathing, and it seemed he hadn't made much progress. With each new portion of rock that he removed, the ceiling continued to collapse on his progress. No word from Scarface.

And then, just as he was finishing the last gulp of water from his canteen, he heard the shouts from the other side of the cave-in: his men.

Two hours later, back at their FOB, he showered, collapsed onto his rack, and lay there, staring at the tent's ceiling. He'd just finished giving his report to the CO, along with the captain and the team sergeant. The intel guys and another CIA field agent believed that of the four men Walrus had killed (two by rifle fire, two by rifle and grenade fire), at least one guy had been a training camp instructor.

So Snake had not died in vain. The mission had been partially successful. The tunnels would be destroyed. But the battle had hardly been won. Strike up another one for the critics.

And all Walrus could do was swear and ball his fists in frustration.

"Karl?"

Captain Paul Jacobson was leaning over Walrus's rack. He sat up. "Hey, Paul."

"Can we talk?"

The team sergeant with whom Walrus shared the tent was grabbing a bite, so they had their privacy. "Sure. What's on your mind?"

"I tried to take command of this team with an open mind. Learn what I could from you and the team sergeant, and then move on. That's what command wants me to do."

"Absolutely. I know I'm not the best teacher sometimes."

"We both have our shortcomings. Can we talk man-to-man?" The captain's baby face and bright blue eyes made it difficult to consider him any more than just a kid.

So speaking man-to-man was, in Walrus's much more experienced eyes, an impossibility.

Not that he'd say that. "Yeah, I asked what's on your mind."

"To be honest, I've been thinking about ways I can earn your respect, and the respect of the team sergeant."

"Oh, that's something that, you know, when you're new it just takes—"

"Time?"

"Yeah, yeah, you'll get to know the ropes. It's only been a few weeks."

"Unfortunately, I don't believe you."

Walrus slowly got to his feet and leveled his gaze on the captain. "I'm a little confused here."

"Karl, you and the team sergeant have been around a long time. I'll be here for twelve months. I won't ever earn your respect. Especially yours."

"That's not true. I thought we got off on a real good foot. First-name basis. You've been tight with everybody. No one's got a problem."

The captain chuckled under his breath. "Let's get real here. I need an assistant who's not going to overstep my authority. You want a captain with a little more experience. I think we can solve both of our problems *and* make the CO happy—because he owes a favor to an old friend."

"What are you talking about?"

"A transfer."

"You want to leave?"

He snorted. "No, a transfer for you."

"We lost Snake out there this morning. We're already short an operator, and now you want to get rid of me?"

"I think it's for the best. For our mutual benefit. There'll be some reorganization here anyway."

"Oh, that just puts the cherry on it, doesn't it?"

"I didn't think you'd be upset. Rumor had it you wanted off this ODA anyway."

Walrus rolled his eyes. "Where am I going? Baghdad?"

"No, you'll stay in country. Triple Nickel just lost their assistant."

"If you're talking about Bull, that was a while ago. They sent an old buddy of mine, Church, to replace him."

"I'm sorry to tell you this, but Reggie Church was killed last night."

"Aw, Jesus. What happened?"

"I don't know the details. Just KIA is what we have so far."

"Where were they?"

"Little town called Londo in the southwest, near the Helmand River."

"They're operating out of Lashkar Gah right now."

"I believe that's correct."

"So I'll be the third assistant detachment commander under their captain."

"It would seem so."

Walrus's mind began to race back and forth between the present . . . and the past. "Paul, just tell me this: Is Zulu still on that team?"

"Zulu?"

"Master Sergeant Robert Burrows. The team sergeant. He's been there forever."

"I'm not sure. Why do you ask? Is that bad?"

Walrus sighed deeply. "It's bad. Very, very bad."

7. SCARS

The two little girls, both no more than five or six, burst out of the house and clung to Zulu's legs as he fired at the two al-Qaeda gunmen roaring forward in the pickup truck.

Rounds boomed and drummed into glass and metal as sparks arced into the night. The windshield shattered and blood sprayed as the truck veered left and crashed into the nearest hut, mud bricks tumbling onto the hood. The girls shivered and screamed, gripping Zulu so tightly that he thought they'd cut off his circulation.

He'd shouted for them to say in the hut, but they hadn't listened, so he wrenched them off, screamed in Dari that he was taking them back.

Grabbing each by her tiny wrist, he dragged them to the hut, kicked open the door, and shoved them inside. "Don't come out!"

Breathing a shallow sigh of relief, he charged forward to engage the others, as the rest of the team swarmed in from the flanks.

He fired once more, keeping a few other gunmen across the street at bay. Just as he released his trigger, the hut behind him—the hut with the little girls inside—took a mortar hit and exploded, the blast wave knocking him to the dirt, rocks and burning wood raining down on him. He looked up, saw a delicate little hand covered in blood and soot.

Then everything locked up. Every muscle.

And a scream began to form in the back of his throat.

Zulu shook awake, his head snapping back, the dusty windshield orienting him to time and place. He, Pharaoh, and Borokovsky were on the road again, heading back to Londo to sniff around for clues regarding Church's death. Damn it, he'd fallen asleep.

"Zu, what the hell was that?" asked Pharaoh. "You were saying you had to get them back into the hut."

"I was just daydreaming."

"More like a nightmare. I've never heard you talk in your sleep before."

"Yeah, that's weird, huh? Maybe I need therapy," he said sarcastically.

"Maybe you do," said Borokovsky from the backseat.

"Those little boys who were throwing rocks at us?" Zulu began, turning his gaze back to Pharaoh. "I think they reminded me of a bad night. That's all."

"What happened?"

Zulu sat there, considering whether he wanted to go there or not. Then he blurted out, "You ever think about getting married?"

"Maybe someday."

He craned his neck, catching the medic's eye. "How 'bout you, Steve?"

"I was, for about a year. Then I went from the ten percent minority to the ninety percent majority."

"I hear that," said Pharaoh.

"I mean, that's pathetic," the medic went on. "A ninety percent divorce rate in Special Forces? Why don't they just come out and say it. You want this? Then don't waste your time with rings and fake promises. I don't know how the guys who are married even do it."

"Hookers and booze," Zulu quipped. "Same as us single guys."

"What about their wives?" asked Borokovsky.

"Same thing," Zulu answered with a wide grin. "Hookers and booze."

"I think every operator's got a mistress. Her name is the U.S. Army," said Pharaoh.

Zulu and Borokovsky said, "Whoa . . . ," nearly in unison, to tease the captain.

Then Zulu went on. "Me? I've never even thought about getting married. I couldn't subject a woman to that much alone time. And I'm *never* having kids. I couldn't imagine something ever happening to them. You know, that's got to be it right there. Greatest pain on Earth: a parent losing a child."

"I'm going to agree with you," said Borokovsky.

After a long moment, Pharaoh said, "Me, too."

Zulu took a deep breath and remembered the parents of those two girls. They'd been in the hut right next door to the one that had taken the mortar. Their older son, twelve, had been shot, and they were tending to him, completely distracted, unaware that their daughters had run outside.

After the firefight, they'd come to Zulu, the mother falling to Zulu's knees and wailing, the father screaming at the top of his lungs and raising a fist at Zulu.

Their little girls were dead. And their son had bled out and joined his siblings.

They would never get past the loss. Never.

And neither would Zulu. He had many scars, but two ran deeper than the others. Much deeper.

Losing those girls was one.

The other scar he would keep in check by denying it had ever happened. Better to lie to himself and feel better. At least temporarily. Yes, he knew it was eating him alive, but pretending it had never happened was the best way to move on—because you had to move on.

But every time someone mentioned Bull's name, Zulu

would grow cold, as though Bull's ghost were breathing on his neck . . .

"There's the truck," said Pharaoh.

A couple of HMMWVs, along with a Black Hawk, were positioned around the flatbed truck. All of the concrete blocks had been offloaded and inspected.

They got out and met up with Hojo and Gator, who were still hanging around, sweating like pigs and waiting for the team to finish up their inspection.

"Hey, guys," said Hojo. "You didn't come out here for us, did you?"

Zulu shook his head. "We're going back to Londo. You guys ride home with them and catch a few Zs."

"No kidding. We need it."

"The load was clean?" asked Pharaoh.

Hojo nodded. "Just blocks. Weird."

Zulu chuckled under his breath. "Yeah, it's weird when you actually find law-abiding citizens."

"Those guys were punks," said Gator, stroking his long beard in thought. "I don't trust them."

"There was one thing I noticed," Hojo said. "They had some maps in the glove box. Two of them were for Iran."

"The truck could come from Iran," said Zulu. "Doesn't mean anything."

"Well, that's all we found. Why you guys going back to Londo?"

"Just a little mopping up," Pharaoh said quickly.

Hojo got the message: Don't pry further.

"All right," said Zulu. "You monkeys get back and get cleaned up. You smell like garbage."

Gator made a face. "Just like home."

Two dusty roads later, Zulu, Pharaoh, and Borokovsky were standing along the river at the precise location where Chief Warrant Officer Church had died.

They crouched down, staring at the sun-baked mud.

The bloodstains looked more like oil now, more like the river itself, dark and unmoving.

Two of the village elders, black turbaned guys and former members of the Taliban, had come down to meet them, and Pharaoh explained that they were just making another inspection—a formality. He also asked if they would go back and put out the word to see if anyone else had information. He bribed them with the promise of cash and MREs.

No, they didn't trust the elders, but you could pay them to do some of your bidding. If you expected betrayal, you'd be all right. Zulu had taught the young captain well in that regard.

While Pharaoh took the old men back to the truck to pay them off, Zulu studied Borokovsky. The medic looked as though he would vomit any second. "Hey, Steveo, you all right, man?"

"Yeah, I'm good."

"Seriously."

The medic nodded. "Hey, Zu, you ever think about quitting?"

Zulu grinned. "Dude, you're getting me depressed. Do I think about quitting? Every time some idiot's got a gun pointed at me."

"I was looking at Church, you know, and I just—"

"Steve, what the hell you talking about? You're a Special Forces operator, for God's sake. We don't whine and think about quitting. Just get squared away and deal with it. Hey, man, it's all for our entertainment pleasure. One big circus. And we got front-row seats."

"You're right."

"I'm always right, except when I'm wrong. And when I'm wrong, that really sucks, because people get hurt. Now, you done feeling sorry for yourself?"

"Yeah. Thanks, Zu."

"Come on, tough guy. Let's go poke around town."

* * *

It took a while, but Zulu was determined to find the two little boys who had been throwing rocks at them the night before. That didn't take long, and it turned out the boys were brothers. Their parents looked on with suspicion as Zulu hunkered down and spoke to them, very slowly in Baluchi, one of the many languages of Afghanistan that he'd been studying for the past couple of years. While many of the villagers spoke Dari because they had migrated from the north, Zulu had learned that the majority of locals in the Nimroz Province did not.

"We're soldiers. We came here to take away some bad men. We came to help you get the bad men out of your village. Do you understand that?"

One little boy just looked at Zulu. The other shook his head, then said, "Every time you come, the bad men come. You bring the bad men with you."

"No, that's not true."

"If you want to help us, two of our cows are sick," said the father.

Zulu glanced to Borokovsky, who often spent as much time helping treat a village's animals as he did their people. When an entire village grew sick, you could often find the root cause in their livestock.

Ten minutes later, the medic was examining the cows as Pharaoh returned with the village elders.

"Well, no big surprises so far," said the captain. "I found a bunch of guys who saw Church. And they saw the same thing: He was running, slowed down a little, then suddenly exploded. No one saw anyone throw a grenade."

Borokovsky peeled off a pair of rubber gloves. "I've got some stuff in the truck I can leave them for these cows. I'll be right back." He jogged off.

Zulu pulled Pharaoh aside, away from the family and their livestock. "So what do you think?"

Pharaoh frowned. "I just don't know."

"Well, if he popped the grenade himself, what did he do

with the pin? They searched him. There was no pin on him."

"Was he missing one of his grenades?"

"Who knows. Sometimes I carry three, five, six, whatever I happen to have. No way to tell."

Pharaoh sighed, rubbed his temples. "When Steve's done, we're leaving."

Zulu nodded, stepped over to the little boys. "See, we'll help your cows. We're the good guys."

The one boy just stared again. The other shrugged.

Zulu crouched down, proffered his hand to both of them, but neither would take it.

"Zu, don't push."

"Shake my hand," he told the boys.

They would not.

"Zu . . ." Pharaoh warned.

"Come on, shake my hand," he urged them, raising his voice.

Their parents stepped forward, the father looking daggers.

Pharaoh's hand came down on Zulu's shoulder. "Zu, that's it. We're going back to the truck."

He rose, whirled around, and started off.

What kind of an idiot am I? he wondered. Did he really believe that making friends with these boys would balance the scales? Or was he just a fool groping for ways to ease his conscience?

8. BAD BOOTS

Two days after the night Chief Warrant Officer Church was killed, an EFP had gone off in Kabul, killing three American servicemen aboard a Stryker and two nearby private contractors at a checkpoint just outside the city.

Pharaoh was reading about the story online when Major Nurenfeld came into his tent and sat next to him.

"I think Church just killed himself," said the major.

Pharaoh nodded. "It's the only explanation."

"But the pin. That pin . . ."

"Yeah. Would've been on him—or on the ground. Nothing. Weird. Unless someone rigged up a frag to be remote-detonated."

"I was thinking the same thing. I just finished grilling Borokovsky and Grimm again. They don't know anything."

"And like I said, McDaniel and Weathers saw it themselves. Church just blew up."

The major nodded. "Well, as far as we're all concerned, he was killed by enemy fire. And that's in writing."

"Agreed."

"But, James, I don't want you to drop this. Someone's not telling you everything."

Pharaoh began tugging nervously on his beard, which had thickened over the past few months. "I don't know. I can't be looking at them and wondering. They'll pick up on that. It undermines the integrity of my team. With all due respect, I think I *need* to drop this."

The major opened his mouth, but a chorus of shouts from outside sent both of them to their feet. For a moment, Pharaoh thought they might be under attack.

And no, this wouldn't be the first time that FOB Cobra had taken fire. Two weeks prior, two insurgents had driven a small car toward the base's main checkpoint and blown the vehicle up. Just four days ago, sporadic mortar fire had come in from the garbage dump, the insurgents having set up their positions on the mountains of trash.

Pharaoh bounded out of the tent first and jogged down the row, where in an open area adjacent to the motor pool Zulu had been training a half dozen Afghani Army personnel in knife-fighting tactics. He'd been doing this voluntarily for the past month, and the soldiers really appreciated his instruction. He was teaching them Martial Blade Concepts (MBC), a four-level program developed by his friend and mentor Michael Janich, covering all aspects of employing knives and personal defense tools.

At the moment, though, Zulu was on the ground, having been dropped by another man whom Pharaoh did not recognize, a scrubby-faced operator with a Fu Manchu mustache and droopy eyes. He looked about forty-five or fifty, with blond, gray-streaked hair pulled back in a ponytail, though he was mostly bald up top.

Zulu was on his knees, his arm twisted behind his back by this stranger, whose karambit—a hooked folding knife shaped like a talon or tiger's claw—was less than an inch from Zulu's neck. However, the blade was a trainer, rounded off and with holes through its center; it could not cut Zulu.

"Get off me, Walrus!" cried Zulu.

And so Zulu knew this guy Walrus. And damn if he didn't look like one.

"I'm not kidding," Zulu added.

"What's the matter? I thought you were going to show these guys how to escape an attack—not fall victim to one."

"What's going on here?" shouted Major Nurenfeld.

"Nothing, sir. I was actually on my way to see you." Walrus suddenly released Zulu, quickly folded up his knife, and started toward the major, but Zulu, still on the ground, swung himself around and hooked his boot around the taller guy's ankle.

Walrus dropped like a drunk.

Zulu sprang up and moved in, but Pharaoh cut him off before he could get his hands on the guy. "Are you crazy?"

"He is," cried Zulu.

"Hey, just having a little fun. Zu, what happened to you? You are way too serious, bro."

Walrus got to his feet and proffered his hand to the major. "I'm Chief Warrant Officer Karl Kowalski. Most people call me Walrus, sir."

After hesitating, the major accepted Walrus's hand and said, "Well, Chief Warrant Officer Karl Kowalski, you make some entrance."

"Sorry, sir." He grinned, flashing two chipped teeth. "It's just, I know Zulu."

Zulu rubbed his sore shoulder. "I was in the middle of a demonstration." He glowered at Walrus. "What the hell's the matter with you?"

"Just having some fun. And it seems you're a knife geek who's lost his edge—bad pun intended."

Zulu was ready to retort, but Pharaoh silenced him with a look. The team sergeant rose, turned back, and waved over the Afghani Army guys, who formed a circle around him and began asking questions.

"You're James Pharaoh," said Walrus, offering his hand. "I saw you at a meeting back in Kabul."

Pharaoh shook the heavily calloused hand with a feeling of dread.

It couldn't be.

But apparently it was.

"Kowalski was cut loose to become your new assistant," explained the major.

"I know I've got some pretty big boots to fill. Dennis Bull was one of the best Special Forces operators I've ever worked with, bar none. And he was a good friend. We can only hope to be half the operator he was."

"You know I recommended him for the Medal of Honor," Pharaoh said.

"I'm aware of that."

"Well, gentlemen, I'll let you guys get better acquainted. I have a meeting with the spooks in a few minutes. Afterward, I'd like to meet with you alone, Walrus."

"Yes, sir."

They watched the major walk off.

"So how long have you known Zulu?" Pharaoh asked.

Walrus laughed under his breath, as though over some private joke. "Long time."

"Do we have a problem?"

Walrus glanced off in Zulu's direction. "I don't think so. Well, maybe."

"What's that mean?"

He shrugged. "Church was a friend of mine, too. How did he die?"

Pharaoh paused. "We're talking about Zulu."

"We'll get there."

"That's an interesting tone you have."

"Captain, I don't mean to be rude. I'm just too damned old to be subtle. What happened to Reggie?"

"He died from an enemy grenade."

"No question about it, huh?"

Pharaoh pretended to be surprised. "Yeah, of course."

"I see."

"Why . . . why are you asking that?"

"Oh, no reason. You know what they say about friendly fire. It isn't."

"What's your problem with Zulu?"

"Ah, just a clash of egos. I'm sure we'll work it out. You know, if you want, you can call my old captain, and he'll tell you about how difficult I am to work with. I think he's the one who orchestrated this little transfer. Tried to tell me our CO owed your CO a favor. That was BS. He just couldn't handle me telling him what to do."

"You're right. Subtle you ain't. I won't bother calling anyone. Our team needs you, and you and I need to be on the same page. Zulu has been an incredible team sergeant, and he's taught me a lot. He fights this team. Not me. Not you. No one else. Are we clear on that?"

Walrus smiled. "We most certainly are. But I think you may have put a little too much trust in your team sergeant. No man is infallible. Mister Knife Geek over there is just as capable as anyone else of stabbing you in the back."

"You just said you were too old to be subtle. You have something to say about Zulu, say it."

"I got nothing else, Jimmy."

"I prefer James. Or Captain."

Walrus nodded. "You mind showing me where my luxury accommodations will be? I'm sure they'll smell as good as the rest of this place."

"Okay."

As they walked back to the tents in silence, Pharaoh had an even greater appreciation for what he had lost in both of his chief warrants. He already had one loose cannon in Zulu. Now he'd have to contend with a double barrel.

At dinner that night, Pharaoh and Zulu sat together in the mess tent, while Walrus hung out with the rest of the team. Ondejko and Gator knew Walrus, as did Sullivan and

Figueroa. The talk from their table was loud and punctuated by bursts of laughter.

"That guy's quite a character," said Pharaoh.

Zulu didn't look up from his plate. "He's an ass."

Pharaoh snorted. "Why doesn't he like you?"

"That's the funny part. I don't have a clue. Last time I saw him, we were cool. Now he's got some kind of problem with me, and I don't know why."

"Well, you guys need to clear the air before we head out again."

Zulu gritted his teeth and glanced over at Walrus. "I'll give it a try."

"I was surprised he took you down."

"Whoa, you didn't see the whole thing. He comes up, interrupts me, acts all happy, reaches out to shake my hand, I reach out, and boom, next thing I know I'm on the ground, knife to my neck. That wasn't skill, just dirty pool."

"But he had you. You couldn't get out."

"Take a guess who taught him that move?"

"Well, if it's any consolation, we didn't get off on the right foot ourselves. He said something that bothered me. He asked about how Church died, and he seemed to imply that he knew something about friendly fire. It was like he had his own suspicions about who killed Church."

"He's got a big mouth is what he's got. I never knew him to stir things up like this. Maybe something's snapped with him, I don't know."

"But why would he think Church got killed by friendly fire, if he didn't know anything about the incident?"

"Who knows. Maybe he's got connections."

Pharaoh groaned, shook his head. "Maybe I'm just cursed."

"What?"

"I'm oh for two on assistants, and my number three guy is Satan himself."

"Don't worry about him. I'll take care of it."

Pharaoh stole a look at Walrus's table and accidentally caught the man's gaze.

Walrus nodded, then turned to the others, launching back into his conversation. Suddenly, the men laughed once more.

Before that laughter died back down, Rock was seated next to Zulu, pushing Zulu's tray out of the way with his own. "Uh, excuse me, but the Central Intelligence Agency has already secured this table."

"Negative," snapped Zulu. "This is a restricted area. Authorized personnel only."

"Me and my fresh intel need no authorization—or invitation." The spook dug into his green beans.

"What do you got?" asked Pharaoh.

"Well, nothing yet on why our al-Qaeda targets weren't in Londo. And that's still a huge problem."

"For you and your credibility, yeah," said Zulu.

Rock smirked. "Let me ask you something. Who's the highest value target in this entire hellhole?"

"Well, that'd be Sheikh Abu Hassan," said Pharaoh. "But he hasn't popped up his head for months. He went to the Osama Bin Laden school of keeping out of sight."

"That's where you're wrong. I've got good intel that indicates he's on the move. Might even be heading into Iran, coming right through here."

"Here we go again," moaned Zulu.

"This intel is solid."

Zulu's lip twitched. "You said that last time."

Pharaoh pointed his fork at Rock. "After that misfire in Londo, you'll have a tough time convincing higher of this."

"I doubt that. They'll move on it. That smuggler's waypoint up on the Helmand, Chahar Borjak? That's where we think he's heading before crossing the border into Iran. We can get him there. But we'll need to move tonight."

"Damn, Rock, you must be hard of hearing," said Zulu. "This is the same scenario: HVTs stopping at a village along the Helmand. Been there, done that, got burned."

"Yeah, but this intel doesn't come from my people. It comes from yours, SIGINT. Cell phone calls. And look at that." Rock raised his head at Major Nurenfeld, who had just entered the tent and approached Walrus's table. "He just got word. Better hurry and finish your meals, boys. We'll be rolling out in a few hours."

"If he's right, you get with Walrus beforehand," Pharaoh told Zulu. "Okay?"

Zulu nodded.

"Something I should know?" asked Rock.

Pharaoh widened his gaze. "No."

9. THE WALLS CAME TUMBLING DOWN

During the entire briefing by Major Nurenfeld, Zulu noted how Walrus would turn his head slightly, meet Zulu's gaze, then turn back, as though probing for something.

Afterward, outside the tent, while the others were heading off to gear up and load the SUVs, Zulu pulled Walrus aside and said, "You got something on your mind. Let's get it over with before we head out."

"I got a lot on my mind."

"Last time I saw you, we shook hands, wished each other good luck, and that was that. No bad blood. What's your problem?"

"That a lot of work?"

"Is what?"

Walrus took a step closer. "Maintaining that cocky demeanor, even when guys like us know that it's the quiet professionals who get the job done. Not the big mouths."

"Look who's talking."

"Tell me, Zu. Was he threatening to tell them? Is that why you killed him? You thought it mattered that much that you had to kill him?"

Zulu stiffened. "Excuse me?"

"Good old Reggie Church. Even his name sounds religious. Not an immoral bone in that guy's body. I guess maybe he let it slip. And maybe you got scared."

Zulu seized Walrus by the collar. "You think I killed Church?"

Walrus gripped Zulu's wrist and applied pressure. "I don't know. Did you?"

"You fool. Where is this coming from?"

"Zu . . . I know . . . *everything.* And so did Church. He was the only guy I told—because when I heard he was coming here to replace Dennis, I wanted him to have a heads-up on things."

"What things?"

"You know exactly what I'm talking about."

And deep down, Zulu did, but there was always a scintilla of doubt—and he wanted to hear it from Walrus himself. He released the guy. "I have no idea what you mean."

"Well, I guess she's partly to blame, isn't she? It takes two to tango. But how could you do that to another brother? How could you sleep with a fellow operator's wife, literally cause the breakup of their marriage, and do it all behind his back? How could you do something that low?"

Oh my God, thought Zulu with an internal gasp. *He knows. Somehow, he knows.*

"You forgot that Melissa was my sister-in-law, didn't you? You forgot all about that. What would the rest of the team think of you if I told them that you were having an affair with Dennis Bull's wife for nearly two years? That you caused the breakup of their marriage? That you might as well be pissing on his grave right now? That's the kind of man you are, Zulu. And maybe Church told you the same thing—and he got fragged for his efforts."

"I didn't kill Church. He never came to me. He never said anything. I didn't even know he was aware."

"That's your story."

"What do you want to do? Ruin my career? Is that what'll make you happy?"

Walrus steeled his voice. "Did you kill him?"

"I was with the captain when Church got fragged. He'll vouch for that."

"Means nothing. You could have paid off one of the locals to frag Church. That investigation could be interesting— special agents from Fort Belvoir running around here, poking their noses into everything, questioning you for days on end. Picture a full-blown CID investigation, with you bent over, and all those agents trying to pin the tail on the donkey."

"Walrus, you're scaring me, dude. Have you lost it? Have you finally lost it? I slept with another guy's wife. I made a huge mistake. I didn't commit murder."

"I just want two things. I want an explanation of why you did what you did. And I get to fight this team. You make Pharaoh think you're doing it, but you don't make a move without my approval. I run the show. Not you."

"Otherwise you'll tell."

"Very good. I like a monkey who pays attention."

"You want to know why I did what I did?" Zulu turned away. "You think I planned it? You think I felt good about it? She had no one. I had no one. We happened to be there. That's all it was at first."

"You plan to see her when this tour is up?"

As a matter of fact, he did, but he wouldn't admit that to this idiot. "None of your business."

"You better start explaining."

"I don't owe you anything."

"If I spill the beans, the guys won't respect you anymore. That's a fact. And if I add in this little theory I have about Church's death, well, yeah, that could put a dent in your career. At the very least, they'll transfer you out, and you've been on this team a long time. I've heard some people say that Zulu *is* Triple Nickel, which is unfortunate, because we are an ODA team, not a one-man operation."

"Who told you about me and Melissa? She'd never say anything. Never."

"That's where you're wrong. You know how some women are. They can't keep it bottled up inside. So she went to her sister."

"Your wife."

He grinned. "And my wife can't keep a secret to save her life. I found out at Bull's funeral. Ain't that ironic? And a shame."

"None of this was planned. We didn't mean to hurt anyone. Like I said, it just happened one day. I went over there to drop something off, she was alone. She hit on me first."

"And you didn't have enough self-discipline and respect to say no. You didn't care enough about your fellow operator to honor his marriage."

Zulu's eyes began to burn, and his mouth had already gone dry. "I don't know what to say. If I owe anyone an apology, it's Bull's daughters. It's too late for him now."

"That's a good idea. That'll be the third thing I want from you. Thanks for reminding me."

Zulu snorted. "Right."

"Another thing," Walrus continued. "I've written this all down in an e-mail that I sent to my wife—just in case something happens to me."

"Jesus, do you believe I'd do something like that? I've given my blood, sweat, and tears for this. We all got our weaknesses, but I am an operator above all. Maybe I'll save you the trouble and go to the guys myself, tell 'em everything. Tell 'em how you're trying to blackmail me and take charge of the team. How low is that?"

"I'll deny it, and you'll still be the lowlife cheater who can't be trusted."

"I don't believe this."

"Believe it. Zu, we don't live in reality. We live in army reality, which means those guys need to believe you're a god out there. They've trusted their lives to you. Would you want to trust your life to a liar and a cheater who undermined the hero of your team? You are the guys who saved the president of Afghanistan's life. You are part of the most famous Special Forces team in this country, maybe even in the world. What a disgrace you are . . ."

Zulu stood there, and in his mind's eye, he saw the walls of his world collapse, swallowing him in the dust cloud. He began to speak, caught himself, opened his mouth again, and finally said, "You can't say anything."

"Then you do what I say. Everything I say. You buck me, and all the dirty laundry comes out. Are we clear, Sergeant?"

"Yes, we are."

"Very well. Let's haul some ass. We have a long ride ahead of us."

Zulu's cheeks sank in nausea. He turned away and gagged.

Back in his tent, Zulu drank some water then grabbed his gear and was about to step out when Pharaoh slipped inside. "You clear the air with Walrus?"

"Yeah. We shouldn't have any problems."

"Why don't I believe you?"

"I talked to him. He's just mad at the world because Church died. They were friends, too."

"This guy knows everyone and everything."

"You can say that again."

"You want to drive?"

"I'd rather not, if you don't mind."

"All right, but the fun's about to begin. We got reports of a big storm rolling through the desert of death. Not sure what it means for us, but we're going to find out."

The wind had already picked up as they headed outside and climbed into the Pathfinder. As usual, the team was split between the two SUVs, and Rock rode along with them in the backseat, his face cast in an eerie glow from his computer.

As they pulled out of the FOB, Zulu put on his NVGs and stared out into the distance, toward the dump, where the usual two idiots sat in their beat-up old car and spoke on their cell phones. Every time vehicles left the base, these scrawny young bastards would make their reports. There wasn't anything the army could do about them except get the signals guys to trace their calls. Technically, "Fred" and "Barney," as they'd been nicknamed, weren't doing anything illegal. What signals had learned was that these guys played a sophisticated game of phone tag that became increasingly harder to trace and ultimately link back to them.

After swearing under his breath, Zulu asked Rock, "You get us any more satellite imagery I don't have here on the BFT?" He was referring to the Blue Force Tracker computer through which their own CO would feed them intel.

"Same as what I showed you earlier."

During the briefing Rock had explained that he'd been down to Chahar Borjak a few times.

The town had recently been bought by a new sheikh, a kid really, in his twenties, who went by the nickname of Dr. Lucky. His family had come into a lot of money from the drug trade. His father had actually bought him the town. He had a harem in his brand-new house, a mini palace of sorts. Higher immediately concluded that Hassan would be staying there.

Pharaoh jerked the wheel as a strong gust buffeted the SUV. "Damn, it's really blowing out there!"

"It's only going to get worse," said Rock. "Any of you guys ever been in a real sandstorm?"

"Not me," said Pharaoh. "Missed all the big ones."

"Well stay tuned, buddy. You'll be picking sand from parts of your body you didn't know you had."

Zulu sighed back into his seat. He was barely listening to the conversation now.

Walrus was seated next to Rock, arms folded over his chest, the heat of his gaze burning Zulu's neck.

"Captain, before we get to the town, I have a couple of changes to the plan we went over," Walrus began. "I've already discussed them with Zu, here, and he agrees."

Zulu was about to say something. Didn't.

"Uh, Major Nurenfeld was pretty emphatic about the way this should go down."

"I understand," said Walrus. "And we need to be emphatic about one thing: not failing this time. So here's what I have in mind . . ."

Zulu sat there and cringed as the man went on and on about their little split-team raid on the town.

And no, he wasn't fond of the new plan, but he would sit there, and nod, and tell the young captain that yes, this was the best course of action, not because it was, but because he had made a terrible mistake in a moment of weakness, and now all of them might pay for his sins.

10. THE CALM BEFORE THE SANDSTORM

The prostitute disrobing before Saeed Hanjour was much prettier than some of the others he'd had, and she seemed stunningly young in the flickering candlelight. Behind her, cobwebs spanned the walls and ceiling of the old hotel room, and the worn wooden bed creaked as Hanjour adjusted his weight and shuddered with anticipation.

He knew she'd be worth every *rial*—40,000 of them to be exact. That was a pittance, really, for such a lithe and beautiful thing.

She was one of a group of girls who had come down from Qom to satisfy Hanjour and his fellow al-Qaeda fighters. The sheikh had taken care of their every need, and Hanjour's breath began to grow shallow.

Once naked, she folded her arms across her small breasts and asked, "Can I come onto the bed?"

He nodded, and as she approached he could smell her now, clean and fresh, the scent similar to a soap his mother had used so many years ago. "How old are you?"

"Sixteen."

"And you've done this before?"

"Many times."

"Why?"

Suddenly her tone shifted from a demure little girl to a businesswoman. "Do you want to talk or have sex?"

He smiled. "I'm just curious."

"If you really want to know, my mother used to beat me, and she wanted me to marry a man twice as old as you. This is better than begging in the streets."

"Do you enjoy the work?"

"Sometimes."

"I think you will tonight."

"Maybe."

A sharp beeping came from the nightstand: Hanjour's satellite phone. He cursed under his breath and snatched up the phone. It was the sheikh. He put his finger to his lips, and the girl nodded.

"I'm in Chahar Borjak," the sheikh explained. "I should be there tomorrow."

"Tomorrow?" Hanjour's voice had cracked.

"Yes. I want to see for myself why there are so many delays. You people have promised me many things and delivered little. Maybe I can speed up production."

"Crossing the border is quite a risk. I can assure you there will be no more delays."

"I'm coming. I will see you tomorrow. I hope you will be ready for me." He ended the call.

Hanjour burst from the bed, his heart ready to explode.

"What's wrong?" the girl asked.

"He's coming here," Hanjour thought aloud. "The engineers need to get back to work! They need to work all night!" He grabbed his shirt, began putting it on.

"Are you leaving?"

"You'll stay here. I'll be back in one hour."

"If you're not, I won't wait. I have other appointments."

He grabbed her by the throat. "Stay. Or I will find you. Trust me." He shoved her back toward her pile of clothes on the floor. "Get dressed and wait."

* * *

Once Hanjour had left the room, Fatima muttered, *"Elif air ab tizak,"* which was an Arabic phrase that involved Hanjour's posterior and the application of one thousand male genitalia. She rushed to her bag and fetched her cell phone. She called the old woman Ezzat, who cared for and protected her and the other girls. "He just left to go back to the factory. He wants me to stay here."

"Do that," Ezzat said. "We'll follow him from our end. Just remember, Fatima, the people I'm working with will pay much more for the information they want than you could make in an entire year sleeping with these dogs. You must do exactly what I say. No mistakes."

"I understand."

"Good. Now I have to go and tell the others. Did he say if he was coming back?"

"In one hour."

"Wait for as long as it takes."

"Yes, Ezzat."

Pharaoh and his men were about fifteen minutes away from Chahar Borjak, running with the lights out. Sand blasted into the SUV and formed long trails off the hood as he wrestled with the wheel. The vehicle was taking a serious pummeling, with the occasional small rocks slamming into a door or ricocheting off a window, threatening to break it. "See if you can get another weather report," he cried.

"I can't reach the satellite," said Rock, typing fast on his laptop.

"Neither can I," said Zulu, doing likewise on the BFT's keyboard. "No GPS yet."

"I still have good contact with our gunship," said McDaniel from the narrow third-row seat. "But they're maintaining a very high altitude because of the storm. They don't think they can get in low enough for weapons, so they might pull off."

"No surprise there," said Walrus.

Even with the NVGs attached to Pharaoh's helmet, the road repeatedly vanished as the cloaks of dirt rose and lowered. He kept in close contact over the MBITR radio with Ondejko, who was driving the other SUV, pulling up the rear. Ondejko had it easier, since all he had to do was keep Pharaoh in his sights. But it was like the blind leading the blind. And for a few moments, Pharaoh wasn't even sure he was still on the road.

"Sounds like a freight train," said Zulu.

"If this storm doesn't let up, we might be forced to—"

"We don't want this to let up," said Walrus, cutting off Pharaoh. "This is beautiful. Helps our cover and misdirects Dr. Lucky's security guys. We're going to walk right up to his little fortress and bust down the door."

Pharaoh sighed. "You might be right, Walrus, but I'm worried about mistakes. Hard to hear over the radio. Hard to ID friendlies. Hard all around."

"That's the way we operators roll. Easy is for the other guys. We'll be okay. I got it all covered."

"You mean Zulu," Pharaoh corrected.

"Right . . ."

They rode in silence for the next ten minutes, save for Pharaoh's occasional swearing as the gusts came in and tried to push him off the road.

Soon angles began to form in all the blowing sand: rows of mud huts and even a few more modern-looking structures, along with power poles and a few vehicles parked outside—the entire scene tinted grainy green in Pharaoh's goggles.

"All right, we're getting close," he announced.

Walrus keyed his mike. "Triple Nickel, this is Tacoma. Perimeter team breaks off and parks in the northeast corner, near the last few huts." Walrus had used his new call sign for the first time. He was actually from Tacoma, Washington, thus choosing a call sign beginning with the letter "T" had been simple for him. That Zulu still insisted upon being different and going with "Zulu" annoyed Pharaoh, but he allowed the team sergeant his eccentricities because he made up for them with interest on the battlefield.

Hojo, Ondekjo, Gator, Figueroa, Sullivan, Grimm, and Weathers—"The Magnificent Seven" as Hojo had dubbed them—would establish the outer cordon around Dr. Lucky's elaborate and newly constructed house.

Meanwhile, Pharaoh, Walrus, Zulu, Borokovsky, McDaniel, and Rock were the inner cordon entry team who'd knock on the door and ask if the sheikh could come out to play.

As they drew closer to the village, gusts began delivering one-two punches to the truck, as though trying to coax them to turn back, and Pharaoh could barely keep the Pathfinder on a straight line. He thought several gusts had actually lifted the wheels. They wove haphazardly down the long road, past the scattered mud huts, to the larger beacons of light ahead.

By Afghanistan standards, Dr. Lucky's was, in fact, a palace, with two stories, ornate columns, and across the second story, large glass windows from which shone all that light piercing the dark and fluctuating clouds of sand.

"It's like Las Vegas," said Zulu as he tied his *shemagh* over his head and face. "Mo's Palace in the middle of nowhere." He and the rest of the team had already donned their Blackhawk ACE tactical goggles, and they sure as hell would need them now.

"This is where we ditch the truck, boys," said Pharaoh, turning down a narrow alley between mud huts. They'd gone over this part twice at the briefing, making sure everyone could identify each key point on a detailed satellite photograph of the town taken twenty hours earlier.

Before Pharaoh had the key out of the ignition, the men were bounding out. He flipped up his NVGs, slipped on his own goggles, and then began tying his *shemagh*.

"I can already see people on the second floor," said Rock, coming around to the driver's side. "Let me get in close for a look before we move. Maybe I can ID the sheikh."

"Sounds good, but you won't have much time," said Pharaoh as he finished with the *shemagh* and climbed out.

"I'd advise against it, Captain," said Walrus. "We can't take any chances of him being spotted. We all move in together and stick to the revised plan."

"Do you want to raid another empty house?" Rock asked. "Let me confirm. Spare us both the embarrassment."

Pharaoh turned to Zulu. "What do you think?"

Zulu tugged down his *shemagh*. "Walrus is right. We need to move fast."

Something wasn't right about Zulu's tone. Pharaoh couldn't put his finger on it, but he didn't have time to pry. He got on the radio and said, "This is Titan 06. Outer cordon team check in with Thunder when you're set. Inner cordon team, hold off for now. Rock moves in for a look through those second-story windows. Stand by."

As the outer cordon team began to sound off to Hojo, their team leader, call sign Thunder, Pharaoh cocked a thumb back at himself, then pointed at Rock: *You and me— let's go.*

Walrus raised a gloved index finger. "Don't do this. You're making a mistake."

"Get in position," Pharaoh snapped, then he waved to Rock, and they took off running.

Rock smiled beneath his own *shemagh* and jogged off, taking the lead from the young captain. They skulked along a windswept alley, completely obscured by the storm. Only a few dim lights came from the mud huts whose walls were already covered by growing drifts of sand.

A rickety wooden ladder tied to the side of a hut directly opposite the house caught Rock's attention. He went for it, mounted the ladder, and gingerly stepped onto the hut's stone roof. This was a much sturdier structure than some of the others. He and Pharaoh moved to the west side and lowered themselves onto their bellies.

Ironically, dozens of shell casings lay across the stone. This was obviously a good firing position or perhaps even a makeshift guard tower for the house.

Just then, a door creaked open below, and Pharaoh shifted over to the roof, pistol drawn. He shouted down to an unarmed old man glancing up, shielding his eyes from the sand. "Go back inside. We're friends, just here for security."

The man shook his head then, unable to take the sand in his eyes anymore, fled back inside.

Rock used a pair of high-power binoculars by Darpa, a prototype nicknamed "Luke's Binoculars," after the character Luke Skywalker in the *Star Wars* films. The binoculars had electroencephalograms (EEG) electrodes that monitored his neural signals, cueing him to recognize targets faster than his brain alone could. It was all science fiction to him, but as he removed his goggles, pressed the binoculars to his eyes, and the electrodes slid into place and began reading his signals, he immediately saw the tiny warning flashes in the display, alerting him to threats.

Several armed men were standing near the windows. He didn't need some expensive high-tech toy to realize that.

But as he zoomed in, he consciously realized what his unconscious mind had already taken into account:

That a pair of familiar men were seated on a long, leather sofa, along with three scantily clad women.

Rock rolled up the magnification.

"Got anything?" Pharaoh asked, lifting his voice above the storm.

Rock gritted his teeth. "Wait!"

And then the images grew clear. All too clear.

Oh, you're kidding me, he thought. *You guys are absolutely kidding me.*

Seated on the couch were Rock's bestest buddies— Jersey and Libra, the contacts who could no longer be contacted, the men who had fed him information regarding the botched raid in Londo.

And standing behind them, holding a glass, was the man himself, Sheikh Abu Hassan, nearly as tall as Bin Laden, though heavier and with a thinner beard that fanned out like frayed coils of electric wire. He was talking and laughing with Rock's old friends.

No, it couldn't be, could it? Had Libra and Jersey actually joined al-Qaeda?

"Rock, what do you see?" Pharaoh demanded.

"Oh, man." He groaned. "You don't want to know."

At that, the sound of automatic weapons fire boomed from somewhere behind the house.

Two more salvos answered.

And then an urgent-sounding voice crackled in Rock's earpiece. "Titan 06, this is Thunder. We've been spotted!"

Rock glanced back to the windows. The sheikh, Libra, and Jersey were already gone.

11. VANISHING ACT

Zulu, McDaniel, and Borokovsky were crouched down near the back corner of a hut directly opposite the grand entrance of Dr. Lucky's "pimped out crib," as McDaniel called it, when the shots had gone off.

Three minutes prior, Walrus had taken two of Hojo's outer cordon team men, Grimm and Ondejko, around the back of the place, working along the walls of the surrounding huts. He'd told Zulu that since Rock and Pharaoh had gone off to play cowboys and Indians that he would need a couple of extra men for the entry team. "Cowboys and Indians?" Zulu had asked. "Dude, you are really old school."

Walrus had disappeared with Grimm and Ondejko around the west side, and from their position the shots had resounded and were followed by the distinct *thump* and *rat-tat-tat* of a machine gun.

Cursing now, Zulu got on the radio. "Thunder, this is Zulu. Who's firing, over!"

"Zulu, this is Thunder. We got some guys with a fifty-cal mounted in the back of a pickup truck out here! They're hosing down the northern perimeter, just firing wildly. Got a bunch more guys coming out of the house, over."

"Roger that! Inner cordon? Move in!"

Zulu flipped down his NVGs as McDaniel and Borokovsky did likewise. They rushed toward the front of the house, where a pair of carved wooden doors were centered between four columns as thick as oak trees. Above them spanned the large, second-story windows. Zulu raised his rifle and sent a panning salvo across all that glass. They slowed as several huge shards tumbled and crashed to the dirt a few feet ahead of them.

Once they hit the front porch, McDaniel began arming his flashbang grenades and lobbing them through the broken windows while Zulu and Borokovsky covered the front door, the wind and sand blasting everywhere.

Two seconds . . . *bang!* Two more seconds . . . *bang!*

McDaniel lobbed up his last grenade, then Zulu motioned them away from the door and dropped a fragmentation grenade at its base. Walrus had the Blackhawk entry tools in his pack, and he was probably using them on the back doors.

They crouched down, near the far corner, and the front door exploded inward, sending showers of splintering wood across the floor. Before the smoke cleared, Zulu announced on the radio that he and the other guys were entering.

And just as they did, team engineer Figueroa, who was working somewhere out on the perimeter, completed the first part of his mission.

All power was cut to the house.

In went Zulu, taking point, ready to clear the first room, the Gladius attached to his SCAR-H rifle casting a brilliant strobe light into a fancy entrance foyer with expensive tile and twin staircases heading up to the second story.

Muzzles flashed from somewhere above, but before Zulu could even look up, McDaniel fired two bursts and dropped a pair of gunmen, one of whom came tumbling over the railing and hit the floor not a meter from Zulu's boots.

At the same time, Walrus and his two guys charged into a large kitchen area in the back. "Clear here," the old warrant cried.

Zulu signaled for Borokovsky and McDaniel to head upstairs with him.

Breathing hard into his *shemagh*, and with every nerve ending tingling, Zulu mounted the stairs and led them up as the sand blasted in through the shattered front door and continued whipping through the house.

Suddenly, a gunman appeared at the top of the staircase, his movements slowing in Zulu's strobe light. He was already blinded by the flashbang grenades and coughing hard, but he managed a quick glance through burning eyes at Zulu and raised his rifle.

Before Zulu could react, McDaniel was at his side, delivering a three-round burst that drummed the guy to the floor.

What Zulu should have said to the young commo guy was "thanks"; instead he reacted instinctively: "Jesus, can I get off a shot myself?"

But McDaniel failed to answer. He probably hadn't even heard Zulu.

They continued up the steps, reached the landing, and shifted down a long hall toward a pair of doors hanging ajar. Those led to the entertainment room where they'd seen people from outside. Waves of smoke escaped from between the doors. Tensing, keeping close to the wall, Zulu led the others forward, his trigger finger aching.

Assistant Operations Sergeant Michael "Hojo" Johnson came in from behind the meathead manning the .50-caliber machine gun. The pickup's driver had rolled up alongside two huts, and despite the heavy wind, the gunner, who wore a black turban and a pair of goggles, continued to fire recklessly toward where he thought two of Hojo's men were hiding behind the four-foot-high brick wall of an empty livestock pen.

What the gunner didn't realize was that the men he and his buddy sought were close. Very close.

Right behind them.

And Hojo was exactly three heartbeats away from making them realize their fatal mistake.

Crouched over, he and Figueroa reached the back of the truck, and just as Figueroa tossed a grenade into the flatbed, Hojo opened fire on the driver, turning his door into Swiss cheese a second before—

They turned and ran as the grenade went off behind them with a solid bang, sending them both to the sand.

The .50-caliber ammunition box that had been sitting beneath the gunner began cooking off a second later, shots pinging into the shattered bed, the entire vehicle lost behind a thick chute of fire.

Hojo smiled at the noise.

Then he looked up. "Aw, no."

Behind the truck in the distance, multiple pairs of headlights glowed like UFOs navigating through the sand. He got out his binoculars as Figueroa continued to cover the area behind them. "I see lights," he cried.

"Yeah," said Hojo, zooming in.

Great. They had more pickup trucks loaded with heavily armed militants on the way. He counted four.

Dr. Lucky, it seemed, had lots of friends, smugglers no doubt, who were at his beck and call.

"Come on," he told Figueroa. "We're running out of time on this target. I hope the captain knows that."

Pharaoh hadn't been able to catch up with Rock. The spook had suddenly rushed off the roof and headed down to sprint for the house, with Pharaoh hollering after him.

Now Pharaoh was shifting over the shattered front door, rifle at the ready. He'd alerted Walrus that he was moving in, and just as he was about to head upstairs, in search of Rock, Hojo gave him bad news over the radio. At least twenty bad guys in four vehicles en route, ETA: less than five minutes. Pharaoh responded immediately by addressing everyone:

"All right, this is Titan 06, listen up. You heard Thunder. Those guys will be here soon. Typhoon, see if our gunship is still available to get on those trucks. And you also report stragglers. Tacoma, SITREP?"

"Titan 06, this is Tacoma," began Walrus. "We've rounded up four detainees, including the young sheikh we think is Dr. Lucky. No Hassan, though. He pulled some kind of a vanishing act. Got these guys out back, but now we have three, maybe four snipers on the roofs out there, northwest side, in the huts along the river, and they're taking potshots at us. Killed one of our detainees already, over."

"Titan 06, this is Typhoon," interrupted McDaniel. "No go on the gunship, over."

Pharaoh cursed. It was all going to hell. Their high value target was gone.

Again.

And now they were under attack without backup.

"All right, Tarzan and Tomahawk, I want you guys to get some 240s between us and those trucks," he told the pair of engineers. "I have an idea."

Zulu had finished clearing the entertainment room. He was going to fire off some orders to set up a defense against those oncoming trucks, but Pharaoh beat him to the punch, which was just as well because at that very moment a shadow passed near the doorway, and Zulu swung around, rushed to the door, and jammed his rifle point-blank into a man's face.

It took just another second for Zulu to recognize Rock beneath his goggles and lowered *shemagh*. "Dude, I almost shot you!"

"Almost is good. Is the room clear?"

"Clear."

The spook cursed and hustled off, back toward the stairs.

"What's wrong? Where you going?"

He didn't answer.

"Zulu, this is Walrus, over."

Zulu winced. "Go ahead, Walrus."

"Get to the damned window and help us out with these snipers, over."

"Roger that."

But before he did that, he got back on the radio to call Gator and Ondejko, told them to get on the roof with their sniper rifles to see if they could find the shooters harassing Walrus. Then he called out to the engineers, asked for a SITREP to see if they were set to intercept the oncoming trucks, per the captain's orders.

"We're good, but fat ass Tomahawk broke the ladder on his way up, over."

"Just get set!"

Only then did Zulu move to the window, hunker down, and observe a muzzle flash in the distance near a mud hut.

The damned windowsill exploded into dozens of pieces, sending him flying onto his back.

He cursed, rolled up, and switched grips on his SCAR-H rifle to the EGLM (enhanced grenade launcher module) attached beneath the main barrel.

Just as another shot cracked below, he took aim, and hollering a long string of expletives, he put a 40mm period on the end of that sentence. *Thump!* Off arced the grenade . . .

It exploded on a rooftop with twin thunderclaps, but the wind and sand robbed Zulu of appreciating the explosion.

Not ten seconds after the detonation, more enemy sniper fire chewed into the outer walls.

"T-Rex, this is Zulu, over."

"Go ahead, Zu."

"You up top yet, man?"

"Just getting ready."

"I can't see jack from here. Snipers are still out there."

"Not for long, bro. Not for long."

Figueroa knew that the second he and Sullivan opened fire with their machine guns at the oncoming trucks, they'd turn into magnets for enemy fire.

So he came up with a little surprise for the fighters below.

Since he and Gator had positioned themselves on the very roof where Pharaoh and Rock had been, one that gave them full view of the yard in front of the house, he decided that they'd wait until the lead truck neared the yard so they could take full advantage of that operational space.

As Hojo had initially indicated, there were four pickups in all, and once the lead truck bounced forward after hitting a deep rut, Figueroa gave Sullivan the high sign, and they both double-teamed that truck, delivering so much 7.62mm fire on target that the entire vehicle burst into flames, sending the driver and several militants in the back arcing into the sky, their burning bodies flickering like fireworks.

Of course, seeing their comrades explode sent the guys in the other three trucks leaping out and directing their fire at Figueroa and Sullivan, who were already leaping down from the roof, hitting a sand pile that rose like a snowdrift behind the house.

Meanwhile, Hojo, recently recruited for their little plan, began hurling grenades at the remaining trucks as they screeched to a halt.

And that sent the fighters whirling back toward him, crouching down beside their trucks to fire.

Figueroa sprinted along the mud huts, coming around

the pickup trucks from the west side, with Sullivan right behind him. Having left their big 240s up on the roof, they now had their SCAR-Ls ready for business.

Keeping low to the walls, they drew up on the row of pickups as the guys continued taking shots at Hojo.

Just as Figueroa dropped to his gut and began firing at two guys huddled behind the second truck, the third and fourth trucks suddenly took off, heading toward the back of the house. Figueroa shouted to Sullivan, "Call Zulu and tell him!"

The two guys firing from behind the second truck were dead now, but a third was screaming and running right toward Figueroa, his AK-47 blazing.

Figueroa rolled onto his side, out of the guy's bead, and squeezed his trigger, but not before several pings hit his helmet, knocking his head to the left.

And in that terrible moment, he knew he'd been shot. "Sully, get 'em!" he cried.

12. LUCKIEST MAN ON EARTH

Staff Sergeant Larry Sullivan knew that if he didn't drop the oncoming fighter, Figueroa would be dead.

Jonathan Figueroa was a longtime friend from boot camp and a fellow engineer who had taught Sullivan more about combat operations in the last twelve months than Sullivan had learned in his entire career in the army.

Figueroa was a hard-drinking, short-tempered operator, but Sullivan got along with him because he was always the easygoing, less emotional, and more logical of the two, which made him a natural for his favorite game: sudoku.

That Figueroa initially teased him about his obsession with the game was understandable. After a while, the guy had accepted Sullivan's thick sudoku books and electronic versions of the game as though they were just field manuals or Nintendo DSs lying around their bunks.

Neither of them was married and they figured they'd remain single—unless they got hurt and discharged. Trouble was, hookers were getting more expensive, no matter where they went. One smart-ass prostitute in the Philippines had said her rates were tied in to the price of crude oil.

"What does oil have to do with your rates?" Sullivan asked her.

"You're an American," she told him. "You should know that already."

"Oh, yeah," he'd said, pretending she hadn't stumped him.

Only weeks later did Sullivan learn that he'd been "Punk'd." Figueroa had put the girl up to it, and she had taken the extra money she had collected from him and given it to Figueroa, who'd cut some other deal with her to keep her "honest."

Yes, they were the two musketeers, wiring stuff to blow and taking names, both on an express route to Hell with a connection in Atlanta, as they liked to say. That's the way they rolled. And if you didn't like that, then you'd best clear the area, because the fire was most definitely in the hole.

And now, barely able to see through his sand-filled goggles, it was up to Sullivan to save his best friend's life.

All he could do was open fire, empty his entire damned magazine if he had to, so long as Figueroa had time to get out of the guy's bead.

Yet something else quite unexpected happened that sent Sullivan diving face-first into the dirt:

A grenade exploded at the bad guy's feet, shredding him with exquisite efficiency before he could fire again.

And just as the smoke began billowing hard and fast in all the wind, Hojo appeared, a silhouette in goggles and *shemagh*, running past the torn, wet remains of the fighter and dropping down beside Figueroa.

Sullivan burst to his feet and joined Hojo. He didn't realize he'd stopped breathing until he arrived beside his friend. "Jon? Jon, you all right?"

"Oh my God, dude, look at that," said Hojo, tracing his finger over Figueroa's half-head ballistic helmet, where a round had penetrated the front, dug in a few centimeters, then emerged about four inches higher—without penetrat-

ing all the way through. The round had come in at a remarkable and life-preserving angle.

"Who's the luckiest man on Earth?" asked Sullivan.
"Dude, you are!"

"What happened?"

"We'll show you later," said Hojo. "Sully, help me get
him up."

They hauled Figueroa to his feet as a sudden booming
of gunfire rose from behind the house and Walrus began
yapping over the radio.

In a near panic, Rock was tearing through the house, looking for anything: tunnels, secret passageways, any avenue
of escape for Libra, Jersey, and Sheikh Abu Hassan.

Somehow, someway, his former colleagues and the most
wanted man in all of Afghanistan had slipped through
their fingers.

There'd be more than hell to pay.

He went back into the kitchen, opened up all the cabinets, jammed his knife into the backs, probing for doors—
as rounds suddenly tore through the back window, sending
him ducking for cover.

Back up on his hands and knees, he keyed his mike.
"Titan 06, this is Rock. Do you have the situation con-
trolled out there or what?"

No response. But Pharaoh was on the channel now, ex-
changing curt reports with Walrus and Zulu.

Rock went to the back living room, where Borokovsky
and Weathers had the remaining detainees lined up on the
floor, all sitting cross-legged, their hands bound behind
their backs with zipper cuffs.

Having dealt with Dr. Lucky before, Rock moved to the
young sheikh and cried, "Where are they?"

Automatic weapons fire ripped through the windows,
sending showers of glass across the room as Rock flinched

and the detainees began screaming and leaning forward, the glass tumbling over them.

As the guys outside returned fire, Rock screamed his question again.

"What are you talking about?" asked Dr. Lucky, wearing a smirk. He'd been educated in California, and his English was quite good but not quite as honed as his attitude.

"I saw them. They're still here, aren't they?"

The kid began to laugh. "As the lieutenant colonel likes to say, this is my house, but this is his ground. And when he finds out how you've treated me, he will not be happy."

Rock cursed and seized the punk by the neck. "Where are they?"

Borokovsky grabbed Rock's wrist. "Don't cross the line, Rock. We're taking them back anyway."

"Let me go." The sheikh groaned.

Gritting his teeth, Rock squeezed the sheikh's neck once more then shoved him back.

Hassan panted, bared his teeth. "You'll pay for that."

"You might have the battalion commander in your pocket, but you got me breathing down your neck. And that won't stop. Not ever."

The sheikh exaggerated a shudder. "I just got a chill."

"You'll get a bullet in your head when I'm done with you."

"I thought we were friends, Rock. We've done a lot of business together."

"Is that it? If I pay you off you'll talk?"

"Not this time, my old friend. You could never pay me enough. In some ways, I'm sorry. In others, well, I think your time here in Afghanistan is finished."

Ondejko and Gator were on the house's flat roof, propped up on their elbows and leaning over the small, concrete ledge with their SCAR-H Sniper Variant (SV) rifles.

They were close to each other and could talk without mikes.

After shifting his aim toward the last muzzle flash coming from the collection of huts directly ahead, Ondejko stared through his scope, with his breath held, scanning for the target.

Oh, yeah, there he was, a little guy lying on his belly across a thatched-roof hut. That was a nice piece he had, too. Looked like a Dragunov.

"I got one sighted," said Gator.

Ondejko smiled. "Mine's lying on his side, thatched roof. You don't got the same guy, do you?"

"Nah. Mine's on a tin roof."

"Let's go on three. You got him?"

"Yep. Waiting on you."

"One, two . . ."

With all the wind and sand still blowing, there was a sizable chance their shots would miss, but Ondejko had worked in similar conditions before. In fact some of his best instructors had deliberately taken them out in the worst weather imaginable to demonstrate how the wind and rain affected their shots.

And so, with hundreds of hours of that kind of training under his belt, he squeezed his trigger.

Both of their rifles brought a tremendous booming to the village, and Ondejko watched as his guy blew apart, limbs hurtling end over end.

"Got mine," he cried.

Gator cursed. "Wait, wait . . . He jumped down, he's running, I got him!"

Boom!

The hoot coming from Ondejko's buddy told him enough. Three shots, two kills. Not bad. "All right, keep scanning. Let's see if they're taking us on or bugging out."

* * *

Zulu tilted his grenade launcher to the right, exposing the breach. He shoved another shell home. Turning back to the window, he aimed down ahead of the pickup truck roaring past the house.

Wait, wait, fire!

The grenade shot forward and hit the ground. The truck rolled over it.

Even Zulu couldn't believe his lucky timing as the round exploded, heaving the truck several feet into the air, shattering all the windows and sending flames licking up from beneath both sides of the hood.

Two guys who'd been riding in the flatbed and firing at the house were blown out of the back and hit the ground, probably pincushions for shrapnel, but Zulu couldn't tell from his vantage point. One rolled over but remained down. The other was lying on his back, dead or unconscious.

Walrus, who was below, ran out in the open and put three rounds in each to be sure.

Pharaoh's voice broke into Zulu's earpiece: "This is Titan 06. We got one more pickup left, but he's heading down toward the river, over."

"Titan 06, this is T-Rex," called Ondejko from the roof. "We see your truck. Tombstone and I will take care of him from here, over."

"Roger that."

"Titan 06, this is Tacoma. Still have at least five or six guys back here behind the huts taking shots at us. We're pinned down pretty good. We need to move in there and take them out, otherwise I can't move the detainees to the trucks, over."

"Titan 06, this is Zulu. I'm coming down. Tacoma and I will flank those guys behind those huts, over."

"Roger that."

"Titan 06, this is Tacoma. I suggest you get up to the roof with T-Rex and Tombstone to observe from there, over."

Zulu snorted. Walrus was now telling the captain what

to do and turning him into a bystander, which was what he always did. He never allowed his captains to do anything, and he always got with his team sergeants to ensure that.

Zulu had a different philosophy. Let the captain fight. Teach him everything. Make him an ally.

Pharaoh, who probably didn't want to make waves—given the urgency of the moment—just responded affirmatively.

Zulu whirled away from the window, ran out of the entertainment room, and bounded down the stairs. He jogged over the front doors and met up with Walrus on the left side of the house.

"Screwed this pooch pretty good, didn't we," said Walrus. "The kid should've listened to me and not the spook."

"Who fired the first shots? Them or us?" Zulu asked accusingly. "Sounded like us."

"You think I fired the shots?"

"You didn't get to play it the way you wanted it. Maybe you wanted to speed things up. You must've said 'time on target' a hundred times."

"You think I fired to spite them? Man, you are so lost." Walrus gave him a black look, then motioned him on.

The sporadic rifle was coming from their right, and they ran down a long, sand-swept row between three huts, then came up behind two individuals crouched near the corners of the huts, one firing at the left side of the house, the other the right.

Still more fire came farther up the row, and Zulu knew that if they took out these guys quietly they'd have a better chance of nailing the rest. A loud, sloppy takedown would most certainly send the others running.

He gave Walrus hand signals: He'd take the guy on the right.

Walrus had already slung his rifle around and had a thin wire garrote extended between his gloved hands.

As much as Zulu now hated the guy, he had to admit he was a smart operator, a mind reader even.

They moved in.

Zulu might have given his first and most precious Jani-Song knife to Pharaoh, but there were more where those came from, and his friend Mike Janich had personally shipped him a new one. He flipped out the blade and inner handle and did a lightning-fast up-down-up opening, locking the blade in place. Though similar to a Filipino balisong or butterfly knife, the Jani-Song was safer and more practical for Special Forces ops. The satin-finished D2 blade didn't reflect much light, either.

Silently coming up behind the gunman, Zulu reached around, cupped his mouth in one gloved hand, then sliced open the guy's neck with the other.

As expected, the guy didn't fire but dropped his rifle in an attempt to get Zulu's hand off his mouth—but the blade across his neck made him realize that was a fatal error.

One more kill shot to the spinal column finished him. Zulu let him drop.

But then a glance over at Walrus stole Zulu's breath away.

The old warrant was in a hand-to-hand death grip with his guy, who had apparently heard his approach and gotten his hands around the garrote before Walrus could slip it in place.

The guy had wriggled himself around, still holding the garrote, and was about to shove Walrus back, it seemed, so that he could reach down with one hand for a pistol holstered at his hip.

And for an agonizing moment, Zulu wondered what would happen if he picked up his own enemy soldier's rifle, which was lying right behind the guy. Zulu could take care of two problems at once.

13. BITE THE BULLET

"All right, there he is," Ondejko announced to Gator as he sighted the truck bouncing over the road. But then blowing sand erased the green image in his scope. "Lost him. You got him?"

Gator hesitated, then cried, "Got him."

Ondejko set his teeth and took a long breath, raising the rifle slightly to adjust his aim—just as the blurriness faded into a more distinct image of the pickup. "I'll take the driver. I shoot first. Ready?"

"Ready . . ."

With that Ondejko fired, and a heartbeat later, the driver's head exploded, just as Gator's shot came like an echo and blew a gaping hole in the truck's side panel, taking out a rear tire. The truck slowed, veered to the right, then crashed head-on into a hut, where it stopped beneath the tumbling bricks and began to leak fluids, sans any dramatic explosion.

Ondejko lowered his rifle and leaned over, laughing with relief as he gave Gator a high-five.

"Sorry I missed that earlier shot."

Ondejko raised his brows. "It's the hits that count."

Captain Pharaoh, who has crouched down beside them, lowered his binoculars and crawled over. "Beautiful shot. Just awesome, man!"

"Thank you, sir!" Ondejko turned back to the huts below. "Looks clear now."

Pharaoh got on the radio. "Get those detainees to the trucks. Use the southeast street."

Walrus looked at Zulu, and something in Zulu's gaze seemed wrong. Very wrong.

In fact, for just a second Zulu looked toward the bad guy's gun, as if he wanted to pick it up and satisfy multiple accounts in one fell swoop.

Realizing that he might very well be alone in this moment, Walrus mustered all of his anger.

And, screaming at the top of his lungs, he swung his guy around and suddenly released the garrote, sending the thug flying.

As Walrus reached back to swing around his rifle, the guy hit the ground, rolled, and was reaching for his pistol, while Zulu reached for his.

For a split-second, Walrus wasn't sure who to shoot first. Then he took aim.

Zulu's gaze switched from the bad guy to Walrus. Why was the warrant shifting his weapon away?

In the span of a second, Zulu had his hand wrapped around his gun.

In the next second he had it out.

And before the next second rolled around, he shot the thug in the head, and with a loud gasp Walrus flinched and shoved the man away.

With the gunfire still ringing in their ears, Zulu went

right up to Walrus, who was standing there, caught in the headlights of the moment. Zulu had both hands on his weapon and aimed it at Walrus's head. "You were a little slow there, buddy."

"So were you. And if you're going to shoot me now, why don't you do it with his weapon, not yours. You'll never learn to cover your tracks, will you? And you call yourself a Special Forces operator? Jesus . . ."

Abruptly, Zulu lowered his pistol. "Am I saving your life so you can ruin mine?"

"You did that to yourself."

"Why don't you just get off my back?"

"Because there's a ghost whispering in my ear, telling me to do what I have to do."

Zulu just shook his head in disbelief.

"Well, I bet we just lost the last two guys with your shot. You want to talk or try to catch them?"

The old warrant sprinted away from the hut, and Zulu fell in behind him, still pumping with adrenaline and aching to shoot the fool in the back.

Walrus's arrogance knew no bounds, and Zulu wondered how long he could control himself.

And maybe that's just what the guy wanted. He was chumming the waters, trying to draw out the worst in Zulu.

Rock took Dr. Lucky by the back of the neck and practically threw him into the Pathfinder, along with two others from Lucky's little band of smugglers and whoremongers.

The storm was beginning to subside, and for a few moments here and there, the stars shone through the mottled canopy. Rock coughed and raised his *shemagh*, leaving Weathers and McDaniel with the detainees.

He charged back to the house for one last look.

There just had to be some carefully hidden escape route or hiding place within the building. There was no way in hell that Hassan, Jersey, and Libra had just waltzed out of the house within seconds and not been seen.

Inside, Rock raced up the stairs, went through two small bedrooms, then a larger one. He pushed furniture out of the way, checked under the bed with his light. Nothing.

Back in the kitchen, he checked the walls and cabinets once more, then swore and stood there, his heart and thoughts racing.

You're here. You're right under my feet somewhere, you bastards. I know it.

He cursed, beat a fist into his palm, spun around, picked up a glass on the counter, and hurled it across the room; then he charged outside, to the smaller hut serving as the outhouse. There was a toilet in the room, but it led only to a deep hole in the ground (no plumbing), and the place absolutely reeked. Rock took one more look, then started back for the main house.

Gunfire tore into the dirt at Zulu's feet. He dove to the ground, realized the fire originated from the roof of a hut to their left.

Blindly, he returned fire and heard Walrus doing the same, though he wasn't sure exactly where the warrant was until he rolled onto his side and saw him there, lying on his side, rifle blazing as rounds ripped into the cement behind him.

Zulu craned his neck as something heavy came down on the back of his head.

Pharaoh jumped down from the rooftop and ran over to the house, where he found Rock in one of the back bedrooms, knocking over a bookcase loaded with hundreds of DVDs, probably bought on the black market. "We're out of time."

"I know."

"The battalion commander's going to send in a site exploitation team. If you're looking for something, those guys will find it. We don't have time now."

"I'm telling you, I saw them. They were here."

"I believe you. But they're gone. Hell, they got out within the first couple minutes."

"No."

"Look, we had no gunship. That's the way it goes. Come on . . ." Pharaoh spoke into his mike. "This is Titan 06. Everybody rally back on the trucks. We are out of here!"

Hojo, Figueroa, and Sullivan were running along a narrow alley when Figueroa caught sight of a muzzle flash somewhere ahead and dove into a sand drift for cover.

Hojo and Sullivan were right behind him, Hojo already returning fire.

"Damn, the truck's right around the corner, and this fool's got us pinned here," said Sullivan.

"Hojo, I owe you one. Let me go around, get him from behind . . ." said Figueroa.

"We'll keep him busy here," said Hojo. "Be careful."

"Dude . . ." said Figueroa with mock surprise as he tapped on his bullet-scarred helmet. "On three. One, two . . ."

Just as he barked the last number, Hojo and Sullivan opened fire, delivering a vicious barrage of steel that left the thug crouching behind the corner for cover.

Figueroa bolted back down the narrow alley, came around the first mud brick hut, then hung a sharp right turn, running directly into an old man waving his arms, knocking him onto his rump.

The old guy was as surprised as Figueroa, and all ninety-eight pounds of him went skidding across the dirt.

"Get back in your house," Figueroa ordered him in Dari, shouting against the *shemagh* concealing his identity.

"No, my son!"

"Get back to your house!"

Figueroa rose and took off.

Hojo and Sullivan ceased fire from the next alley over.

Figueroa spotted the bad guy ducking back into the alley, moving now to get in behind Hojo and Sullivan.

But the bad guy didn't realize that Figueroa had already moved in behind him.

And just as the guy turned his head, Figueroa fired, kicking the guy up for a second, then pounding him onto his back, his chest riddled with rounds.

A shuffling of feet came from behind Figueroa, and he spun to spot the old man, who didn't even look at him. He raced forward, toward the thug, and dropped to his hands and knees, screaming, "My son! My son!"

Shuddering with adrenaline and confused, Figueroa screamed, "What the hell was he doing out here? Did he work for Dr. Lucky? Why was he firing at us!"

The old man ignored Figueroa and took his son into his arms, the wind swirling around them.

Figueroa got back on the radio and called Hojo: "Thunder, this is Tarzan. Alley is clear. The guy's down, but I'm not sure if he was working for Lucky or not. Got an old man who claims to be his father out here, over."

"Roger that. Just get the hell out of there. We'll meet you at the truck, out."

"I'm sorry," screamed Figueroa over the wind. "I'm sorry!"

The old man just looked at him with tear-filled eyes and shook his fist.

Cursing away his guilt and frustration, Figueroa spun around and ran off.

Pharaoh and Rock reached their truck, and Pharaoh got Hojo on the radio to make sure everyone was present and accounted for.

"We're good to go here, over."

"We're still waiting on Zulu and Walrus," Pharaoh told

the assistant ops sergeant. "But I want you out of there. Get moving now."

"Roger that, I'm out."

Pharaoh sighed and shifted closer to the Pathfinder to stay out of the wind. "Zulu, this is Titan 06, over."

Static.

"Tacoma, this is Titan 06, over."

He waited, swore, then turned back for the truck. "Borokovsky? McDaniel? Get out! We're going back to find Walrus and Zulu."

Someone dabbed the sweat from Zulu's brow with a cloth. He flickered open his gaze and saw Melissa leaning over him, smiling. "They hit you pretty hard."

"Where am I?"

"You're home. With me."

"What happened?"

She frowned. "What do you mean, *what happened*? You've been running a fever since this morning. Guess that flu shot didn't work." She went to the window. "It's snowing again."

He bolted up in the bed, felt a wave of dizziness and nausea pass through him, and was forced to lie back down. "I was in the 'Stan. We were raiding a village. I think someone hit me on the head."

"Oh, that one again. I thought you worked that out with the therapist. We'll schedule you another appointment. Don't worry, sweetheart." She sat on the bed and placed a hand on his cheek.

He reached up for her hand, realized his long beard was gone, then shifted the hand farther up to his head. His hippie locks were gone. He sported a crew cut.

"No, we can't be together. Ever. It's wrong. You're Dennis's wife."

"Bobby, Dennis died over fifteen years ago. What are you talking about?"

"What are you talking about? What happened to me?"

"I'm going to call Dr. Roberto right away," she said, rising from the bed.

"No, don't go."

"I can't . . ." she stammered. "I can't do this anymore, Bobby. It's too much. You always say bite the bullet, but I'm not a good caregiver."

"I'm sorry."

"I think this is the best for both of us." She crossed around the bed, reached into a nightstand, and produced his Special Forces pistol.

"Melissa, what the—"

She raised the gun. The muzzle flashed. The bullet penetrated his skull and knocked him hard into the pillow.

He gaped at her as she began crying, tossed the gun to the floor.

The shot echoed away, and suddenly he was thumping up and down, his stomach aching, head raging, back straining, until he realized that he was, in fact, being carried across someone else's back.

And the horribly familiar voice came: "This doesn't make us even, Zu. You got that? I should've left you back there."

Zulu craned his head, stole a look up, saw that Walrus was carrying him down another alley between the huts. Gunfire ripped across the walls. Walrus cursed and double-timed even faster.

"You're going to turn over a new leaf." Walrus grunted. "You're going on a diet this year."

Zulu opened his mouth, but he could barely speak.

Walrus continued. "I don't know how much farther I can . . ."

And with that he dropped to the ground, and Zulu went tumbling off his shoulder.

A fresh spate of gunfire came in, and Zulu rolled onto his stomach, looked up, saw a wall ahead, and began to crawl toward it, as Walrus returned fire.

14. NO LUCK AT ALL

Hearing Walrus's voice over the radio struck Pharaoh with relief, but two sentences later, that relief turned to an urgency coursing through him like electricity.

He, Borokovsky, and McDaniel sprinted in a line past several fences nearly buried in sand. They turned left, toward the sound of the gunfire, then kept low near the huts.

McDaniel, who had taken point, raised his fist, and they settled down near a corner.

With hand signals the commo guy indicated that there were two men on the roof of a hut around the corner.

From what Pharaoh could gather, Zulu and Walrus were at the far end of the street, keeping low near a wall but trapped there. If they rose to bolt, the two gunmen would have them clearly in their sights. And those thugs let them know that with sporadic fire that echoed into the howling wind.

Pharaoh sent Borokovsky around the corner after Walrus and Zulu, wanting the medic to be out there first since Walrus had reported that Zulu was injured, though the warrant had not been clear regarding the extent of the injuries.

McDaniel pointed toward an old cart parked beside one of the huts. They could use it to scale that hut, reach the roof, and perhaps have a level firing position on the bad guys. Pharaoh nodded, and they rushed off.

Once at the cart, McDaniel went up first, then he reached down and helped Pharaoh to the top.

While the worst part of the sandstorm was over, occasional gusts swept in, and a particularly strong one nearly knocked Pharaoh off his feet, the sand crackling across his goggles.

He dropped down to his hands and knees, and crawled up near McDaniel, who had already flipped down his NVGs. "I see them, Captain. But they're in a nest, sandbags, the whole nine. It'll be hard to get a bead on them."

"Well, we're not sitting around till they leave."

"It's a pretty far throw, but I played a lot of ball in high school. Third base."

Pharaoh grinned. He had first met McDaniel back at the JFK Special Warfare Center and School, Fort Bragg. They'd hit it off pretty well, so when both of them were assigned to the same team, there was some concern from Bull and Zulu that Pharaoh would show favoritism—but he had allayed those concerns. He rode McDaniel as hard as anyone else.

And the commo guy, although hardly the most experienced staff sergeant of the group, was a professional whose even temperament had a calming effect on Pharaoh.

"Third baseman, huh?" asked Pharaoh, surveying the two men through his own pair of binoculars. "Well, let's see what you got. You frag 'em, I'll fire."

McDaniel rolled back and fished out a fragmentation grenade, while Pharaoh moved forward into a firing position, elbows propped, the small wall of sandbags in sight.

After McDaniel flashed a thumbs-up, Pharaoh turned away from his gun sight and keyed his microphone. "Walrus, this is Titan 06, over."

"Go ahead, Titan."

"Triage should be there, over."

"He is."

"How's Zulu?"

"Banged on the head, but okay."

"Could've told me that earlier. Listen up. When you hear the frag, get out of there. Back to the trucks."

"Roger that."

Pharaoh craned his neck. "All right, Rudy. Ground ball to third base."

McDaniel pulled the pin, wound up, and with a slight groan made his toss. The grenade arced into the darkness . . .

The gunman behind the sandbags barely heard the metallic *thump* behind him.

But he did, indeed, hear something.

So he turned his head, straining against the sand blasting into his eyes . . . and saw the grenade.

His mouth dropped open.

He had one thought: *I'm dead.*

Then, in the next moment, every part of his body grew stiff with utter fear as the frag detonated, bursting his eardrums and sending a thousand points of pain rocking through his body.

Pharaoh nearly lost his aim as the first guy blew apart, pieces of him tumbling over the side of the hut. The second guy, who had been positioned near the back of the roof, along the far edge of the bags, staggered to his feet, having been torn up by shrapnel, no doubt.

Pharaoh delivered two salvos that knocked him off the ledge to join his friend.

McDaniel began hooting and hollering, laughing with relief. "The runner at first is out!"

"Hooah!" shouted Pharaoh, getting back on the radio. "Walrus, you better be moving!"

The warrant didn't reply, which was good. That meant he was too busy getting his butt out of there.

"Hey, Rudy, you're the man," said Pharaoh, scrambling to his feet.

"I've been accused of that, sir." The commo guy draped his legs over the ledge and jumped down onto the cart, which suddenly broke under his weight, sending him tumbling to the sand.

Pharaoh cursed in surprise and added, "You all right?"

"Damn, yeah. Guess I ain't the man anymore!"

Zulu had his arm draped around Borokovsky's shoulder. There was still a drunken swagger to Zulu's gait, and he had a thick lump on the back of his head. Wasn't that special? He had a hangover and hadn't touched a beer.

According to Walrus, Zulu had inadvertently surprised a guy on the ground, who had reacted with the butt of his AK since he couldn't get it into firing position in time.

As Zulu had gone down, Walrus had shot the man. Bang.

At that moment, the gunfire from up top had started to rain down, and Walrus had scooped up Zulu and tried to evac him.

That's the way the warrant told it. He didn't sound as though he were lying.

Damn, when word got out that Walrus had tried to carry the injured Zulu to safety, the old warrant would be a true hero to the others, and the bastard would milk the moment for everything it was worth.

I have no luck at all, Zulu thought with a groan.

If he could take back what he'd done, he would. Every time he and Melissa had been together, he'd felt the guilt—an itchiness that started on his back and spread across his shoulders—begin to overwhelm him.

Sure, all the sneaking around and the sex had been exciting at first, but then every conversation he'd had with Bull seemed forced—and a few times Bull had even asked what was wrong.

And deep down, in the ugliest part of Zulu's heart, he had been glad that Bull died—just so he wouldn't have to face the man anymore. A damned horrible truth.

He and Borokovsky finally turned down the last alley, where the Pathfinder was idling. Borokovsky helped him into the backseat as Pharaoh and McDaniel came jogging up.

"We good to go?" asked the captain.

"Good to go," cried Walrus.

Zulu sat squashed in the backseat with Walrus and Rock. He gripped the back of his head and closed his eyes.

Pharaoh fired up the truck, wheeled around, and they rumbled off into the wind. Every bump sent needles through Zulu's throbbing head.

Rock shifted in the seat and cursed under his breath.

"It ain't all bad, Rock," began Zulu. "Only ninety-nine percent."

"Know what the joke is?" asked the spook. "Those guys are still there, and we're driving away because the clock's against us."

"It always is," reminded Zulu. "We strike. We leave. We don't give 'em time to figure out who we are. Have you not been paying attention?"

"Oh, come on, Zu. You think there's any doubt what happened? They know American Special Forces hit their village. If we would stay there and tear up the place, we'd find Hassan. He's there."

"You don't know that for sure."

"The hell I don't."

"Those guys are long gone."

"No, they're not. But they will be. That's just the way this war works." Rock swore again.

"We went over it at the briefing," said Pharaoh. "Time

on the target is everything. We either accomplish the task or we don't. Every time you stick around to put Band-Aids on the situation, it only gets worse. At least you confirmed they were there. We got that far."

"Captain, no offense," said Walrus. "But you let the spook take point, and, well . . . I don't need to finish."

"No, you don't. We'll talk about it when we get back."

Rock sang a string of epithets, then added, "Hey, Walrus. If your team hadn't been spotted, maybe we wouldn't be having this conversation."

Walrus raised his voice. "You limp Langley boys are all the same. Always bad timing. What are you now, oh for two in this province? Hell, they'll be pulling you out pretty soon. You don't know any more than we do."

Rock opened up his laptop, thumbed a button, then growled. "Quiet now, fat man. Some of us have to work."

Walrus chuckled—more of a cackle—then finally calmed himself and said, "You haven't done real work in twenty years."

"That's it," snapped Pharaoh. "Nobody talk."

Zulu leaned back in his seat and closed his eyes once more.

In his mind's eye, Melissa stood there in that bedroom, gripping his pistol.

Then Bull came up behind her, smiled, and took her into his arms.

But before he went in for the kiss, he glanced across the room at his two college-aged daughters, who were scowling, then he slowly faced Zulu. "This is what you took away from me."

"Not just me. Her, too."

"I forgive her. But you, never."

"I'm sorry. I'm so sorry."

"No, you're not."

Zulu shuddered and grimaced.

"You all right?" whispered Rock. "Sounds like you're losing your breath."

* * *

Back at FOB Cobra, Pharaoh and Walrus marched Dr. Lucky and his men into a detention area, where they'd remain under guard until higher and the other interrogators were ready to question them.

"You have no idea what a mistake you've made," said the punk sheikh.

Pharaoh shifted up to him, tensing. "You need . . . to be . . . more diplomatic. Understand?"

Lucky cursed.

Pharaoh shook his head. "Someday you'll learn."

"And you know what'll happen on that day?" asked Walrus. "We'll bomb his village, bulldoze the whole place, and turn it into a parking lot for one of our new Walmarts. And we'll give him a job as a greeter. Welcome to Walmart!"

"Shut up, man," said Pharaoh.

He and Walrus left the tent and headed out to see Major Nurenfeld. Pharaoh hoped the debriefing would be, ahem, brief. In the morning, he would write up the after action report, regretting every keystroke. Right now, he just wanted to sleep it all off.

"This should be interesting," said Walrus.

"Do me a favor, Kowalski, just keep your mouth shut in there."

Walrus winked. Whatever that meant. They entered the CO's office, and Nurenfeld, obviously fueled by a pot of coffee, rose from his desk and came around it, champing at the bit.

Before they could even salute him, he was talking: "We're going to go over it not once, not twice, not three times—but as many times as it takes for me to understand how you had a visual on the highest value target in this entire country, and then you lost him."

Pharaoh felt sick to his stomach.

Walrus snorted. "Well, sir, there was some delay in our initial move on the house."

"What do you mean?"

If Pharaoh could have melted Walrus with his gaze, he would have. "Sir, if I—"

"Let him speak," said Nurenfeld.

Walrus wriggled his thick brows. "Well, sir, Agent Rock seemed to think that it'd be better to positively ID the target before we entered. I believe this delay caused the mission to go south, sir. Our intel was good. The target was there. If we'd hit them hard and fast, maybe we would've got him."

Pharaoh was ready to turn and drive his fist down Walrus's throat. The bastard was hanging him out to dry, and what was Pharaoh supposed to do? Stand there and take it? "Sir, that's not exactly what happened."

Nurenfeld's gaze remained locked on Walrus, and the CO began to pant. "Don't mince words. What the hell happened down there?"

"That's exactly what I want to know," cried Lieutenant Colonel Richard Kazzer as he pushed past the half-open door and paraded into the office. His broad chest tented up his army digital pattern uniform, and he removed his ACU patrol cap to rake fingers across his salt-and-pepper crew cut.

Kazzer was the battalion commander, and Chahar Borjak was his ground. He'd made that quite clear during the briefing.

"Sir, Detachment Commander Pharaoh and Assistant Detachment Commander Kowalski were about to enlighten us," said Nurenfeld, a slight crack in his voice.

"Well, Major, before they do, let me express my understanding of the situation so far. You sent this ODA into my village, and for all I know shot up the place, maybe killed a bunch of my good informants, took my best guy, Dr. Lucky, pissed him off, dragged his ass back here, and now you got what? Nothing to show for it? Am I missing any part of this?"

Kazzer was a New Yorker whose accent really came out

when he was angry. If Pharaoh hadn't known better, he'd have assumed that someone in the room was about to get "whacked."

Nurenfeld raised his chin. "Sir—"

"I'm not finished yet. I'm already putting together a QRF. They're going in there to mop up your mess."

Kazzer's quick reaction force would perform a site exploitation, piecing together exactly what had happened. What they couldn't discern from their own investigation they would buy from the locals, paying them in large sums of U.S. greenbacks for the information.

The colonel went on: "You guys have no conception of the amount of time it takes to nurture those relationships. Now I want you to get a couple of men and drive Lucky and his buddies back home."

"Sir?"

"You heard me, Major."

Pharaoh couldn't take it anymore, and his incredulity came out in his tone. "Colonel, Lucky was seen with Hassan. He was there, in Lucky's house. And we're going to let him go?"

"Captain, I believe you. But do you think he's going to tell us anything? He's more valuable down there than detained up here. We got our eyes on him. But he's also very well connected, and if we step on his toes, my stream of intel gets cut off. We hold him, and no one talks. That's just the way it is."

In Chahar Borjak and other villages, Kazzer's soldiers were like the beat cops. Special Forces were like SWAT teams. The beat cops had one-on-one daily relationships with the locals. The SWAT teams only came in to solve bigger problems, which sometimes involved a lot of collateral damage and casualties.

Consequently, Pharaoh, like many Special Forces operators, often found himself caught between three worlds: his own, the battalion commander's, and the average Afghan's.

You could never make everyone happy.

And at the moment, no one was. Damn.

"Sir, I understand what you're saying, sir," began Pharaoh. "But I still can't believe we're letting this guy go. Doesn't aiding and abetting count for anything? Can't we at least try to question him? Jesus . . ."

"Son, if it's any consolation, I don't believe it either. But this is a little bigger than all of us. The longer we hold him, the more the turbans get ruffled."

Walrus gasped through a curse.

"You got a problem with that, Kowalski?" asked Kazzer.

"No, sir. I am in complete agreement with the army's policy to release bad guys for the greater good."

"God damn, you are a wiseass."

"Yes, sir."

"All right, then. Since you like talking. Why don't you tell me all about your little party tonight?"

Kazzer crossed over to a chair and sat. He motioned that Nurenfeld do likewise, leaving Pharaoh and Walrus standing like a couple of privates being reprimanded.

"Well, I wasn't happy with the initial plan—so we made a few revisions . . and I'll tell you why . . ."

Pharaoh held his breath. *Here we go. I got no luck at all.*

15. GUNMETAL GRAY

Marwan Ali, who still preferred to use his old CIA code name "Libra," sat cross-legged on the floor of the musty, six-foot-diameter concrete pipe. Beside him was Junaid Qureshi, aka "Jersey," and farther down stood Sheikh Abu Hassan, who had just finished cleaning his pistol.

The pipe was about ten meters long, and its depth and thickness helped conceal their heat signatures from coalition forces' aircraft. At one end of the pipe they'd found enough food and water for several days, as well as folding beds and blankets and a half dozen battery-powered lights. Hopefully they would not need the food or blankets and be out of the pipe before sunrise.

Access to the shelter had been carefully concealed by a nondescript panel in the floor, hidden beneath the kitchen stove. Lucky had also constructed a similar hiding place beneath the outhouse, which stood near the river and about ten meters north of the main house. In the event that he or the others were attacked while outside, they could flee there and disappear, swallowed as it were by the commode itself.

Libra, Jersey, and Hassan had been waiting in the pipe for three hours and thirteen minutes now, according to Libra's watch, and their cell phones indicated that no signals were present. Hassan had insisted that they wait until someone came for them. That had always been the plan. Impatience and frustration would lead to their capture.

Still, Libra had wanted to argue about that. Their most cordial host, Dr. Lucky, could have been captured or killed, leaving them to rot in the hole. But Hassan, it seemed, was assuming that someone else would come for them.

With his heart beginning to race again, Libra took a deep breath and calmed himself. Although several pieces of PVC pipe extended through the concrete pipe and up into the house to provide them with air, the claustrophobia had already set in, and the dank odor repeatedly made him grimace.

But who was he to complain? This was the life he had chosen for himself. No wife. No kids. Just guns, high stakes, and adrenaline.

He'd been all over the world gathering intel for the past twenty years. And he wouldn't have it any other way.

He and Jersey were partners in crime, so to speak, joint owners and sole employees of the Global Intelligence Group (GIG), a private military contractor of epically small proportions for whom no job was too big, they liked to joke.

Libra could not have imagined a few years ago that he and his buddy would be sitting in a pipe, in Afghanistan, with the leader of al-Qaeda. Nope. He wouldn't have taken that bet.

He turned to Hassan and, in perfect Arabic, said, "I think we should take a look now."

"Have more faith. And more patience. Besides, our delay getting to Zahedan will allow Saeed to better prepare for me. I know right now that he is screaming at the top of his lungs, trying to get those engineers to work more quickly."

"Yes, you're right. And your trip there will inspire the

men as well. They need to know that you recognize their hard work."

Hassan grinned. "I will be sure to reward each of them. But I will also remind them that I will not tolerate further delays."

A scraping noise from above drew their attention. Someone was moving the stove.

"They're coming," cried Jersey, his eyes seeming to rise from the depths of his face.

They drew their pistols and aimed up, toward the wooden panel with the rope ladder extending below.

Bright light shone through the hole, temporarily blinding them, as Jersey cried out, "Lucky?"

"Not him! But he sent me to come get you! The truck is waiting. We must move now before the sun comes up!"

"Let's go," ordered Hassan.

They mounted the ladder, were helped up into the kitchen by a small group of Lucky's men, then were rushed outside to the rumbling truck, a large tarpaulin-covered flatbed whose exhaust pipe shook so hard it had already broken several of its mounts.

Libra and his partner had been courting Hassan for the past year, posing as arms dealers from Pakistan who wanted to join al-Qaeda and fight with him in Afghanistan. Unfortunately, gaining Hassan's trust involved several million greenbacks and thousands of crates of rifles and ammunition.

The world Libra and Jersey resided in now was gunmetal gray, and they were—depending on who you asked— traitors who had aided a terrorist organization.

But sometimes, as they'd learned during their CIA years, you have to fatten up the pig before you slaughter it.

And even gunmetal gray always had a tint of true blue.

For their part, Libra and Jersey had been tasked with infiltrating Hassan's group and monitoring all of his activities. They needed to ensure that Hassan established clear ties to the Iranian government.

The men that Libra and Jersey worked for were, to come right out and say it, war hawks in Congress whose undisclosed and unyielding aim was to take military action against Iran. The country's off-again, on-again nuclear weapons program needed to be abolished once and for all, and this clandestine group, who operated under the guise of the American Readiness Committee, needed definitive proof that the Iranian government was aiding and abetting al-Qaeda and directly responsible for the recent surge of terrorist activity in Iraq and Afghanistan.

The U.S. had invaded Iraq and found no weapons of mass destruction. That debacle could not be repeated. This time, the congressman had said, we need hard, irrefutable evidence. Then we go in and seize control.

Libra and Jersey would provide them with that. The concrete factory in Zahedan was owned by seven members of the Iranian Parliament, all of whom knew exactly what was going on there. In fact, two of them were scheduled to meet with Hassan once he arrived.

Libra piled into the truck with his partner. Hassan sat up front, in the cab, features concealed behind a new *she-magh*. The driver was a heavyset Arab and heavily armed.

Clutching the side rails, Libra adjusted himself on the splintered wood and glanced out, across the desert, where on the horizon the sky glowed a deep sapphire.

Jersey looked at him. Libra knew that look. It was time to send another text message via their satellite phone. The other three guys on the flatbed with them would not suspect anything. The message would be sent to their office, and their liaison, "Jimbo," would relay it back to the committee chairman, Senator Greenfield, at his office in Texas: "LEAVING CHAHAR BORJAK NOW. EN ROUTE VIA TRUCK TO ZAHEDAN."

Libra nodded to his partner.

This was arguably the most dangerous contract Libra and Jersey had ever accepted. And they had no allies to speak of—except maybe one.

Good old Rock. Libra knew that if push came to shove, he would confide in Rock, let him know exactly what was happening. They could count on Rock to do what he could. Yet there was a distinct possibility that even Rock, with all his contacts, could not save them now.

Better not to think about that. Better to focus on the mission. And the money.

Yes, indeed, the bill for their services, excluding gratuity, was a cool $10 million.

Those old war hawks wanted their war.

Libra and Jersey would give it to them.

16. TOO HARD TO KEEP

Rock's satellite phone woke him out of a sound sleep. He checked the time: 0627. Damn, he'd barely had three hours of rest. Jack Andropolis was calling from Langley, and Rock was desperate for any kind of news.

"I know it's early and you've had a long night," his friend began.

"Long?" Rock chuckled under his breath. "You got my message, huh?"

"I did. Just what the hell are those guys doing now?"

"That's why I called you."

"Well, I've been running with this as far as I can, but so far nothing. And Rock, there's always the possibility that they—"

"No. No way. They were always in it for the money, yeah, but they wouldn't sell us out. That line is pretty damned clear to them."

"Times change, Rock."

"Don't even go there. Look, they always keep it small. Fewer leaks. But their client has to be somebody huge."

"And that's the part that scares me."

"Yeah because that somebody is paying big-time to keep them in Hassan's pocket."

"Jesus, Rock, I have to tell you, something like this could cost me a lot. I don't know if I can be involved anymore because—"

"Hey, I'll do what I can from here, but I'm oh for two, and three strikes you're out. You can't bail on me. I'm calling in every favor you owe me—right now."

"This isn't just a favor, Rock."

He hesitated. "I know."

Now it was Jack's turn to think about it. The silence on the other end left Rock uneasy, then, finally, Jack cleared his throat and said, "Aw, hell. We got some Predators in the air right now. I'll get back ASAP with their intel."

"I know who my friends are. Thanks, man."

"Might be worthless. Tri-border traffic has tripled over the past month, and every vehicle looks suspicious."

"I know, I know. Hassan's heading into Pakistan or Iran. If you can point me in the right direction, that'll be a start. I'm not asking for blood."

"Yeah, yeah. And I hate to say it, but you should tap Colonel Kazzer's men. They have the pulse in Chahar Borjak. Lucky won't give you anything, you know that. And he probably doesn't know anything. He was ordered to entertain the sheikh for the night. That's it. But Kazzer's men know the locals, and if you're right about them taking off after you guys left, then those old men would've seen that— and they'll know which way those guys are headed."

"Which means I need to drag my overtired ass back down there. I knew it."

"Yeah, you do. What about Pharaoh and his guys?"

"They don't know anything."

"Keep it that way."

"You don't need to remind me. Call me when you got something."

"All right, buddy."

"You hang in there."

"I'm trying. And like I said, Rock, I'll push for you, but I've been doing this a long time, and the second I feel like I need to look over my shoulder, I'm done."

"You've been looking over your shoulder your whole life."

"You know what I mean."

"Just give me a little help. Been there, done that. And you know you owe me."

He sighed deeply. "I'll call you."

"Thanks."

Rock thumbed off the phone, sat up in the small bed. He shuddered.

Even Jack, who seemed to feed off intelligence like a piranha, was troubled by this news. Rock rubbed the grit from his eyes, pulled his hair back into a ponytail, and pulled on the rubber band. *Time for this old hippie to get back to work.*

Zulu watched as Rock left the FOB, traveling back to Dr. Lucky's house with a couple of regular army guys in a little Ford Ranger pickup truck, then he slipped on his sunglasses against the noonday sun and headed off toward the mess.

The lump on Zulu's head was now only half as big as his bruised ego; both still ached. The four aspirins he had taken an hour ago had barely helped.

He found the heavy-eyed Ondejko and Grimm waiting for him at a table in the back. Zulu grabbed his chow and joined them, keeping his voice low. "All right, guys. I need a straight answer."

"Zu, before we get into this, I want you to know that Grimm and I are one hundred percent behind you and that we would never do anything to undermine this team. But, man, it's hard. It's like you got a lot on your mind. I know Bull's death messed us all up. Then Church came on real heavy and got fragged, and now everyone's looking at everyone else, you know?"

"Whoa, slow down there. What you trying to say?"

"I'm just saying if Walrus has a problem with you, it might be because we've all been through a lot. He's just a real hard-core asshole. But you know how it is when we're out there. He's the guy you want. I didn't know it was possible to meet someone meaner than you."

"You're defending him?"

"Not defending, just—"

"I'm going to throw up, and I haven't eaten yet." Zulu faced Grimm, and the assistant medic recoiled. "What about you, Tony? You going to sit there and tell me I'm crazy and that Walrus is right?"

"He did save your life. That counts for something."

"Jesus God."

"Zu, we're just thinking about you, man. You don't make mistakes like that—letting guys come up behind you. Walrus told us about it."

"I'm sure he did. Why don't you tell me which one of you jokers fired last night?"

Grimm frowned and faced Ondejko, who shrugged and said, "What're you talking about?"

"Steve, Rudy, and I were out in front of the house, and the first shots we heard were from a SCAR. Not an AK. A SCAR."

"You must've been hearing things," said Grimm.

"No, I wasn't. The shots came from behind the house, where you guys were. So . . . we can only conclude that those shots came from one of your rifles." Zulu raised his index finger. "The first shots came from you . . . or you," he added, pointing at Ondejko, then Grimm. He cocked a thumb over his shoulder. "Or Walrus."

Their gazes dropped to their laps.

Zulu slammed his fist on the table, startling them. "Is there something you want to tell me?"

"So I screwed up, okay?" said Ondejko. "Got trigger happy. Walrus wanted to tear my head off, but he covered for me."

"Or are you covering for him? He didn't fire the first shots?"

"No, he didn't. I saw a guy, and I thought he saw me. But he didn't. I just reacted."

"That's funny. Because I know Walrus wanted to prove the captain wrong more than anything. I wouldn't put it past him to fire off a couple of rounds. He's always got to be right."

Ondejko shook his head. "See, Zu, it's that kind of thinking, man. Why do you hate him so much?"

"He's a know-it-all and a showboat. We don't need a guy like him."

"He's got a lot of experience," said Grimm. "So maybe we make the best of it."

Zulu snorted, then bared his teeth. "Did you hear what he did to the captain last night? Totally embarrassed him in front of Kazzer. The way Pharaoh put it was, 'He hung me out to dry.' Yeah, it sounds like we should really make the best of it. I'm sure the captain would agree with that."

Ondejko made a face. "Zu, what do you want from us? He's the warrant. You're the team sergeant. We fight for you, man. You want us to say we'll listen to you first? We're caught between a rock and a hard place. I mean, what do you want?"

Zulu sat there, contemplating his reply. It was a very good question: What did he really want?

Ondejko was able to quietly organize the men for a brief meeting. All were present in his quarters save for Walrus, Zulu, and Captain Pharaoh. Hojo, being the assistant operations sergeant, led the conversation, after Ondejko had carefully filled him in on everything he knew.

"All right, guys, we're here because we have three problems. Walrus is really coming on strong. Zulu's head is not in it, and we don't know why. And, well, something happened to Church back in Londo, and if anybody knows anything at all—"

"Damn it, Hojo, we've been down that road a million times," said Borokovsky. "Grimm and I have told the same story over and over. Just drop it. The official report is in, and that's what it is."

Hojo looked surprised. "Getting a little defensive there, Steve."

"I'm just tired of talking about it. Let the guy rest in peace. Show some respect for his family. For his memory."

"We are. We are. But everyone's still thinking he either fragged himself or one of us got to him."

"What is this? A Spanish inquisition, for God's sake?" cried Grimm. "Steve and I were there when he died."

"And you told us you didn't know what happened," said Ondejko.

"That's right," snapped Borokovsky.

An uncomfortable silence followed, lasting about five seconds until Hojo lifted his voice and said, "All right, no matter how hard it is, we're going to put that issue to bed. Church is gone. We'll have to leave it at that."

"Can I say something?" asked Ondejko.

Hojo nodded.

"I don't know if he told anybody else this, but Walrus seems to think that maybe Zulu had something to do with Church's death."

"No way," said McDaniel. "Zulu wasn't even around. He was with the captain. I was there. I saw everything."

"So did I," added Weathers.

"Look, I'm just saying what Walrus told me. He seemed to think that Church might've been blackmailing Zulu over something, so Zulu got rid of him first. Maybe he rigged up some kind of remote detonator, or something on a short timer, I don't know."

"This is crazy!" cried Hojo. "And we're not even going

there. We know Zu. We know that man. And the EOD techs would've found parts from a remote detonator."

"Maybe they just missed them," said Figueroa, the engineer and expert on such matters. "Sometimes that stuff is so small after an explosion . . ."

It was clear to Ondejko that the others were entertaining the scenario, their minds already working overtime.

Hojo glanced around at the others, then added, "What we need to do now is put out the fires, not fan them—before the next warning order comes in. Understood?"

"And we need to keep the captain out of this mess," said Ondejko. "Looks like he's already got enough stress."

"Seems like we all do," said Hojo. "But this team's got a history of overcoming."

Senior medic Steven Borokovsky left the meeting with assistant medic Anthony Grimm at his side. They headed in silence back to Borokovsky's quarters, and once there, despite the somewhat early hour, they both shared quick and secret swigs of whiskey—for medicinal purposes only.

"I told you this wouldn't work out," said Grimm.

"I didn't think it'd get this far." Borokovsky took a deep breath, then moved to his bunk and collapsed.

"We can't let it go on."

"We don't have a choice."

Grimm came up to the bed, wide-eyed. "Walrus is going around trying to blame it on Zulu. I don't want to fight with these guys if they want to kill each other more than the bad guys. Steve, we're the only ones that can make this right."

"We're making it right. And we're not going to say a goddamned thing."

"It's just too hard to keep, man. I don't know if I can do it."

"You've done it already. It's too late." As the words left

Borokovsky's lips, he could almost taste them: bitter and stale, the way lies always tasted.

Maybe Grimm was right. Maybe they had made a promise too hard to keep. "Just don't let it get to you. Just lay low. Another mission will come in, and everyone will forget all about it. Hojo's pushing for that."

Grimm gave a halfhearted nod. "I need another drink."

17. KNIFE IN THE BACK

When Rock arrived at Dr. Lucky's house, he found the punk himself standing outside under guard and shouting at the quick reaction force that was still aggressively searching (see: tearing apart) his little Shangri-la.

Rock climbed out of the pickup truck and marched past the sheikh, wearing a broad grin.

The sheikh began to say something, but Rock held up his hand. "Save it."

Dr. Lucky spoke anyway. "I'm coming for you now, Rock. You're on my radar."

"I'm on your radar? Where'd you hear that? You think your life is an action movie?" Rock snorted, hustled away, and showed his ID to the soldiers posted outside the front doors. He strode into the house, toward the kitchen, where he'd been told he would find Captain Jones, a tall black man in his forties, an expert cynic who had once helped Rock nab several drug runners.

The captain stood near a wall, flicking a light switch up and down and wearing a deep frown.

"Hey, Leo. They tell you I was coming?"

"Oh, yeah, they did. And I couldn't wait for you to get here." The sarcastic lilt in Jones's voice made Rock grin—because Jones sounded just like him. "Would you like command of this search?"

"Absolutely. Cigar?"

Jones winked and accepted the stogie. "I thought you'd be a problem."

"I'm good people, Leo. I tell myself that every day because being here makes it easy to forget."

"That's right. But let me ask: You guys only show up when you want something. So I can only assume you want to help us dig through your mess."

"Me?" Rock chuckled. "Let me tell you something. This is a whole lot more important to me than those two Mohammeds we nailed last year. You read me?"

"No kidding."

"Yup. Have your men questioned the old guys yet?"

"They're out there now."

"I think our HVTs got off sometime this morning. Probably by car or truck. I'm just looking for a direction. Tell 'em I got the cash for good intel."

"You always do." Jones took a long pull on his cigar. "Now, let me tell you about my world. I'm standing here, wondering why I got a light switch on a wall that doesn't turn anything on. I found it by accident after we got the power back on. I wouldn't think twice about this, but when it comes to our boy Lucky . . ."

Rock frowned.

"Also, we've been tearing through this place, and this is the only thing that's caught my eye."

Rock stood there a moment more, smoking his cigar, then a slight shimmer on the tiled floor made him lean in closer. He shifted his angle, the light now playing over the tile at a steeper angle—

Revealing scrape marks extending out from the stove.

He practically dove for the appliance and dragged it away from the wall, revealing a perfect square of newly spread grout along the perimeter of four tiles. "Give me your rifle!" he cried to Jones, who complied.

Rock slammed the butt of the weapon into the center of the four tiles. They smashed apart, revealing a thin piece of plywood. Rock cleared the broken tiles, dug in the corners of the wood, and lifted it away like a hatch.

"Wait a second," cried the captain. "Let's see."

As Jones flicked the switch on and off, light flashed from below.

Rock gasped. "Son of a—"

"Lieutenant Reese," shouted Jones, cutting off Rock. "We found the rabbit hole. I need two men over here right now. And tell Yanez to get the major back here."

Rock practically fell down the ladder to get into the concrete pipe.

"Hey, man, don't touch anything down there," warned Jones.

"Relax, bro. And do me a favor? While you're calling in the cavalry, why not bring Lucky along. I want him to explain this. That should be entertaining."

"Oh, yeah."

The single bulb dangling by a wire into the pipe barely illuminated the hole, so Rock dug out his Gladius, thumbed on the light, and directed it forward. "Whoa . . ." His beam stretched off into the darkness and seemed to dissolve away before the pipe ever ended. From the distance came the faint sound of trickling water.

He started forward, minding his head, carefully letting his light play over the floor until he spotted some gear ahead: blankets, boxes, and a few crates.

Someone had dropped an empty book of matches on the floor. On the cover was the logo of the Avari Towers Hotel in Karachi, Pakistan.

Avari Towers. He knew the place all right. And so did his friends.

He picked up the matchbook, opened it. Inside were

three letters handwritten in pen: GIG. They knew Rock would come. They wanted him on their tail. They were leaving bread crumbs—but why? How bad was it? What did they think Rock could do for them? He held the match-book tightly in his fist. Yes, it was a message, and the message had been received.

Now that Walrus was bound, gagged, and blindfolded, Zulu dragged him out of his quarters and out behind the billet, to where he had an HMMWV waiting.

With considerable effort he loaded the fat pig into the back, stole a quick look around, then hopped into the driver's seat and took off.

He glanced at himself in the rearview mirror, his eyes bloodshot, his hair a lion's mane of coiled chaos.

Just as he left the main gate, he glanced once more in the mirror as Pharaoh sat up in the backseat, shocking the hell out of him.

"What are you doing, Zu?" the captain asked matter-of-factly.

And for some strange reason, Zulu grew calm and answered just as routinely. "Hey, Captain. I'm just going for a drive."

"Why is Walrus making those grunting sounds?"

"I don't know. I gagged him?"

Zulu checked the rearview mirror as Pharaoh turned back and glanced at Walrus. "Yeah, he's gagged. Blindfolded, too."

"Yeah . . ."

"So where we going?"

"Over to the dump."

"Ah, I see, you're taking out the trash. That's very poetic, huh?"

"Well, I don't mean to be poetic."

"What do you mean to be?"

"I don't know." Zulu hung a sharp right turn, heading down a heavily pockmarked dirt road that terminated in mountains of rubbish.

The captain sighed, almost sounding as though he were bored. "So . . . you going to kill him?"

Zulu took in a long breath. "Yeah. I bought a Glock from that guy in the city. Remember that idiot?"

"Yeah. He was pretty weird, but he had some nice pieces. I liked that Glock, too. And that's good. You got the ballistics covered. But what if they go to that dealer?"

"He won't talk because he ain't here anymore. I sent him on a little trip to see Allah."

"Damn, Zu. I'm proud of you. This is a first class murder right here."

"Well, I'm not stupid. What it's going to be is just another soldier whacked in Afghanistan. And it sounds like you're okay with this?"

"Absolutely. I want him dead as much as you."

"You kidding me?"

"No. I want you to shoot him ten times. I want to see the fat bastard's body jump every time you shoot him."

"I can't do that. Then it'll look like an execution."

"Who cares?"

"I care."

Pharaoh began laughing, slowly at first, then he broke into a fit that nearly robbed him of breath. "You got a conscience or something? Come on, Zu. You're a cold-blooded killer. Nothing bothers you."

"I wish."

Zulu shivered hard, snapped open his eyes, and saw Walrus leaning over him, framed by the late-day sun filtering in from the open door behind him.

"What time is it?"

"Nearly eighteen hundred."

He cursed, realized he'd been sleeping the day away. And not really sleeping at all but battling his way through the nightmares.

"Let's go, sweetheart, nap time is over. We got big news from Rock and new orders down from CENTCOM."

Walrus left the room, the door slamming after him. Zulu lay there a moment more, shivering through his breath. Damn, he had plotted Walrus's murder—and the captain had condoned it all. Part of him wanted to confess his sins to someone; the other part wanted to go to Pharaoh and firm up those plans. Together they would share the guilt of removing a fellow operator from the equation. Now that sounded so much more clinical and palatable than murder.

What am I thinking? I'm insane . . .

A knock came at his door, and Pharaoh stuck his head inside. "Hey."

"Big news."

"I heard. Can I come in?"

"Yeah." Zulu sat up.

Pharaoh entered and took a seat at the small desk. "We're going to meet in fifteen minutes."

"Nurenfeld say anything?"

"Before we get into that, I've just had a really interesting conversation with Rudy."

Zulu dragged the hair out of his eyes and sniffled. Damn, that dream had sucked the life out of him. "Yeah?"

"What we talk about here doesn't leave this room."

"All right."

Pharaoh pursed his lips. "The other guys had a meeting without us."

"What?"

"Rudy told me. He didn't want to, but he did."

"We always knew you were bestest buddies."

"No, I've never cut him any slack. You know that's not fair."

Zulu rubbed his eyes. "You're right. So now what?"

"Rudy says they were talking about something Walrus put out there. He's saying you might've had something to do with Church."

"Of course he did."

"You have to tell me right now what's going on."

Zulu raised his voice. "There's nothing to tell! I was with you the entire time."

"They're talking about remote detonation. They're throwing all kinds of crap out there."

Zulu shot to his feet. "Where is Walrus? We'll put an end to this once and for all." Zulu was shaking, because in his mind's eye, he already saw the old warrant announcing to everyone what had happened.

"Sit down."

Zulu stood there a moment more, then nervously reached into his pocket, pulled out his Jani-Song, and began to unconsciously open and close the blade, his hand working furiously.

Pharaoh eyed the knife, then said, "I don't believe any of that crap. I trust you, man. But you have to trust me. You have to tell me what this is about, because it needs to end, right here, right now. He might have saved your ass, but he's still got it in for you. I did a little research, and there's nothing officially that indicates you guys have had any problems."

Zulu grew even more tense. "You're like me. You don't like to talk about your personal life. All I know about you is that you're single, an only child, and that story about your dad dying two days after you got promoted to captain. I mean, I don't know anything else. I mean I heard you once say you like blondes. That's it."

"What are you doing, Zu? We're not talking about me."

"I'm just saying, you know . . ."

"No, I don't know. What do you want to tell me?"

"I was sleeping today. I had a dream that me and you took Walrus out to the dump." Zulu made a pistol with his fingers and fired it.

"That's great." Pharaoh was beginning to grow pale, and his eyes, once so young and naive-looking, bore a heavy, heavy burden.

Zulu smiled crookedly. "Relax. I woke up before we killed him. You know who woke me up? The fat man himself."

Pharaoh snorted. "Uh, good?"

Zulu took in another long breath, released it slowly, and considered telling Pharaoh everything.

After all, the kid was, in the grand scheme of things, still pretty new, and maybe he would be more forgiving than the rest of the men would. Maybe his youth would allow him that. Maybe he would just blow it off and not think any worse of Zulu. People are weak. Mistakes happen.

Or maybe he wouldn't. Maybe his image of Zulu as the great trainer and mentor would shatter like windows under mortar fire.

Thanks to Zulu, Pharaoh was already an officer whose hands were calloused and dirty.

And when Pharaoh got promoted, he would still lobby on behalf of the little guys like Zulu—because he'd been there and knew what ODA teams went through. Zulu had worked very hard to instill that in the young captain.

Yet all of Zulu's work would be for naught if that image—that all-important image—were tainted.

It wouldn't have been so bad if Zulu had been cheating with the wife of one of the other guys, say Gator or Ondejko, who were just average Joes.

But Dennis Bull was the Jesus Christ of Triple Nickel who had sacrificed his own life to save them all and the president of Afghanistan.

Dennis Bull would forever be known as the most famous member of Triple Nickel, a man who had been recommended for the Medal of Honor by Pharaoh, a man who had lived by the Special Forces Creed because he believed in it to the marrow.

Dennis Bull would rise again in some garden somewhere as a towering statue gazed upon with respect and admiration and awe by all those fortunate enough to encounter his legend. The plaque at his boots would detail his heroics, and grandfathers would read those words to their grandkids, and some might even say, "I fought with that man. I knew him well."

And Master Sergeant Robert "Zulu" Burrows would be remembered as the guy who had put the knife in that great man's back.

That was what he should tell Pharaoh?

Not on his life.

Zulu vowed right there to never admit it. Ever. Let Walrus try to rake him over the coals, but he would never, ever admit to anything, not because he was afraid to accept responsibility, but because he would protect Bull's memory. Bull deserved no less.

And Zulu was already suffering enough, although Walrus and the others would never know that.

"I have to get cleaned up before the briefing," he told Pharaoh.

"So, Walrus hates you for no reason at all."

"Pretty much."

"And if I go to him now and demand an answer, that's what he'll tell me."

"I have no idea what he'll tell you."

"Then why don't you soften the blow?"

Zulu shifted his tone, suddenly becoming terse and formal. "Captain, I need to get ready."

"All right. But, Sergeant, if this in any way interferes with your performance and our mission—"

"I respect that, sir. If I were you, I'd do the same."

"See you there." Pharaoh rose and left.

Zulu fell back onto his bed. Maybe the only way out of this one was to immortalize himself, the same way Bull had.

Maybe it was time to push it just a little harder, a little further than any sane man would.

They were already chanting his name in Valhalla.

Or in Hell.

18. AT THE REQUEST OF THE PRESIDENT OF THE UNITED STATES

Saeed Hanjour held his breath as Sheikh Abu Hassan and the two arms dealers hurried into the concrete factory in Zahedan. They all wore *shemaghs* and were well armed with rifles and pistols.

A rumbling came from out back where Hanjour's engineers worked furiously to produce more EFP parts, and Hanjour intended to show the sheikh a large shipment that had already been disguised inside the bricks and was bound for Afghanistan.

Perhaps that would ease the blow of the bad news that Hanjour must now tell the sheikh. The members of the Iranian Parliament who were supposed to meet him this evening had been delayed and would not arrive until the following evening. If the sheikh wanted to thank them in person for their help and support, he would need to wait another day.

Hassan looked exhausted as he removed his *shemagh* and glanced around, squinting as his eyes adjusted to the facility's bright light. Outside, the sun was just setting, and Hanjour's daytime security crew was being relieved.

After brief introductions, the sheikh frowned and asked when the members of parliament would arrive.

"I'm afraid they've been delayed until tomorrow evening," said Hanjour. "Assuming you want to stay, I've already arranged for entertainment and accommodations for you and your associates. But praise Allah, that is the only bad news I have. Come with me to the back and I will show you some very good news."

One of the sheikh's associates, Marwan Ali, whispered something into the sheikh's ear, and the sheikh reacted strongly and whispered something back while scowling at the man.

The atmosphere grew even more tense for a moment, but then, finally, the sheikh faced Hanjour and said, "Show me this good news. And I hope for your sake that you've made a dramatic increase in production. Because I am exhausted. Because I was almost caught by the Americans. And because now I'm forced to stay here another day. This does not please me. Do you understand?"

Hanjour gasped and imagined his own demise at the sheikh's hand. "Yes. Now please follow me."

Fatima, who had been up on the roof of the old warehouse from which large shipments of rice were transported, lowered the digital video camera and turned to Ezzat, who had been crouching down beside her.

"Do you get a good picture of them?"

"Yes."

"All right. I will call the man and tell him where to meet us. They said he will pay a lot for those pictures."

Fatima seized the old woman by the throat and said, "Tell me the number."

"What . . . what are you doing?"

"Tell me the number, old woman, otherwise you'll die!"

Ezzat dug her fingers into Fatima's wrist. "I don't know it. I've . . . written it down . . ."

"Where is it?"

"In my pocket."

With her free hand, Fatima dug into the old woman's pocket and produced the small slip of paper.

On it was written a satellite phone number and a single name in English:

Rock.

Fatima reached back into the pocket and pulled out the woman's satellite phone—the one "they" had given her.

Then she shoved Ezzat, scrambled to her feet, and darted for the staircase on the other side of the rooftop. Ezzat was screaming after her, but Fatima was confident that the old woman would never catch up.

Rock stood beside a wall of sandbags at FOB Cobra, and the second Jack Andropolis answered the phone, Rock fired off his question: "Why did you sell them out?"

"Rock, shut up and listen to me."

"Why the hell did you sell them out?"

"I didn't do that."

"Then how did Army Intelligence learn that two, as they're calling them, 'rogue contractors' are aiding and abetting Abu Hassan and have crossed the border into Iran?"

"Rock, you have no clue what's going on right now. I told you the second I had to watch my back, I was out. This is, Jesus, this line could be tapped. But you know what? It doesn't matter anymore. It doesn't matter."

"What are you talking about? They were our friends. And you sold them out."

"Shut up, Rock! No one forced them to do what they're doing."

"Christ . . ."

"Listen to me, in case we don't talk again."

"What do you mean?"

"Just listen. I dug up one good source, just a kid, really

an intern—but they already got to him. No body of course, but trust me, he's dead."

"What?"

"Pay attention! Libra and Jersey were hired by a group of congressmen who want to go to war with Iran. It's huge now. The director had to go to the president himself, tell him he's got two former employees who are now renegade contract agents working for a congressional cabal. The White House is involved."

"I heard. The orders came down. I didn't know why."

"But listen, my source talked. And I'm the only leak left. They've already trashed my condo. I can't go home."

"Oh my God. Call Bryan."

"I did. And you know what he said? There's nothing he can do. They got to him, too."

"I don't believe this."

"Believe it. So don't talk to me about selling out friends."

"Who are these congressmen? Tell me everything you know. Make me the next leak. I don't care."

Just then another call came in, and Rock almost dropped the phone: The number belonged to Jersey.

"Hang on," he told Andropolis. "Hello?"

The voice on the other end was female, the words Arabic. "Is this Rock?"

"Yes," he answered in Arabic. "Who is this?"

"I have pictures you want. You will meet me here in Zahedan."

Pharaoh took a seat around several portable tables set up inside the Tactical Operations Center. Every man of ODA-555 was present and accounted for, and even Zulu, who'd plopped down next to Pharaoh, looked clear-eyed and alert.

Major Nurenfeld was the only senior officer present,

which was very odd, and he stood beside Rock. Both of them wore grave expressions.

"All right, gentlemen, I want to get this show on the road before the quixotic nature of our current president decides to rear its ugly head."

"What the hell is that supposed to mean?" Gator whispered behind Pharaoh.

Pharaoh craned his neck and put a finger to his lips. Nurenfeld was tossing his word salad again, and Gator, though quite familiar with the major's manner of speaking, was poking fun as usual.

"You might be wondering why Agent Rock and I are the only ones present. Well this one's black, all right. There's no official WARNO. Nothing in writing. And only a few people inside CENTCOM are even aware of it, let alone our own people—just to give you an idea of how important this is.

"Now listen up. The President of the United States, at the request of the director of the CIA, has written a Presidential Finding authorizing ODA-555 to cross the border into Iran. Let me say that again: The president wants you boys in Iran."

Pharaoh glanced down the row of men to Walrus, who was already wearing a broad, evil grin. Most of the other guys were mouthing the word "whoa," or just letting their mouths fall open. If they were captured in Iran, they'd be treated as spies and beheaded. There would be no negotiations for their release.

"Uh, excuse me, sir, but the president picked our sorry asses to go into Iran? What's he got against us?" asked Walrus, drawing a few snorts from the others.

"He picked us because we're the best," snapped Hojo.

"Damn right," said Ondejko.

The major widened his eyes. "Gentlemen." Once he had regained their attention, Nurenfeld turned. "Now Agent Rock will elaborate."

Rock regarded a small screen upon which Nurenfeld had displayed a map of the tri-border area where Afghanistan, Pakistan, and Iran all met. "Intel I gathered back at Chahar Borjak suggests that Abu Hassan and two rogue American contractors were still present after we left, hiding in a concrete pipe below the house and accessed beneath the stove. They traveled southwest and headed to Zahedan."

Walrus cleared his throat. "Rock, that's some pretty specific intel you got there, but what makes you think they're in Iran in the first place? If I were them, I would've gone directly south to Pakistan. More allies there."

"Hassan, we believe, is on a diplomatic mission, trying to drum up more support with the Iranian Parliament, meaning he must be carrying a serious amount of cash. Some signals intel we intercepted indicates he's scheduled to meet with two members of parliament within the next day or so. The meeting will take place in Zahedan."

"So we go in, and we take him out." Walrus grunted.

"Were it that easy," Rock retorted, then glanced to Nurenfeld.

"So here it is," said the major. "You're to engage in a direct action mission to terminate the American contractors and Hassan. You will terminate them with extreme prejudice. The purpose of this mission is to prevent the discovery of those contractors aiding and abetting Hassan and operating in Iran. If word gets out of this, those Americans will be used as a propaganda tool by the Iranians. It's critical to the welfare and security of the U.S. that you succeed."

"Who are these damned traitors?" cried Zulu.

"We don't have much on them," answered Nurenfeld, switching the image of the map to the photos of two bearded, dark-skinned men. "Guy on the left is Marwan Ali. Guy on the right is Junaid Qureshi. They can pass for Middle Eastern, but they're both Americans. They started a little company called Global Intelligence Group. And oh yeah,"

Nurenfeld added with a bit of sarcasm, "they both used to work for the CIA."

"Friends of yours, Rock?" asked Zulu.

"More than that," Rock answered in a deadpan. "We were lovers."

That generated some serious hoots and laughter, so much so that Nurenfeld had to shout for the men to get serious again. "This mission was ordered by the President of the United States, for God's sake!"

The room went silent.

"Sorry," Rock said. "Fact is I met those guys once or twice. Never worked directly with them. They're not friends. Just acquaintances."

"So you think they turned, got bought out, or what?"

"I don't know what to think. But I do know Langley wants me to hitch a ride with you boys and kill them."

Something in Rock's uneven tone bothered Pharaoh. Moreover, there was a slight crack in his voice, and a barely perceptible tremor. It would be naive to believe that Rock was telling the whole truth and nothing but the truth.

Ex–CIA agents gone private and now working with Abu Hassan?

There was much more to that tale.

"Captain Pharaoh, your men and Rock will take a Black Hawk approximately three kilometers from the Iranian border. Your pilot will have the grid coordinates. From there you'll infil via ground vehicle, dressed as smugglers and packing opium and greenbacks to buy your way out of any trouble en route."

"We already have two CIA contacts in Zahedan en route to meet us at the designated rendezvous point," Rock added.

"What about the exfil, sir?" asked Pharaoh.

"It'll be up to you to make it back across the border— into Afghanistan."

"Let's be clear," interrupted Walrus. "You won't cross the border to pick us up."

"We're not authorized to do that."

Walrus rolled his eyes and snickered.

Zulu leaned over and grinned. "Makes it more interesting that way."

"What about Pakistan?" asked Pharaoh.

"I can't guarantee we can extract you from there. That'd depend on which way the political wind is blowing, and right now we're downwind from a pile of dung. You get across the border, I'll have an extraction bird there within thirty minutes. Keep in mind we'll have full access to all our eyes in the sky, so you won't necessarily be alone."

"We will be if we screw up," said Walrus, tossing an exaggerated gaze in Zulu's direction.

"You won't," retorted Nurenfeld.

The rhythmic drone of an incoming chopper sounded overhead, and the major nodded and switched off his laptop projector. "Gentlemen, that's your taxi right now. I hope you all enjoy your little vacation in Iran."

"We sure will," said Walrus.

They filed out of the TOC and Zulu was already barking orders for the men to grab their gear and meet back at the chopper.

Pharaoh motioned Walrus aside, and out behind the TOC he said, "Once we cross the border, this'll be a split-team op."

"Easy, Captain. Let's see what we got, once we get there."

"I don't care what we got. I'll be doing my best to keep you and Zulu separated."

"That shouldn't be an issue."

"Come on. You guys won't talk, but it's obvious."

"Captain, rest assured we'll be there for you. We might have our differences, but when it comes to an op like this, we're on the same page."

"We're not playing games here, Walrus. I am as serious as a goddamned heart attack right now."

"Understood, sir. Tell you what, we all make it back

alive, I promise you, I'll tell you why there's no love lost between me and your buddy. Deal?" He proffered his hand.

Pharaoh narrowed his gaze and sharpened his tone. "Get your gear." He turned away, leaving Walrus standing there with his hand extended.

Half a world away, inside the oval office, President James Gallagher glanced over at Secretary of Defense Dennis MacIntyre and said, "Christ, Dennis. What a mess. You think this kid Pharaoh can pull it off?"

MacIntyre rubbed his sleep-deprived eyes. "After what they did up in the mountains last year? Of course he can. And you know Pharaoh isn't his real name, right? He had it legally changed when he was a kid."

"Why'd he do that?"

"Because he's Rick Bradley's son."

"I don't follow."

"Major Rick Bradley? First Gulf War?"

The president thought a moment, then he remembered the headlines. "Wow, that's too bad. I can see why he did that."

"His father's still sitting in Leavenworth."

"Aw, Jesus, why didn't you tell me this sooner?"

"Just found out myself. And because the kid is good. And his NCOs are great, so I'm told. And because the kid must have one huge chip on his shoulder."

The president nodded. "I see. He's out there to prove that he's better than his old man. He's already saved the president of Afghanistan."

"Now he's going to save our political asses."

19. INFILTRATION

The Black Hawk thundered through the night, the rhythm of its rotors and the vibration of its turbo shafts filling Walrus with a sense of raw power. He loved flying. He should have been a pilot. Alas, he'd made different choices in his life.

The entire team and Rock had been jammed aboard the chopper, and the four-man crew of "Night Stalkers" from the 160th Special Operations Aviation Regiment hadn't been thrilled about a couple of extra guys beyond the usual eleven. Their expressions said it all.

Walrus sat crunched up in the rear, helmet and headset on so he could listen to the pilots, crew chief, and other radio chatter. Pharaoh, who sat next to him, was also listening in, as was Zulu. The rest of the team kept their heads lowered, some stealing a quick nap. They had all donned their "drug smuggling duds" as Walrus liked to call them—the tattered clothing of local Afghans—and toted AKs and other assorted Russian-made weapons.

Just fifty feet below, in the grainy night, the dunes rolled by, an endless brown sea broken here and there by long lines of crests formed by the winds. The locals had nicknamed the entire area the "desert of death," and with good reason.

"Captain Pharaoh, we're about five minutes out now if you want to get your men ready," said the pilot.

"Roger that. Do you see our taxi?"

"Not yet, sir."

"All right. Maybe they're late, but we're getting off either way." The chopper began to bank as Pharaoh passed word to get set.

Walrus glanced over at Zulu and barely caught his gaze in the scarce light. The team sergeant just eyed him stoically. Walrus wanted to say, *Hey, I could told have told them already.*

He wondered what he really hoped to gain by dangling Zulu on a string. Maybe teach the guy some humility? Maybe teach him a hard lesson about being a true Special Forces brother? Would Zulu really learn those lessons?

With a shrug, Walrus removed his helmet and headset, donned his goggles, and adjusted his grip on his rifle.

As the engines roared, the Black Hawk's nose rose, and the bird thumped down for a landing below an absolutely stunning dome of stars.

One by one they jumped down into the blinding rotor wash, the sand stinging Walrus's cheeks, his eyes protected by the goggles.

The team immediately split in two to form a defensive perimeter around the drop zone in case they had been observed and might suddenly fall under attack.

Pharaoh signaled the crew chief, and the Black Hawk immediately dusted off.

While every operator was lying prone, a radio check commenced. No problems with the MBITRs. Amazing.

They remained in position for a few moments more, as the dust began to settle and Rock and Pharaoh scanned the western hills with their NVGs.

"Titan 06, this is Rock. I see two trucks coming, lights off, over."

"Roger that. People, let's move out."

The two men who had been hired to drive the trucks were well-paid and loyal CIA informants whom Rock had known since the days right after 9/11. They operated in and around the tri-border area, gathering intel for him and other agents in Iran and reporting back. They were used to crossing the border, knew a few shortcuts off the beaten path (there was but one main road heading south to Zahedan), and Rock felt confident that they were the best men for this simple but very dangerous job.

What did bother him, though, was that they had his satellite phone number and had been instructed to call him upon their approach to the rendezvous point.

Thus far, they had not, and Rock chalked it up to an unforeseen but harmless delay. They were probably in a mad dash to make the point at the scheduled time.

The team took up positions along a little rut, and as the truck came within a quarter mile, Rock fished out his Gladius and gave the customary three quick flashes.

He sighed as the lead truck flashed its headlights once. "All right, guys," he called into his mike. "Got a good signal."

"Roger that," said Pharaoh. "Everybody hold position until they stop."

Rock tensed as the trucks drew even closer, long tails of dust wagging behind them. The pair of dilapidated pickups with caps over their beds were probably twenty or more years old. He zoomed in with his *Star Wars* binoculars now, but he still couldn't get a clear image of either driver, though the beards and body types looked familiar enough.

He would head out first, along with Hojo, to ensure that everything was all right.

That part he didn't like. But the arrangements were his.

Once the trucks reached the crest of a slight hill, they stopped, and Pharaoh gave the order.

Rock burst from his position, along with Hojo, and they both headed off to the trucks.

Even as he ran, Rock's satellite phone began to ring. He snorted and thought, *Now you call me? I'll be there in a minute.*

So he let the call go directly to his voice mail and kept on. As they neared the lead truck, the driver climbed down, along with another man, as the rear truck suddenly roared around it, heading directly for the team.

A gunshot rang out.

The driver of the lead truck had been shot in the head by the other guy.

"Titan 06, this is Thunder!" cried Hojo. "Ambush! Ambush! Ambush!"

Rock dove as the rear truck roared by and a guy in a black turban leaned out the window and fired a salvo at him, then turned his bead on Hojo.

Rock's satellite phone rang again as he rolled, came up, then brought his rifle around to return fire, but a half dozen pops echoed behind him, and he realized that three guys had just come from the parked truck and were running toward him and Hojo.

"I got the rear!" he screamed and whirled around to deliver a half dozen rounds of his own that sent those men to sand.

He knew if he didn't move, they would advance and finish him. They had him outnumbered and out in the open.

But if he did move, he'd be even more vulnerable, presenting a much larger target.

Rock shuddered with the desire to act, as behind him, every guy on the ODA seemed to be firing, rounds thudding and ricocheting off the truck.

"Rock, go, I'll cover you!" cried Hojo. "Now!"

Without a second thought, Rock burst from the dirt, heading off to flank the other guys, while Hojo thoroughly hosed down the three. But then his weapon went silent, and Rock hit the ground, just as incoming rounds chewed at the sand no more than a few meters from his boots.

He returned fire, caught one guy, wanted to scream in triumph, but the other two opened up on him, and he flinched and ducked as the bullets whirred overhead.

Zulu ran directly at the oncoming truck, firing madly at the driver, rounds shattering the windshield and punching the guy back into his seat, blood spraying.

The truck turned abruptly to the left as two guys bailed out the back, both spinning around to face Zulu.

For an instant he knew he couldn't shoot both in time—

But before they fired, dozens of rounds coming from behind Zulu tore up their chests and drove them onto their backs, all of it happening in the faint light. Zulu wasn't sure they were dead until he ran forward and shot them again himself.

"Walrus, Gator, Ondejko? Get the truck!" Pharaoh shouted. "The rest of you move up!"

Zulu was supposed to be fighting the team, but his mad dash forward had left Pharaoh no choice, it seemed. He'd catch hell for that later.

Two gunmen were still firing at Hojo and Rock, and a few more muzzle flashes woke from behind the parked truck.

Zulu broke off to the left in a wide arc, hoping the bad guys were too intent on targeting the rest of the team coming straight at them.

He made it past the first two guys, but piles of sand kicked up by incoming rounds began spewing over his boots, and it was only then he realized that at least one guy out near the truck had seen him.

"This is Titan 06. Take out these guys but save the trucks, you read me? Save those goddamned trucks!"

Zulu had been in his share of firefights, and this one offered few advantages. There was scarce cover and no good chance to frag the bad guys, because as the captain had just reminded them they needed the vehicles. It could quickly turn into a time-wasting standoff, and they needed to be across the border before daybreak.

So the hell with it—he kept on toward the idiots behind the truck, returning fire at the guy who had spotted him, surprising the bastard by continuing to fire and run right at him, even as the guy adjusted position, trying to get down near one of the tires.

But the fool's movement betrayed him, and Zulu took him out quickly, though at least one of Zulu's rounds punctured a tire, the air hissing. Damn.

Zulu reached the truck, spotted the other two guys lying on their bellies near the back tires, their popping guns drowning out his approach.

In a heartbeat he had his XSF-1 combat dagger in a reverse grip and plunged it home in a spinal-shot kill to the guy nearest him.

His left hand, now clutching his little Makarov, turned slightly, and he aimed the pistol at the other guy's head, pulled the trigger. Game over for him.

Just ahead, Hojo and Rock had finally finished off their guys and were breaking from cover.

Zulu rose, panting, blood dripping from his dagger. He checked inside the pickup truck's cap: empty. Then he went around the truck to the driver's side, wrenched it open. The cab was clear. He moved over to the guy who'd been executed, probably Rock's contact.

That guess was confirmed as Rock jogged up and dropped to examine the guy with his light. "Aw, man, what the hell happened?"

"We can't count on you for anything, can we?" Zulu asked through his teeth.

"Zu, that was crazy, man!" cried Hojo, who'd come up behind Rock. "You ran right into that fire."

"No, I didn't."

"Yeah, you did. I saw you."

Zulu grabbed Hojo's shoulder and squeezed. "No, I didn't. The guy with the best covers wins the fight."

"Uh, okay . . ."

"Zulu, this is Titan 06, over."

Zulu adjusted his headset and closed his eyes, bracing himself. "This is Zulu, go ahead."

"We're clear over here. They're all down. Truck's shot up bad, leaking everything. How's yours, over?"

"Flat tire, otherwise I think okay. We'll get a tire off that one, over?"

"Roger that, I'm sending Sullivan and Figueroa. Send Rock over here—right now, out."

"Hey, Rock, they want you over there."

"Gee, I wonder why," Rock snapped, getting to his feet. Then he reached for his satellite phone and quickly dialed a number, waited, listened to a voice—

And Zulu wished he had a camera. The look on Rock's face was priceless.

Pure shock.

In fact, he'd never seen that face.

"Hey, Rock, you all right?"

"Not now!" he screamed, holding up his hand.

Figueroa and Sullivan came bounding up. "What's up here, Zu?" asked Figueroa.

"Nothing. How you doing?"

"Good. Except I'm feeling a little bloated and a little emotional right now." Figueroa smiled sarcastically. "Boss says you got a flat tire."

"It's right over here."

"Hey, Zu, what the hell happened?" asked Sullivan.

"I have no idea. Why don't you ask him?" Zulu cocked a thumb over his shoulder at Rock, who was still clutching his satellite phone but was now frozen like a darkly clad statue in the fluttering sand.

20. A FAIR PRICE

The voice mail message for Rock had come from Jack Andropolis, who had called from his car to confirm that someone on the inside had tipped off the congressman regarding the intercept plan. They had sent a group to hijack Rock's trucks, head out to the rendezvous point, and intercept the Special Forces team. As Jack had been trying to warn Rock, gunshots had rung out, and Jack had gasped, "I've been shot. Oh my God." And the call had ended.

Sullivan came up to Rock, opened his mouth, and Rock raised a finger. He turned and stared off into the distant dunes. He thought of Jack's family, of how they'd take the loss. Rock had eaten dinner more times than he could remember at Jack's house and had even attended the wedding of Jack's oldest daughter. He had been there when the younger son had graduated from high school. Who would tell them that their father had been murdered? And would Rock ever tell them that he had been the one who had pushed Jack into learning more?

Rock clenched his fists against the guilt. Only Libra and Jersey knew the whole truth, and he shuddered with the

desire to confront them. It seemed Jack had not known anything about the woman who had called to say she had the
pictures he wanted. Nevertheless, Rock had set up the meeting with her. She would not reveal her name, but she might
have been hired by Libra and Jersey and could take him to
them, for the right price, of course.

"Rock," said Zulu from somewhere behind. "What the
hell was this?"

Rock finally turned and approached the man, while the
others began hauling out an old spare they had found below the rusted cap over the flatbed.

With a snort, Rock threw up his hands.

"You'd better start talking," Zulu warned.

"This is bad."

"That's all you got?"

"For you, yeah."

Off to Rock's left, Walrus trudged up looking daggers
at Rock. "Guess we got you to thank for tight security, huh?"
In a blur of movement, Walrus had his paws on Rock's
collar.

Rock ripped at Walrus's hands and cursed.

"Walrus, enough," ordered Pharaoh, who'd just jogged
over.

"Yes, sir," said the warrant from the corner of his mouth
as he released Rock.

But then, to Rock's surprise, Pharaoh grabbed Rock by
the neck and squeezed. "He doesn't get to choke you. I do."

"Damn, Captain, take it easy," said Zulu.

Rock reached up, but Pharaoh was already letting him
go. "Smart move," said Rock.

"Who jacked your drivers?" demanded Pharaoh. "Who?"

"I don't know."

"And your contact in Zahedan? What the hell was his
name, Nasser Abdullah—"

"Nasser Abedzadeh," Rock corrected.

"They get to him, too?"

"I don't know."

"What the hell *do* you know?"

"Listen, I'll call Nasser."

"And he could be answering with a gun to his head."

Rock bared his teeth. "Hey, Captain, if you want, call back the chopper and go home, be my guest. Just leave me the truck. I got my own orders. I'm going."

Pharaoh's tone grew even darker. "We're all going. Our president wants us there. I just want to know if you got a backup plan—because I do."

"You mean like kill everyone and let Jesus sort 'em out?"

"No, wiseass. A plan, as in I don't want my face on Al Jazeera before they chop off my head."

"Just take it easy. I have a little code with these guys. He'll tell me if he's been captured." Rock dialed the number.

Two rings later, Nasser picked up, and Rock spoke quickly with him in Baluchi, mentioning the three code words. Nasser repeated the code. He was okay. Rock told him about the hijacking and intercept attempt. He said he had not heard anything about it from his people and was still standing by to receive Rock and his team.

"We're good there. He's waiting for us."

"Then we'd better move," said Pharaoh. He called out to the men fixing the tire. They had three minutes. He put another team on the bodies. They'd be buried in shallow graves and as many of the shell casings policed up as possible. He'd mark the location on GPS and forward it to higher.

A narrow, unmarked dirt road, approximately five kilometers wide, ran southeast out of Afghanistan and crossed into a small corner of Pakistan before terminating at the Iranian border. The road was walled in by mountains to the north and south, and there were two small checkpoints at each end manned by no more than three or four guards, according to Rock.

The original plan had been to head north, circle around the mountains, and pick up Iran's A78/13 Highway that ran south between Hamark and Zahedan, but Pharaoh had been convinced by Rock that they would waste a lot of time doing that, and might not have enough fuel for the journey, since they'd discovered that the "good" truck's gas tank was now leaking. They'd done their best to plug the leak, but the repair might not last very long. Additionally, they'd decided to use what they had, some 550 paracord, to tow the second truck. Its fuel tank was already empty and the radiator had been torn to shreds, but they needed it, since they could not fit thirteen individuals in one vehicle.

So with their towing operation under way, seven guys in the working truck, six in the tow vehicle, they rumbled toward the border, keeping well west of the nearby town of Robat-e Jali. If they made it past the two border crossings, they would hit the highway just thirty kilometers north of the city.

Pharaoh drove the truck with Rock seated beside him. Zulu was in the narrow backseat, along with Ondejko, while Grimm, Weathers, and Figueroa were in the back. Howling wind gusts of fifty miles an hour or more slammed into the trucks as they pushed on, headlights off in the darkness, with Pharaoh using his NVGs to navigate over the rocks.

"There it is," said Rock, lowering his high-tech binoculars.

Ahead lay two old police trucks parked in a wedge shape, with just enough room for a vehicle to come through. There was no elaborate fence, guardhouse, or long wooden pole for them to smash through. Just a lonely little section of mountainous terrain.

"Flash your headlight once," said Rock.

Pharaoh complied, and a flash came from one of the trucks. Then, two men climbed from each truck, rifles drawn, as Pharaoh eased back on the accelerator and brought them to a stop. The four men fanned out, a pair on each side.

"Stay here," instructed Rock.

"All right, everybody," Pharaoh began over the radio. "Hold fire but stay sharp."

One of the guards, a heavyset, heavily bearded man who, with those characteristics, looked like the average Joe in Pakistan, came toward Rock. They spoke quickly while the other guards worked flashlights on their truck and the one behind. Rock then turned back and came around the driver's side to Pharaoh. "He's asking a lot of questions about what happened to our trucks. I told him we were almost hijacked by bandits trying to steal our shipment."

"Will they let us cross?"

"Sure. For a thousand."

"A thousand? How about fifty bucks?"

"You got ten thousand in that suitcase. Easy come, easy go."

Pharaoh snorted. "Is that even a fair price?"

"Fair in this part of the world is determined by the laws of supply and demand. But I have something in mind that'll make it more than worth the money. That second checkpoint will be much tougher to cross, but I think these guys can help. Just give me a few minutes."

Rock stepped back and began the negotiations.

Zulu leaned forward and said, "I'd rather just shoot them, take their trucks, and storm the next checkpoint."

"Then we'll have everybody and his mother looking for us in the city," said Pharaoh. "Nice plan."

"Bring 'em on."

"That's your new strategy, huh? You know, I saw what you did back there."

"What're you talking about?"

"You ran straight into the fire."

"No, I attacked."

"No, you were hoping to get shot."

Before Zulu could answer, Rock returned with their new best friend, who was now puffing hard on a fresh cigar. "Okay, give me the money. We're good to go."

Pharaoh craned his head toward Zulu. "Dig it out. Get me ten."

Zulu reached under the seat, produced a suitcase, and fished out the cash. "Tell 'em not to spend it all in one place."

Rock took the money and handed it over to the guard, who grinned broadly, pointed to the southern mountains, and began speaking far too quickly for Pharaoh to translate.

After both men chuckled, Rock crossed back to the passenger's seat and climbed in. "Let's go."

Pharaoh threw the truck in gear and slowly moved on, as Walrus, who was behind the wheel of the rear truck, got on the radio and told him to slow up until the paracord pulled taut. Then they rolled on.

"There's another little dirt road coming up on our left. Take it. It'll bring us around a smaller little pass, then farther south, past the checkpoint altogether. It's the one most smugglers use, but it seems the Iranians are okay with it because these Pakistanis give them a little cut to keep their mouths shut and everyone's happy. No one patrols this other road, and there's no checkpoint."

"You had a feeling about that, didn't you?"

"This happens up and down the border."

"They like to play Allah," said Zulu. "They decide who passes into the next life, and who doesn't."

"I think you're reaching there, Zu," said Rock. "These guys are just greedy bastards who play a game. And every once in a while some punk smugglers come down here and shove guns in their mouths. They figure for that kind of danger they should be better compensated. Ain't like the government's going to make that happen. So I don't blame them."

"They're just cowards and thieves."

"So are we. Just depends on the day and the mission."

"No, I don't think so."

Pharaoh thought a curse as the truck dropped hard into a pothole, then came back up. The other truck was already plunging into the hole as Walrus got on the radio and asked for a warning next time. Pharaoh silenced him and described the new route into Iran.

Then, when he was finished, he looked over at Rock and asked, "You're sure we can trust those guys?"

Rock laughed under his breath. "You've already bet your life on them."

21. NIGHT MEETING

Walrus's head snapped back as the pickup truck jerked forward. He felt as though he were on a carnival ride operated by a beer-soaked sadist with a cigarette dangling from his mouth.

It seemed Pharaoh had hit a bump, and slack had dropped in the towline. "You'll break it, you keep that up, sir," he warned the captain over the radio.

"Tell me when that happens again."

Trouble was, Walrus, sans night vision goggles, could barely see the paracord in the darkness. Occasionally, a thin shadow would catch his eye, seeming to rise up from the windswept mountain pass a few seconds before the next jerk.

Assistant Operations Sergeant Hojo rode shotgun, and he continually shifted in his seat and jutted his head out the open window. "Won't be much longer," he said, checking his watch. "Once we hit the highway, should be smooth sailing from there."

"Till we reach the city, and we find out if the hotel Rock booked us in is being run by Hassan."

"Either way, I heard we get free HBO."

Walrus shot him an ugly grin. "Between Rock, an inexperienced captain, and a nut job like Zulu, you boys don't got a prayer, do you?"

"Isn't that why you're here?"

"Absolutely. Somebody needs to take command of you misfits."

Hojo chuckled under his breath. "Damn, I guess Zulu's right about you."

"Oh, yeah?"

"Funny thing is, as an old-timer, you ought to know that the guys who come out here with the biggest egos make the biggest targets."

"Got something you want to say? Say it."

"Lay off Zulu."

"Or what?"

"What's your problem, man?"

Walrus let the question hang for a moment as he concentrated on the bumpy road. Another sharp tug forward had both of them cursing. He got back on the radio, told Pharaoh to slow down a little, then he glanced at Hojo and said, "That man up there in the truck, the guy you call Zulu, the guy you think you know? You don't know him at all. That's my problem." He grinned darkly at Hojo, who returned an equally sarcastic grin.

After a moment, Walrus added, "Hojo? You and me, we'll get along just fine, so long as you understand where I'm coming from. And I think from this point on, you'll refer to me as Chief Warrant Officer Kowalski."

"Excuse me?"

"If you don't like that, you can just call me Assistant Detachment Commander Kowalski."

"Now you're pulling rank?"

"Do not test me, son. Talk to your boy Zulu about what it's like if you do that."

"Chief Warrant Officer Kowalski?"

"Yes?"

"You're an asshole."

Walrus bust out laughing. "Yeah, the worst kind."

Pharaoh stopped the truck about fifty meters away from the highway. He, Rock, and Zulu got out and surveyed the checkpoint which now lay about a half click north of their position. "Your Pakistani buddy was a man of his word," said Pharaoh.

"He's all right," said Rock.

"Good thing," added Zulu. "They got about twenty guys up there."

Pharaoh jogged back to Walrus's truck. The warrant was rubbing his tired eyes with one hand, massaging his neck with the other. "Highway's ahead. We'll be in the city in about a half hour."

"But not before you break my neck."

"Sorry."

Walrus wagged an index finger, waving Pharaoh in closer. "You're not sorry. But let's go."

Pharaoh made a face, called the others back to the truck, and they moved out.

Walrus had been right. Pharaoh was not sorry. The warrant had payback coming with interest.

They thumped up onto the highway and began the remarkably smooth ride toward the city, whose lights soon shimmered up from the black mountains.

Rock had been in Zahedan before and purported to know his way around the city, so they turned off the highway and headed down into the labyrinth of dirt roads intersected by hundreds of dark alleyways between single-story ramshackle homes and businesses. Rock told Pharaoh to turn left here, make another right there. Head down this street. No—you missed the turn. We'll come back around.

They pulled up behind a long row of flat-roofed houses whose forward sections had been converted into businesses, among them a local grocery store and a clothing shop. On the back side were the families' living quarters.

"This is Titan 06, everybody sit tight," ordered Pharaoh. He and Rock got out, and Rock lifted his fist to knock on a rear door. Suddenly, the door opened, and a young man probably in his twenties emerged and thumbed his glasses higher on his nose. He wore a small cap and sported a brown beard as thick as steel wool. A deep scar ran from just beneath his left earlobe and wound down across the side of his neck, vanishing below his collar.

He and Rock embraced a moment, spoke in Baluchi, then Rock turned and in English said, "Nasser, this is my friend James."

"Nice to meet you, James." Nasser's English was heavily accented but clear enough.

Pharaoh nodded and spoke in English. "Can we get inside? And we need to ditch these trucks."

"We'll take care of that," said Nasser. "Just leave them here."

Pharaoh nodded and lifted his voice a little. "All right, everybody. Let's go. Nasser, I need to put a man on your roof. You okay with that?"

Nasser smiled. "No need."

"It's a good idea," insisted Pharaoh.

"Look up."

And when Pharaoh did, he locked gazes with a gunman who rose up from the tall ledge, brandishing an AK-47. "That is my cousin Yousef," Nasser explained. "He is also a policeman and has his radio with him. He will help keep them from interfering with your work."

"Outstanding." Pharaoh looked to Rock. "About time something went right."

"Don't push it. We're just getting started," said Rock.

"Can we go in?" asked Walrus, shouldering his pack.

"This way," said Nasser, pushing the door farther open. Inside they found two small rooms which were, in effect,

Nasser's entire house for his wife and two small children; all three were sleeping—or at least pretending to do so at his request.

Pharaoh and his men filed into a third room about the size of a two-car garage. This was Nasser's warehouse for grocery back stock. Shelves lined the walls, and wooden pallets of boxed stock rose toward the ceiling. The room had a peculiar odor that hinted of something rotten. A rat scurried out from beneath one pallet and raced to a second.

"Forgive the smell," said Nasser. "There was a little dispute at the border, and the produce I ship to Afghanistan has been sitting here three days, waiting to go out. I'm afraid some has already spoiled. We will get it all out of here in the morning."

"Thanks," said Pharaoh. "Where's the toilet?"

"Out back, across the alley. I'm afraid we only have a pit. If you want a real toilet, you have to go down the street, but not tonight. Also, don't drink the piped water. It is not very sanitary."

"That's okay, we've brought our own," said Pharaoh, who then faced the group. "Gentlemen, get settled in, then we'll go back over the recon plan."

"I'll be right back," said Rock. "Got to use the pit."

As he headed back out, Pharaoh asked Nasser if he could post a man at the front door of the grocery.

"Inside, yes, but when we open early, he must go. My customers will know something is going on if they see him just standing there."

"I understand."

Pharaoh put Weathers and Sullivan on first watch at the front and rear doors, then he went over to Zulu and sat beside him. Walrus had positioned himself on the other side of the room, beside a wall of fifty-pound bags of rice piled six high. Grimm and Figueroa were talking quietly with him as they fished out their canteens and MREs.

Attempting to begin the search for Jersey, Libra, and Abu Hassan at night was, according to Nasser, much too dangerous. The only folks out during the wee hours were the police, the Revolutionary Guard, and the local bandits. Anyone else would be stopped and confronted by one or more of the former groups unless he knew his way around the city and could carefully avoid them. Nasser had insisted it was better to wait until early morning.

"I'm afraid we can't do that," said Pharaoh. "The men we're after could be gone by then."

Nasser drew in a long breath. "If you are captured, Captain, there will be nothing we can do . . ."

Zulu, who'd just plopped down his pack, muttered, "I'm going to go use the facility myself."

Pharaoh nodded, opened his canteen, and took a long pull.

Zulu had his Russian-made APB/6P13 silenced pistol jammed into his belt beneath his woolen coat, and he'd already attached the silencer. He slipped out into the alley and hit the opposite wall, watching as Rock left the little outhouse and jogged off down the alley.

"Old man, you're getting too predictable," Zulu muttered, then he fell into Rock's path, keeping close to the building, ducking occasionally into doorways to give Rock a chance to pick up more lead.

Rock hustled down another alley, then craned his neck, nearly spotting Zulu, who slipped back around the corner. Zulu waited for another heart-pounding moment, then he chanced a look around the corner, where Rock stood near an old car that had just pulled up, a Paykan that was an exact copy of the British Hillman Hunter, a boxy-looking sedan from the 1970s. The city was full of them, and many were owned by taxicab drivers. If Rock got into that car, Zulu would lose him.

But, thankfully, Rock did not. As he approached, a lithe young woman, wearing a short, tight-fitting coat, Capri pants, and a short scarf that were hardly the traditional burqa and/or hijab worn by most Iranian women, stepped out, along with a young man who'd been at the wheel. The guy whirled and aimed a pistol at Rock's head.

Zulu dug into his coat and withdrew his own weapon.

"Put that gun back in your pocket, where it belongs," Rock told the punk with the smug expression on his teenaged face. "If I wanted you dead, you'd already be playing hokm with Allah."

The kid snorted. "You speak Baluchi well—for a foreigner."

Rock faced the girl. "Are you Fatima?"

"I am. Let me see the money."

"You never mentioned a price." Rock grabbed her by the throat, and her little boyfriend or whoever he was moved in with the pistol. "Let her go."

"What pictures do you have?" Rock demanded, ignoring the kid.

"Kill him," Fatima told her friend. "Shoot him now."

"He's not that stupid," said Rock.

The kid swallowed, his gaze darting between Rock, the alley, and Fatima.

"He kills me, he wakes up everyone," Rock continued. "They'll find you. Show me the pictures."

Pharaoh glanced up as Sullivan came back into the room, shaking his head. Pharaoh motioned him in closer so the others couldn't hear. "They're not out there, sir. But I did talk to that guy Yousef on the roof. His English sucks, but I got enough out of him. He says he saw Rock take off up the alley, then a few seconds later, another guy followed. Must've been Zulu."

Pharaoh cursed. "Thanks, Sully."

"Yes, sir." Sullivan headed off to his post.

"What's the matter?" asked Walrus from across the

room. "We're still not ready? I want to go over this and catch an hour's sleep."

"Just give a minute." Pharaoh rose and left the room, heading back outside to the rear door. There, he stood beside Sullivan and called for Zulu and Rock on the radio. Neither answered.

"What the hell's going on, sir?" asked Sullivan.

Pharaoh stiffened. "I don't know. But heads are going to roll."

Zulu wasn't sure if Rock saw the other person across the alleyway. Though it was dark, Zulu did make out the figure of a heavyset woman, although, with veil and loose clothing, "she" could easily have been a "he" in disguise. That person edged up along the wall behind Rock and the others, an arm extended. Zulu clearly made out a pistol in that person's hand.

The kid still held his gun on Rock, who was still clutching the young girl by the neck.

Who posed the greater threat to the spook? The kid with the gun or the figure behind them?

Zulu assumed he had two, maybe three seconds to make up his mind.

Rock repeated his question. "Show me the pictures."

"I need to see money first."

Rock shoved her backward into the car, dug into his pocket, and produced a stack of cash. "I have money."

Fatima cocked a brow and glanced back at her boyfriend. "Give me the camera."

As the kid reached into his pocket, a shot cracked.

Reflexively, Rock hit the ground as Fatima slammed back against the car, then shrank to the street beside him, blood trickling down her head.

The kid shouted something as movement came from the

corner. Rock rolled, came up with his weapon, and took aim at the figure darting forward, a figure he immediately recognized as Zulu.

"Zu!" he cried, as the team sergeant fired his silenced pistol, then shifted his aim toward another target, the boyfriend perhaps.

Rock burst to his feet. Zulu had just shot someone across the alley.

The boyfriend sprinted to a corner, turned, and vanished.

"You idiot!" shouted Rock, who wrenched open the car door, saw that the keys were missing, probably with the kid.

"I just saved your ass," said Zulu. "What the hell are you doing here?"

"Jesus!" Rock darted around the car and raced toward the corner where the kid had run.

When he reached that corner, he stared down into the deepening shadows as doors began to open and heads slowly appeared.

"Rock?"

Breathing a loud curse, Rock jogged back to where Zulu squatted down before the first person he'd shot.

Zulu peeled away the woman's veil. "Look, man, she's old. Really old. What the hell?"

"She must've shot the girl."

"I saw her. I was going to shoot her, but she fired first," said Zulu.

"We need to leave—now!" said Rock.

"You mind telling me what the hell this is?"

"This is you screwing up our entire plan," Rock said. "Come on!"

22. SECRETS AND SACRIFICES

"James, Yousef tells me there's been a shooting nearby," said Nasser, his face creased with concern. "It is on the police radio. I hope it does not involve your missing men."

"You're a wishful thinker," said Pharaoh through a groan. "I'm sure it does."

Pharaoh was balling his hands into fists, ready to pound flesh. He glanced over at Walrus, who sat there calmly stroking his Fu Manchu. "Those two meatheads will screw the pooch. And it'll be you and I hanging out to dry. Hey, that rhymes."

"Just shut up."

Walrus closed his eyes, continued stroking his mustache.

Nasser spoke quickly on his cell phone then hung up. "Yousef says Rock and one of your men are on their way. They are running."

Pharaoh rushed to the back door, went into the alley, then raised his finger at Rock as the man approached.

"Rock, what the hell—"

"Not now. Everybody inside!" The spook plowed past him and wrenched open the door.

Zulu came thundering up just behind, his silenced pistol in one hand.

"Took a wrong turn on the way to the toilet?" Pharaoh snapped.

"Captain, listen to me. I followed him out. Rock was taking a meeting with a girl and some guy. I don't know what he was doing, but it all went south. One old lady showed up and shot this young girl, and I had to shoot her. I figured she'd go after Rock next."

"Slow down."

Zulu swallowed, tried to get his breath. "Come on, I'll go over it again." He started for the door.

When they entered the storeroom, they found Rock pressed up against a back wall, with Walrus shoving a pistol into the man's head and growling, "Talk, spooky. Tell us all about it. Right now."

Jafar had watched his younger sister die before his eyes, and he could barely contain his anger as he hunkered down in the alley and dialed the number. He did not know who he was calling, but he needed to tell someone what had happened.

Fatima had contacted him when she had taken the job in Zahedan. She had said there might be an opportunity for him to get work in the border city. So he had followed her from Qom, and then she had called with what she claimed was a plan that would make both of them rich.

He once again pictured her lying there in the street, shot in the head by the old woman she had betrayed.

Fatima had prostituted herself and, worse, had been aiding and abetting infidels. Allah, praise his name, had more ways to exact justice than there were grains of sand in the desert. She had tested Allah and had lost.

A man finally answered the phone. "Hello?"

"Hello. This is Jafar."

"Who are you?"

"I am Fatima's brother."

"And she works for Ezzat."

"The old woman?"

"Yes."

"She's dead. And so is Fatima."

A long pause followed, then the man asked, "What happened?"

Jafar explained, and the man said, "You will call Rock. You must give him those pictures. Tell him Libra asked for him to stay close. Tell him we will be in the city for another day. Libra will call him."

"Are you Libra?"

The line went dead.

Jafar snapped shut the cell phone and stood there, wondering if he should make that call. Rock's number was programmed into the cell phone Fatima had given him. But how could he deliver the pictures and get some money without being killed? He could not simply call Rock and arrange for another meeting without help. And then there was his sister to think about. Where would they take her body? Could he claim her, take her back home? Or would that raise too many questions?

His eyes burned with indecision.

Zulu charged across the room, toward where Walrus was holding Rock at gunpoint, and cried, "Let him go."

"This rat bastard will get us all killed. I'm not going out there till he spills his guts, or I do it for him."

Rock cursed at Walrus, then withdrew an unlit cigar from his breast pocket and shoved it in his mouth, attempting to prove he was unfazed by the gun to his head.

Zulu moved in closer to growl in the old warrant's ear. "Walrus, you asshole, just back off."

"Maybe the spooks recruited you, too," spat the old warrant.

"Secure that weapon," Pharaoh ordered.

"Captain, with all due respect, don't you want to hear him talk?" asked Walrus.

"He will. Lower that goddamned weapon—or I'm going to relieve you of duty and put your fat ass on the next camel back home. *Do you read me?*"

The room fell into utter silence.

Walrus shook his head. "Captain, we ain't playing games here. If you send us out there without being fully briefed and one of us buys it, *you* are responsible."

"Thanks for the tip." Pharaoh's tone grew even more steely. "Two seconds."

Walrus snorted and began to lower his pistol.

But before he could move even a fraction of an inch more, Zulu rushed in behind him, seized the man's arm, twisted it behind the old warrant's back, then quickly tripped Walrus to the dirt floor.

Once Walrus was down, Zulu pinned him with a knee to the small of his back and applied more pressure.

"Two can play this game," said Zulu. "And I think you fall a lot harder than me."

As Walrus grunted, Zulu pried the weapon from his fingers and handed it to Rock. Then Zulu turned to Pharaoh and spoke through his teeth. "Captain, you were right the first time. Relieve this asshole of duty. We can't work with him anymore." Zulu applied more pressure, threatening to break Walrus's arm.

Pharaoh lifted his voice. "Zu, he was standing down. Just let him—"

"You ain't relieving me of duty," hollered Walrus. "You want to relieve someone, relieve Zulu!"

"Shut up, old man!" shouted Zulu.

"Zu, enough!" hollered Pharaoh.

"Everybody, listen to me," cried Walrus. "This bastard on top of me slept with Bull's wife. He killed Church.

That's what he did. That's what your boy did. He's an adulterer. He's a murderer. That's the team sergeant you got, Captain Pharaoh!"

Zulu closed his eyes and lost his breath.

The others gathered around Pharaoh as Zulu tightened his grip on Walrus.

"Zu, get off of him," warned Pharaoh.

Abruptly, Zulu released Walrus and bolted to his feet. "He's telling stories. He just wants to see me hang."

Walrus rolled over and sat up, massaging his arm, his face still twisted in pain. "They don't have to listen to me. Why don't you tell him yourself, Zu? Air out your laundry before we go out that door."

"I didn't kill Church!" shouted Zulu.

Walrus struggled to his feet. "To hell you didn't! He was the only one besides me who knew you were banging Bull's wife. You shut him up for good. And I'm next on your list."

"Jesus Christ." Pharaoh groaned, trying to repress his shock. "All right, listen up. I want the truth—right now. Do you hear me?" Pharaoh turned, letting his gaze fall upon each and every member of the team.

Assistant medic Anthony Grimm tipped his head toward the back of the room and senior medic Borokovsky slowly shook his head. They couldn't move, couldn't do anything.

Grimm wasn't sure he could hold back anymore. He had to say something.

They had lied to protect Church's good name. The captain would understand that.

Or maybe he wouldn't. He was trying to make a name for himself, playing it by the book.

But was it worth it? Zulu was one of the best operators

they had. They would be sacrificing him to protect Church.

Borokovsky widened his eyes: *Don't say a word.*

Grimm could already hear the words exploding from his lips. He stiffened and just stood there. *I'm sorry, Zu.*

"Well, gentlemen," continued Pharaoh. "Official report says Church was fragged by the enemy, and that's the way it'll stand—unless someone here's got proof otherwise."

"I do," said Walrus. "Bull's wife is my sister-in-law. Most of you guys know that. Melissa told my wife she was having an affair with Zulu."

"Who cares?" asked McDaniel. "That's personal stuff. Zulu is the best operator out here. No one will argue with that."

"You new school punks don't understand honor and fidelity and respect," said Walrus. "Not the way we do. You don't do that to a fellow operator, especially one who gave his life for this team. You don't piss on a man's grave like that."

"So you got your wife's word that he had an affair, and you told Church. And you're assuming Church threatened Zulu so he killed him," said Pharaoh. "Sounds like you got nothing, old man."

"You want to call my wife right now?"

Pharaoh frowned. "You still can't prove Church threatened Zulu, so you got nothing but gossip."

Walrus threw up his hands. "You guys can believe what you want, but I'm telling you this guy right here has no respect, no honor, and no right to be on this team."

Pharaoh turned to Zulu and raised his brows.

Zulu had sworn he would never admit to the affair, that he was doing so to protect Bull's reputation, yet he wondered now, given what they were about to do, if his own reputation was more important—if only to instill confidence in the rest of the team. They had doubts about him now. And he wondered if a confession would help . . . or hurt him even more.

His shoulders slumped as he leaned back against the wall and closed his eyes. "I didn't piss on Bull's grave. You have no idea how much respect I had for that man."

"Ha! You're really pushing it now," said Walrus.

"Hey, asshole, you don't have to like me, just work with me."

"Is he telling the truth?" Pharaoh asked Zulu.

Zulu steeled himself, no reaction.

"All right, this conversation is over," Pharaoh said, no room for argument in his tone. "We have a mission. Period. And right now, Rock's going to tell us about his intelligence gathering operation, the one he conveniently forgot to tell us about."

Zulu glanced up, his gaze panning the room, the other operators staring at him awkwardly, as though trying to ferret out the truth from his expression.

Rock removed the cigar from his mouth and said, "Gentlemen, I was about to—at least I think I was—secure the location of our targets. I didn't want or need any help, but you know what? Thank God for Zulu, here. If he hadn't followed, I would've been capped." Rock glanced at Zulu and gave a nod.

Zulu could only frown. Why the hell was the spook trying to bail him out? Did Rock have a soft spot after all?

"Who are your contacts?" demanded Pharaoh.

"That's between me, them, and Langley, Captain."

"Wrong answer. Walrus, would you like to spill his guts now?"

"With pleasure, sir." The old warrant drew his weapon.

Rock smiled and raised his hand. "The police are out there now. We can't do jack for a while, till things calm down. Nasser's boy Yousef will let us know. Meantime, I can make a few calls."

"Great. Now your screwup is wasting our time. Hassan and those spook rats could already be gone. I need to know who your contacts are in case you take a round."

"Captain, you go over your recon plan. I'll let you know what I find out. I don't plan on dying in the next five minutes."

"Don't be so sure," Walrus cut in.

Pharaoh nodded slowly at Rock, then he motioned Zulu to the front of the room.

Zulu breathed a shivery sigh and followed.

23. CAR TROUBLE

Rock stood at the back of the storeroom, and out of sheer desperation, he dialed the Global Intelligence Group offices in Norfolk, Virginia. He expected to get voice mail but was surprised when a man answered.

"Jimbo, is that you?" Rock asked.

"Who is this?"

"It's Rock. I have to talk to you."

Click.

Rock cursed, redialed GIG's number, got the voice mail. He thumbed through his phone's contact list, contemplating who else he could call and bleed for information. The list grew frustratingly short until he realized that the only guy who could really help now was Nasser.

Because ground traffic constantly flowed in and out of the city, and bandits, smugglers, and other assorted criminals were, for the most part, everywhere, it had been impossible for Nasser and his people to positively identify the vehicle or vehicles carrying Hassan, Libra, and Jersey. And they had as of now received no other information from their informants placed throughout the city.

Pharaoh, who would not trust CIA contacts (and Rock didn't blame him for that), was now organizing his team into four three-man recon units that he would dispatch to the more obvious locations: the railroad station, the international airport, the mosque, and the bazaar. It was a logical plan, though finding three people in a city of over half a million was going to be futile if they couldn't come up with better leads.

Suddenly, Rock's phone began to ring, and he recognized the number. "Hello, is this Rock?"

"It's you," said Rock.

"I still have the pictures you want."

"Don't hang up."

"I won't."

"Why should I trust you?"

"Because I have a message from your friend Libra."

Rock gasped. "I need to meet you, right now."

"Not now. The police are everywhere. Tomorrow morning. Seven o'clock. Outside the *hosseinieh* near the Rasouli Bazaar. Do you know where that is?"

"Yes."

"Come alone this time. Bring the money. Otherwise the pictures will be gone." The kid hung up.

The *hosseinieh* was a religious meeting place for the commemoration of the martyrdom of Shia Imam Hossein, and the kid must have assumed he'd be safer there. The challenge now was to meet the kid without the ODA team's knowledge. The old "I have to use the bathroom" excuse no longer had wings. Rock decided he would talk to Nasser to see if they could work out something to their mutual benefit. The guy had lost a lot of money during that border closing. Rock could easily provide a bonus to help the grocer in his time of need.

"We've got about two hours till sunrise," Pharaoh said, checking his watch. "Catch some sleep."

As the others stood and shifted away to the corners of the room to unroll their sleeping bags, Pharaoh opened his laptop computer and linked up with the satellite. Bravo Company relayed real-time thermal and infrared imagery from Predator unmanned aerial vehicles operating along the border. Police cars were still clustered around the area where Rock and Zulu had confronted Rock's contacts.

"Still hot out there," said Zulu, observing the screen over Pharaoh's shoulder.

"Bravo doesn't have anything. Rock is our key to finding them, you know that."

"I know."

"And the reason he's not telling us everything? Well, he knows those two CIA guys. He joked about it at the briefing, but I'd bet a month's pay they're his buddies."

"So what you think? Let's give him a long leash, but you and I tail him."

"You read my mind."

"What about Nasser's guys? Yousef and the rest Rock says he has out there?"

"Not sure about them, but let's make it a point not to piss them off."

"Roger that." Zulu lifted his chin at Walrus, who was alone near the rice bags, preparing his bunk. "Sorry about him. About everything."

"I don't believe you killed Church, but you did sleep with Bull's wife, didn't you? That's why he's got it in for you. He's up on his moral high ground."

Zulu pursed his lips.

"I need to trust you, Zu. You think if you admit it that we'll disown you? Everybody makes mistakes. I've been out there with you. Rudy had it right. The only thing that matters now is having a clear head in the field. You work out that personal stuff on your own time. I need you at a hundred and ten percent. We get caught out there, we're dead."

"I understand."

"And if it makes you feel any better, we all got secrets."

"Oh, yeah?"

"Tell you what, when I get a chance, I'll tell you something about me."

"Okay, but I'm not admitting anything."

"Of course you're not."

"But you do have me interested."

Pharaoh nodded, shut his laptop, then began to prepare his sleeping bag.

Since taking over ODA-555 he had done everything in his power to suppress thoughts of his father. He didn't want to come into this with a huge chip on his shoulder. He wasn't here to clear the family name; hell, he'd legally changed his. No, he was doing this to prove something to himself and perhaps to understand why his father acted so brutally in the face of battle. Pharaoh was too afraid to ever ask the man, so he'd put on the man's boots and was determined to find out for himself.

At first light, Pharaoh and his men checked radios and gear. They were all packing concealed weapons and would leave their rifles in the trunks of their vehicles.

Alpha team, comprised of Pharaoh, Zulu, and Rock, would head out toward the bazaar area, per Rock's instructions. He was meeting with a contact there and would not explain further.

Bravo team members Walrus, Hojo, and Gator were being driven out to the airport by another of Nasser's cousins, to recon the main terminal in the event Hassan and/or the mercenaries Libra and Jersey decided to flee by plane.

Sullivan, Borokovsky, and McDaniel of Charlie team would set up at the railroad station, while Ondejko, Figueroa, and Grimm of Delta would head out toward a cement factory in the northeast corner of the city that Nasser's informants had told him now had an unusual number of security personnel outside. That bit of news had raised Pharaoh's brow since they had personally encountered a cement block truck, though that load had turned up clean. Nevertheless, Pharaoh had decided to divert those men from the mosque and put them on the factory.

Much to his chagrin, senior communications expert Weathers would be left back at the safe house and coordinate with the ODB team back at FOB Cobra in Lashkar Gah and with Nasser's folks to secure transport out of the city and across the border. News of the cement factory had Pharaoh thinking about using a pair of cement trucks for that purpose, and he shared that thought with Delta team, who'd be reconnoitering the factory.

Rock had insisted he drive alone in one of the cars because his informant might flee if he saw others with him. Pharaoh had agreed to that, so long as he and Zulu could follow at a safe distance. Nasser had volunteered to drive them, since he knew his way around the city, should they get separated.

They pulled out of the alley in an old, rusting sedan and drove off, the temperature having risen at least ten degrees in the past few minutes, clouds of dust and the scent of burning motor oil wafting in the open windows.

Gas prices were remarkably low in Iran because of subsidies. Consequently, gas trafficking to neighboring countries like Afghanistan remained heavy. Additionally, individuals set up roadside shops and sold gas in containers to incoming foreigners. One such guy was sitting in a lawn chair beside a cardboard picture of a man holding a jug of Castrol. It was a surreal sight to someone from the West like Pharaoh. He'd seen people selling flowers and boiled peanuts on the roadside but never gasoline.

Zulu, who'd been jammed into the backseat, raised his voice as a dust-covered, black heap with shattered bumper suddenly cut in front of them, blocking their view of Rock, who was up ahead in an old blue sedan. "Get around this guy, Nasser."

"Don't worry, I still see him," said the man. "And I know a shortcut at the next intersection."

"Just stay with him."

"I will try."

Suddenly, the black car in front of them began to slow, and the road had grown too narrow to pass.

"What's he doing? We'll lose him!"

"I think he has an engine problem," said Nasser.

In fact, the vehicle that had cut them off came to a complete stop in the middle of the road, and drivers behind them began honking their horns.

"Zu, see what's up," said Pharaoh as he hit speed dial to call Rock on his satellite phone.

Zulu and Nasser got out and went to speak with the driver ahead, and all three of them began arguing loudly.

Pharaoh got Rock's voice mail and hung up. "Come on, get this piece of crap off the road! We're losing him!"

Rock grinned as he checked the incoming call, saw that it was Pharaoh, then pocketed the phone. Pharaoh's call meant that he and Zulu had been delayed. Nasser's little ploy had worked brilliantly.

As he neared the *hosseinieh* ahead, with the bazaar just around the corner, Rock pulled over, parked, then got out and walked briskly toward the building.

Behind him, another old sedan pulled up, a Peugeot ROA, and the passenger hopped out and jumped into Rock's car, which he'd left idling. That man drove away, and the Peugeot followed. Pharaoh and Zulu would never find Rock.

After a nod to the Peugeot's driver as he passed, Rock reached one of the *hosseinieh*'s side doors.

"Don't turn around," came a voice from behind.

"All right."

The voice wasn't the kid's.

"Do you have the money?"

"Do you have the pictures?" Feeling a little bold and a whole lot reckless, Rock turned around and faced the man. He wasn't a man at all but a baby-faced kid with short, jet black hair and a trace of stubble on his upper lip. His voice was remarkably deep for his age. He had both hands jammed into the pockets of his baggy trousers. No doubt he had a pistol.

"You going to fire that gun or play with it?" asked Rock.

"Give me the money."

"It's okay, it's okay," came another voice. This kid had just come out from the *hosseinieh*'s door. He and the other kid could be brothers: same face and haircut. Maybe they were.

Rock faced the second kid and shook his head. "You told me to come alone. Why didn't you?"

"I needed to make sure. Let's go inside." The kid led them into the building, where they paused inside a small foyer dimly lit by a candle sconce.

"Who is this guy?" Rock asked. "Your brother?"

The kid did not answer and instead reached into his pocket and produced the camera. "The pictures you want are on here."

"I told Fatima one thousand dollars." Rock slowly reached into his pocket and produced a small wad of greenbacks.

As the kid's gaze lit on the money, he shoved the camera forward. Rock took it, but he held back the money, saying, "You want to shoot, go ahead. But let me see what I'm buying."

The kid's buddy finally drew his weapon.

"Wait," the kid said. "Let him make sure."

Rock thumbed several buttons on the camera and began clicking through shots, pictures of the outside of a cement factory; of Hassan, Libra, and Jersey leaving trucks; of the outside of a nearby building; a hotel, with the three men entering. As his pulse mounted, he handed over the cash without looking up. "What was the message from Libra?"

"Libra said stay close. He'll be in the city for another day. He'll call."

"Good. Give me the phone you used to call him."

The kid looked surprised that Rock knew about the phone, but he complied, and Rock slipped the phone into the inner breast pocket of his coat.

"And you can give us the rest of your money now," said the buddy, narrowing his gaze and trying to summon up some intimidation in his naive and boyish face.

"No, let's go," said the kid, grabbing his friend's arm.

"The rest of it," snapped the friend.

Rock narrowed his gaze on the cocky young man. "The only thing more you'll get now is a bullet—if you don't leave."

"Come on," urged the kid, grabbing his friend's shoulder.

"I've been doing this a long time," Rock said, then suddenly dropped the camera, seized the friend's arm, and twisted it behind his back, even as he pried free the pistol. Then shoved the friend back, against the wall. "See what I mean? Go!"

The two bolted past him and out the door. Rock chuckled under his breath as he pocketed the gun. Then he retrieved the camera, as his phone vibrated. Pharaoh was calling again.

For his own entertainment pleasure, Rock figured he'd answer this time. "Hello?"

"Rock, where the hell are you?"

"I'm right here."

Pharaoh cursed. "Where?"

"I'm in a good place. Do me a favor. Don't worry about me. I'll be home tonight for dinner."

"Rock, I'll be on the horn to Langley in a heartbeat."

"Easy there. I need a little alone time to gather more intel."

"What are you doing, Rock?"

"Look, if this works out, I'll have our targets pinpointed by the end of the day. They're still in the city."

"You already know where they are, don't you . . . ?"

Rock winced. "No, I don't. Just stand by. Don't do anything rash, know what I'm saying?"

"You got till sundown."

"I'll meet you back at Nasser's."

Rock hung up and left the *hosseinieh*. He shuffled down the street to catch a taxi.

The day was young, the sun was in his face, and for a moment he imagined that his old friends had not dug their own graves.

24. WATCHFUL EYES

Zahedan International Airport was similar to many small-town airports in the States, with tower, main terminal building, outlying parking lots, and taxis clustering in and around the passenger pickup zones; the only difference was, every third guy could be a drug smuggler, a terrorist, or an intelligence agent from the West, Walrus mused.

Then again, maybe there weren't as many differences, given recent news reports regarding huge gaps in airport security back home.

He and Hojo had taken seats just outside the terminal, while Gator had positioned himself near a long row of cabs with the car Nasser's cousin had loaned them. They were all posing as cabdrivers, and the two uniformed security guards posted outside the main terminal doors had not given them a second glance.

Pharaoh had checked in once already, and Walrus consulted his watch, figuring the kid would call again soon for another report. In some respects, Walrus couldn't blame the captain for micromanaging him. He'd just dropped a bomb on the team, and they were still stunned, no doubt.

Walrus was pretty sure the others believed that Zulu was having an affair with Bull's wife; the murder accusation was another story. However, even the thought of Zulu murdering Church was enough, in Walrus's estimation, to tarnish the team sergeant's reputation. That would be justice enough. What Zulu had done was inexcusable, and he needed to pay for his sins. Because the world was merciless and unfair, it took someone like Walrus, someone with raw courage and intestinal fortitude, to mete out that justice when others wouldn't. Some people just had to be assholes and bad cops. That's the way it was. And despite a few lingering doubts— very few—Walrus still felt fully justified in his position and his actions.

"Whoa, hold on, what do we got here," he muttered to himself as a pair of black Mercedes sedans rolled up to the pickup area.

Walrus called Gator and told him to get in close to those guys to see if he could eavesdrop on any conversation.

The drivers got out, followed by two more men, all well-dressed Arabs in white robes and checkered headgear. They waited near the cars for a few moments, and then a group of four Asian men, either Chinese or North Koreans, Walrus guessed, filed out of the terminal, all carrying laptop shoulder bags and wearing the same short haircut and similar glasses. They looked like clones on their way to a science fiction convention.

A police car rolled up behind the two cars, a splash of green across its side doors and the word "POLICE" spelled out in English and Arabic.

The two officers got out and spoke with the drivers. There was some laughter, then the cops returned to their car and followed the other two cars as they pulled away from the airport.

Walrus answered his ringing phone. "What do you got, Gator?"

"Not much. They spoke too fast. I think the suits are

Koreans. They said something about heading south to the mountains. One guy asked how far, and one of the Arabs said thirty kilometers. They were all pretty excited. That's the most I could get."

"Do me a favor, buddy. Pick me up right now. You and I are going for a little ride."

"But they ain't the targets."

"Not yet. But I think we might have a target of opportunity here."

"I don't know."

"Son, do you ever watch the news? If there are Koreans here, they didn't just come for lunch. I'll call the captain. Hojo can hold the fort."

Walrus's blood was beginning to flow nicely now. That higher had allowed a CIA agent to tag along on a mission to kill two former CIA agents was beyond him, and he was damned sure that Rock would call the shots the entire time, but this . . . this was intriguing. Why the hell were those Korean geeks heading south into the mountains? Walrus was no student of Iranian geography (was anyone?) but he was pretty sure that the finest Iranian souvenir shops and "luxury" hotels were not located in that direction. And Iran was, ahem, not famous for its adult entertainment clubs to be sure. Walrus called Pharaoh to convey the news.

Sullivan, Borokovsky, and McDaniel had spread out within the railroad station and kept close watch over those waiting for the next train.

As Borokovsky stood near the platform, pretending to talk on his cell phone, people began gathering nearby, standing alongside their bags. Borokovsky shifted away from them, closed his eyes, and saw Church once again lying near the river, bleeding out and ready to die. He shuddered.

Did Church know about Zulu? Was Zulu really having an affair? Borokovsky bet that everyone was asking the same questions, though Sully and Rudy hadn't said a word to him, as though the mere mention of it might confirm Zulu's guilt.

And worse, would Grimm finally succumb to his own guilt and confess everything? How would the captain react? Ironically, Borokovsky felt more anxiety over covering up Church's death than he did over being an American Special Forces operator working illegally in Iran. You'd think the latter would present a lot more cause for concern.

Sullivan called, and Borokovsky got embarrassed by the phone ringing, even as he'd pretended to speak into it. He quickly turned away from the growing throng of train riders and answered, "Yeah."

"We're wasting our time here," said Sullivan.

"We have orders."

"I'm going to tell the captain."

"Okay."

As Borokovsky hung up, one of the men on the platform, a wizened old guy with hunched back and brow so deeply furrowed that you could barely see his eyes, collapsed to the gasps of those around him.

Borokovsky tensed. His first reaction as a medic was to rush in and assess. But if he did that . . .

Ondejko, Figueroa, and Grimm had situated themselves on the north, south, and west sides of the concrete factory, and at the moment, Ondejko was sitting inside a parked car with one of Nasser's second cousins, a rotund, multi-chinned man named Kourosh, who could more easily pass for an Italian from New Jersey. There were three men posted on each side of the building, and while none of them openly displayed their firearms, it was clear all of them were packing pistols.

On the loading lock, a team of six Baluchi tribesmen were stacking more concrete blocks onto pallets. Another man rolled up with a forklift and lowered another section of blocks, and this seemed to excite the group. Ondejko raised a pair of digital camera binoculars and began capturing pictures and video of the men at work. He zoomed in on the blocks, which appeared as unremarkable as the others, but the reaction of the men seemed to suggest otherwise.

Abruptly, Kourosh, who was in the driver's seat, cried, "Get down."

Ondejko ducked in the backseat as a car rumbled by. "What?" he asked the old man.

"Police. They don't like men with binoculars."

"Yeah, right."

Ondejko called Figueroa, who would pass on word to Grimm. "Something's going on down there for sure," he said. "They're smuggling something in those blocks. We need to get down there, and get our hands on one."

"Okay," said Figueroa. "You go. Have a good time."

"I'm not kidding."

"And you're not sane, either. What do you think? We're going to walk right up in broad daylight and ask them for one?"

"Wait a minute," said Ondejko. "Maybe we can kill two birds with one stone."

"Negative, negative," Pharaoh told Walrus. "You need to stay there with Hojo at the airport."

"Captain, if you get back to the safe house and call higher, maybe they can put a satellite on those mountains. Who the hell knows what they're doing out there. But in the meantime, let us check it out."

"Hang on," Pharaoh said, then he glanced at Zulu, who was still in the backseat of Nasser's car and who'd been listening to the call via the speakerphone.

"Unless Rock comes through for us, the best we can do

is stake out the major exits like we've done," said Zulu. "We only need one pair of eyes at the airport."

"I don't like leaving him alone."

"Get Weathers back out there."

"That's a possibility."

"All right, Walrus, you tail those guys at a safe distance. I'll call higher, and see if they got anything. You send me GPS updates."

"Thank you, Captain."

Pharaoh shook his head at Zulu. "What the hell are we doing, man? We got Rock calling the shots on this mission, and now we got Walrus chasing secondary targets."

"Yeah, and curiosity will kill the cat—and the Walrus. While we're waiting for Rock, it wouldn't be a bad idea to pick up Weathers, get him to the airport, then lay low somewhere south of the city to link up with that old bastard."

"Sounds good."

Pharaoh answered his ringing phone. "Captain, it's me," said Ondejko. "I need your blessing on a little plan I've just come up with. I think we got something big here at the factory."

"Oh, man, what now?"

Rock slipped into the hotel, showed the concierge a few photos, then paid off the man to tell him which rooms Hassan, Libra, and Jersey were staying in.

"But they're not here now," said the old man. "They left early this morning."

"Did they check out?"

"No."

"Keys to their rooms?"

The man held out his hand for more cash. Rock obliged, and two minutes later was going through each man's room, looking for anything of interest but finding nothing more than a few sets of recently purchased clothes and toiletries.

His phone rang. Well, not *his* phone, but the one he had taken from the kid.

He held his breath, answered. "Hello?"

"Rock, it's me," said Libra. "I know you're in the hotel. Don't say a word. At about seven P.M. tonight two members of the Iranian Parliament are coming down here to inspect production and give Hassan a chance to thank them for their help. We're going to photograph and record this meeting for our clients back in the States. We need you to keep that ODA team off our goddamned backs."

"Marwan, you guys are idiots," said Rock, deliberately calling Libra by his real first name to unsettle the man. "Jack's dead."

"What?"

"You heard me. Your clients got to Jack because he was helping me."

"Aw, man."

"The ODA team's not just here for Hassan. They know about you. They got orders to take you out. Those orders come down from the president himself. Do you understand what you're doing here? You won't survive this. Not this one, buddy."

"Rock, we can't pull out now. They'll kill us. We have to play this hand to the end. All I'm asking for is a little time. That's all I need. And you know what we're doing here is right."

"That doesn't matter. You shouldn't have taken this job, because in the end, they'll say you and Jersey sold out to Hassan. Your clients have already got that covered. You'll help them start their little war, and for what? To be murdered and classified as terrorists—after everything you've done in your lives . . . all those operations."

"We've considered that. And we've made arrangements to ensure that never happens."

"No, you're fooling yourselves. Don't do this. Get out of there, man. I can help you. We'll use the ODA team."

"Rock, you have no idea how much money—"

"Screw the money! You're going to die!"

"Not me, Rock. Not me. I'm sorry."

The hotel room door behind Rock swung open, and there stood his old friend Libra, lowering his cell phone and raising his pistol.

25. THE MOUNTAINS SPEAK AND WISE MEN LISTEN

Walrus and Gator barreled south down the highway, past the university, and finally spotted the two black Mercedes sedans out in the distance, heading toward the towns of Kalateh-ye Razzaqzadeh and Kalat E Razzauzadeh. Four other cars lay between them and the Koreans, and those vehicles helped conceal the fact that the Koreans were being followed.

While Gator drove, Walrus kept his binoculars on the targets, now about a half kilometer ahead.

"I don't know, this could be a huge waste of time," said Gator.

Walrus snorted. "Why you worried? You got dinner plans or something?"

Gator didn't answer. Then, after a moment, he blurted out, "You really think Zulu killed Church?"

"So that's what's on your mind. You're worried about your boy."

"We should be worried, with a guy like you on his back."

"Me? I'm just the messenger."

"No, you're not. I just don't get it. We all make mistakes."

"So you believe he cheated with Bull's wife."

Gator snickered. "You've seen her. That body. And the way she acts around us. Bull didn't mind at all. He thought it was funny. I think he wanted us to lust after her, that way he could feel good about having a trophy wife."

"What? And that excuses it?"

"I don't know what happened. But I think Zulu wasn't all at fault. And I have to tell you, no way did he kill Church. No way, dude."

"Maybe *you* killed him."

"And that's what you want—all of us pointing fingers. I've never met anybody like you. We don't play these games. Not at our level. And we don't talk about this stuff—not the way you do."

"Gator, I'm not all evil, man. But I don't care what Bull's wife looked like or how she acted. I don't care if she dropped her panties in front of Zu, as an operator and fellow brother, you don't cross that line, ever. No excuses."

"Who elected you moral cop? Who said you have to enforce what's right and wrong here?"

"Young man, I've put you on a long leash, but you will still watch that tone. And to answer your question, nobody elected me moral cop. But if nobody enforces what's right here then—"

"Then what? Special Forces operations around the world will come to a halt? Think about what you're doing here, man. That's all I'm saying. Think about your own mistakes."

Walrus pulled the binoculars from his eyes and shot a hard look at Gator, even though what the guy had said was getting to him.

"We're coming up on the next town," said Gator, squinting into the distance. "Doesn't look like they're stopping."

"Then neither are we."

*   *   *

Borokovsky watched the old man die right in front of him, and he did nothing. He drifted away as the medical technicians arrived on the platform, then he turned back toward the cream-colored archways and watched the medics lift the body onto a long backboard and carry it back to their waiting ambulance.

Why the hell was this getting to him? He'd seen enough bloodshed in Afghanistan to grow as numb and detached as the army wanted him. So why now? What switch had been thrown to suddenly make him *feel* again?

He couldn't blow their cover to help the old man. And he couldn't allow a decent guy like Church to be remembered as a suicide victim, whether that was true or not. Then why did all of the "helping" he was trying to do make him feel so miserable? Was it really time to get out?

His phone rang, and for a moment, he didn't answer, until a third chime made him shudder back to the moment.

"Steve, it's James," said Pharaoh. "Anything?"

"No. How come you're not calling Sully? He's in charge of this team."

"I'm checking in with you. You all right?"

"I'm good to go, sir."

"Okay, stand by. There's a chance I might be pulling you out of there sooner than later. Let 'em know."

"Yes, sir."

Borokovsky shared the news with Sullivan and McDaniel, then he moved back into the shade and pricked up his ears as the next train clicked and clacked toward the platform.

A tap came on his shoulder. He craned his head and came face-to-face with one of the uniformed security guards, a man no more than twenty-five, with thick mustache and stubbly cheeks.

"Can I see your identification, sir?"

* * *

Rock could not draw his own weapon in time, so he raised his finger and said, "Easy." Then he reached slowly into his breast pocket and withdrew a couple of cigars. "Marwan, come on. One last pleasure, okay?"

Marwan, better known as Libra, closed the door behind himself and eased farther into the hotel room.

Libra had a long silencer attached to his weapon, and Rock felt a pang in his chest as he imagined the bullet already piercing his heart.

He raised his hands as Libra moved up and fished around to find Rock's pistol, cell phones, and wallet. He tossed them on the sofa. Then he found Rock's lighter and handed it to him.

"Couldn't this wait till later?" Rock asked. "Come on, old friend. Smoke with me."

"No."

"Then shoot me. The longer you wait, the guiltier you'll feel. Do yourself a favor."

"If it's any consolation, we'll kill Hassan when we're finished here."

"Where is he now?"

"Inside the factory." Libra's tone turned sarcastic. "He's giving a little speech to the engineers, inspiring them to greatness."

Rock cursed and lit up his cigar. Then he proffered the second cigar to Libra, but Libra shook his head, his eyes beginning to reflect a deep weariness that Rock had not seen before, and in that moment Rock knew that Libra would not shoot him. There was far too much history between them. Their friendship went far beyond any job. This was all just a formality to let Rock know that Libra was serious about interference. Rock would play along and assume he was already dead.

"We had some good times together, huh?" he asked.

"God damn you, Rock," snapped Libra, his lower lip quivering. "Make your move."

"I'm done here. I've had a good run. If this is what you

want to do with your life, then you need to have my blood on your hands. You need to know this was too far. You need to pay the piper. But you let me ask, what happened to that old line in the sand?"

"Go to hell." Libra's expression had shifted, that torn look replaced by a knot of anger, and it was then that Rock realized with a start that his old friend had finally summoned up the courage.

"I probably will." Rock shuddered and took a long puff on his cigar.

Then he leaped forward, about to knock Libra's pistol hand away, when the weapon thumped.

As Rock gasped, he staggered backward and barely felt the floor coming up as a massive pain woke in his chest, and suddenly it was heard to breathe. He hit the floor, coughed up blood, then lay there a moment before he was lifted and held by Libra.

"Why did you have to get in the way, you bastard?" asked Libra, panting, his voice cracking. "We were brothers, Rock. Brothers."

Rock coughed again, raised his arm, and shoved the cigar back into his mouth. "You really did it," he managed.

"Rock, I'm sorry. I'm so sorry."

As the room grew darker, Rock tried to nod. Tried. All the tension in his neck and back was relieved by an overwhelming numbness that began to sweep up, into his neck.

"This is not what I wanted," said Libra. "You have to know that. Good-bye, brother. Good-bye."

Walrus and Gator followed the cars through Kalateh-ye Razzaqzadeh and Kalat E Razzauzadeh then farther south for another eight kilometers between the Kuh-e Manzalab and Kuh-e Jikuli mountain ranges to their west and east, respectively. There was only one other car now between them and the targets, so Gator held them far back.

The two sedans reached a spot somewhere ahead and

turned left, off the main road and onto a dirt road, leaving thick trails of dust in their wake.

Walrus and Gator waited until the cars were far enough down the dirt road before they approached. A few minutes later they came up to an intersection. The dirt road heading east was beaten down by wide tire tracks and those left by the two cars.

"Pull off. Stop. Then pop the hood—in case they're watching," said Walrus.

Gator complied, and while they stood out in the grueling sun, with Walrus pretending to check the engine, Walrus told Gator to take a closer look at the road.

The weapons sergeant squatted down and studied all the tracks. "You ain't kidding. They've had all kinds of heavy vehicles coming up through here. Looks like some larger construction trucks, maybe dump trucks. They must be building something out there."

"Yeah, out here in the middle of nowhere."

Gator stroked his beard in thought. "Maybe they've set up a top secret topless bar for North Korean businessmen."

"Exactly. That's why we're going." Walrus stepped away from the engine, crossed back into the car, and snatched his binoculars.

The two black sedans began to turn left and disappeared behind the mountains.

"Let's think about this," said Gator.

Walrus slammed shut the hood. "Just drive."

"My identification?" Borokovsky repeated, then reached into his pocket.

This puppy patrolman was in for a little surprise. Borokovsky handed him the ID and turned on his deepest scowl.

The man's face began to lose color. "Uh, yes, very well. Sorry." He quickly returned the ID to Borokovsky, who made an ugly face and shooed the security guy away with an air of superiority.

Borokovsky's credentials, along with the rest of the team's, indicated they were *Sepah* agents of Iran's Revolutionary Guard, intelligence branch. The credentials were genuine, removed from the bodies of agents who'd been taken out by CIA operatives during the past eighteen months.

Despite that, Borokovsky made a call to Sullivan and reported the incident. Sullivan said he'd call back Pharaoh and see if they could get the hell out of there before it got any hotter.

Borokovsky spotted the security man across the station, conferring with a colleague and looking in his direction. Yes, it was time to leave. He reached into his pocket for the car keys Nasser had given him.

"We could be sitting here all day," muttered Ondejko, leaning back into his seat and massaging his neck.

Kourosh took a long swig from his bottle of Zam Zam cola, then exhaled and said, "We could be sitting here all day or another five minutes. You don't like the mystery?"

"No."

"I think you have a good plan."

"I think so, too."

"Then it is worth waiting for."

Ondejko sighed, nodded, and called Figueroa and Grimm, who had left their positions and were seated in another car supplied by Kourosh to help execute the plan. "Anything?" he asked.

"Nada," answered Figueroa. "And these pieces-of-crap cars don't even have air-conditioning."

"Still not as hot as the 'Stan."

"Not yet."

"All right. Don't fade on me. Call's going to come out of nowhere, and we'll need to move."

"Roger that. Still waiting for Sully. He should be here soon."

Ondejko thumbed off the phone and glared at the flatbed truck, fully loaded but still sitting there at the dock. "What the hell are they waiting for?"

Pharaoh, Nasser, and Zulu had picked up Weathers and per their plan dropped him off at the airport to join Hojo in his surveillance there. Pharaoh had then received a call from Sully and told him to take his team out to Ondejko's location and join that party.

After leaving the airport, they headed west across the city, then turned south down to the university area, where they positioned themselves along a row of parked cars and waited for the next report from Walrus.

Meanwhile, Pharaoh tried once more to call Rock, and he left yet another voice mail message for the spook. When he was finished, Zulu moaned in disgust and said, "He's been yanking our chains for too long."

"But he's predictable. He's always going to do what's best for Rock and best for the Agency. They want to clean up their own mess here—to avoid embarrassment."

Zulu sighed. "I guess we all want to bury our mistakes."

"Yeah," said Pharaoh, closing his eyes for a moment. "Let me tell you about my father. He was in the first Gulf War."

Walrus checked his watch. They had waited another thirty minutes before heading up the dirt road, and traveled another ten kilometers before Walrus realized that if they continued, they might simply drive into the enemy's hands. The road curved back to the north, leading around the mountains, and Walrus reasoned that if they could park and scale the first few hills, they might have a good view of the valley on the other side. At least his map indicated so.

"We can't go, man," said Gator. "It's going to take us hours to climb up there."

"Probably."

"No way. Captain won't approve this."

"He will. We ain't driving around."

"And what if we get up there, and we got nothing?"

Walrus raised his brows. "Gator, Gator, Gator . . . I've been following my hunches for over thirty years."

"How many times you been wrong?"

Walrus curled his thumb and forefinger and held up the zero with a sarcastic grin.

"Yeah, right."

"Listen, they got something going on. Maybe it's military, maybe they're enriching uranium, who knows, but this could be a hell of a lot bigger than whacking two old CIA agents."

"Bigger than nabbing Hassan?"

"I think so."

"So you're all about the glory."

"And you ain't? There ain't no fame, there ain't no fortune. This is all we got. Now, listen up, listen." Walrus put a hand to his ear as the wind began to pick up. "I don't hear anything."

"No, listen harder. It's the mountains. They're saying, *Gator . . . Gator . . . don't be an asshole. Come on up . . .*"

Gator shoved him back and Walrus nearly fell. "All right, you bastard, call the captain. Don't blame me if he denies the request."

"He doesn't have a choice."

"Are you going to disobey orders?"

"Never. But this heat. It tends to disorient a man, make him walk . . . in the wrong direction, sometimes uphill."

26. THE HEAT

Saeed Hanjour did not trust either of Sheikh Abu Hassan's associates, so when he'd been asked by Hassan to go find the arms dealer who called himself Libra, Hanjour assumed something was wrong. The man had, according to Hassan, gone back to his hotel room to change, but he'd been there for a suspiciously long time.

Hassan found Libra in his room, freshly changed and washing his hands.

"The sheikh has been looking for you."

"Sorry. I wasn't feeling well. A little dizzy. Must be the heat."

"It is time once again to pray."

"It's unbearably hot in there."

"We've grown used to it," said Hanjour.

"And you, I'm sure, have never spent any time at a luxury hotel—with air-conditioning." Libra dried his hands, grinned tightly, then started out toward the door.

"Wait." Hanjour moved farther into the dingy room and crouched down to glance under the bed.

Libra began to laugh. "What are you looking for? The

women you lost last night? The ones you promised us but
failed to deliver?"

"There were complications. I'm sorry. But we must all
be cautious."

"You're a fool. The sheikh trusts us with his life. If you
do not trust us, then you do not trust him. Should we all
discuss this together?"

Hanjour's breath grew shallow. "No."

"Then let's go."

As Libra left the hotel room, he breathed a deep sigh of
relief. Just minutes prior he had nervously paid off Cyrus,
the concierge, to help him drag Rock's body into a utility
room located behind the hotel's front office. Cyrus was a
narrow-faced man with thinning hair, an even thinner beard,
and small, dark eyes. He said he would bundle up the body
and dispose of it as soon as he could. Libra paid him more
than Cyrus would make in a month at the hotel and told
him he could keep anything he found on Rock's body. Cyrus
said he would keep quiet. Libra showed him his sidearm and
said that was a good idea.

Poor Rock. Libra still shuddered over the thought that
he had actually murdered his friend, but Hassan could not
be alerted to any problems prior to the arrival of the parliament members.

Now Libra wondered if the sheikh's suspicious right
hand would have to join Rock. Taking out Hanjour was too
rash, though, since his disappearance would trigger alarms,
unless Libra and Jersey designed an elaborate ploy. Time
was against them in that regard.

As he and Hanjour crossed the street and headed for the
concrete factory, he noticed two men sitting in a parked car.
There was nothing remarkable about them, save for those
stares. Libra averted his gaze and forged on. A chill woke at
the base of his spine. Had he just been spotted by members
of the ODA team? Or were these men part of the cement fac-

tory's security? He couldn't ask the sheikh or Hanjour, for fear of tipping them off to a problem.

But the fact remained: The ODA team members were still wild cards, and Libra wasn't sure how much Rock had shared with them. After the prayer, he would gather more intelligence. He had Rock's two phones. Perhaps he could make a few calls back to Texas, run a few numbers, and get some help from the U.S. Army and CENTCOM itself . . .

He and Hanjour stepped into the dusty building and moved forward past the offices, toward one of the open loading zones, where everyone had gathered to face the qibla, with their chests facing in the direction of Kaaba.

Libra had a lot to pray about now. He would pray for forgiveness, and for the courage and grace to survive the day. He glanced up at Jersey, standing across the room, and he hoped his expression said it all.

Back at the hotel, Cyrus trembled over the fact that he was now involved in a murder. He called one of his cousins for advice. The man wasted no time coming down and helping him finish with the body. His cousin took the man's cigars and rings, while Cyrus took possession of the dead man's gleaming and expensive watch.

As they thoroughly washed their hands, Cyrus's cousin warned him about the dangers of trying to hide the corpse and that if this man was a member of the Taliban or al-Qaeda or worse, an American, there could be serious consequences. Cyrus agreed and they discussed their options. Another of their cousins drove one of the local garbage trucks. They called him. He could come in an hour or two.

Zulu took a long breath then stroked his beard, deep in thought. Even Nasser, who was at the wheel, had grimaced over the story Pharaoh had just told them.

Pharaoh's father, it turned out, was the infamous Major

Rick Bradley, veteran of the first Gulf War and no relation to the famous General Omar Nelson Bradley, first chairman of the Joint Chiefs of Staff. Rick Bradley had certainly never been compared to that general, but to men such as Lieutenant William Calley who was court-martialed for ordering the March 16, 1968, My Lai Massacre in Vietnam.

During the invasion of Iraq, Major Bradley had ordered his men to "kill every living thing" in a particular village just outside Kuwait. Villagers there were supposedly stockpiling chemical weapons for Iraq's military.

Ironically, Bradley did not deny issuing the order or claim he was acting solely on the orders of his superiors. He simply said that he trusted the intelligence that he had in hand and that when his men entered the village, they were met with small arms fire. His men returned fire, and, in the heat of the moment, after two of his men were killed, an enraged Bradley had issued the order. Given the situation, his men obeyed without question. Thirty-one civilians were killed, some armed, some unarmed, some small children. A modest-sized weapons cache was uncovered, but no chemical weapons were found.

"When people talk about living in the shadow of their fathers, I think they have no idea," said Pharaoh. "I just wonder what sent my father over the edge. Anyway, Zu, I'm telling you this so maybe you can put your own problem into perspective."

"Wow. I'm sorry. I used to think it was so easy for you. College graduate, smart guy on your way up the ladder while we monkeys stay on the bottom."

"Yeah, I guess that's what some people think. I ran into one lieutenant colonel at Bragg who knew my dad, and he'd followed our family and knew I'd changed my name. He gave me a long talk, but he respected my decision."

"Have you ever gone to see your father?"

"Not since I was a kid. I just . . . I can't."

"So you're here to prove a point?"

Pharaoh grinned. "In the beginning I thought, if I do this and do it well, I can make it better for my dad. But I'm not helping him. He doesn't even know I'm in the army, and I'm still not sure if that alone wouldn't kill him. Anyway, I'm just here for me. Making it better for myself, I guess."

"Some guys just do this and don't think about it," Zulu said. "I'm here because this is what I've always wanted to do. I've been playing army since I was four years old. I'm into knives and martial arts, what have you. But you, man. There's something more scary about why you're here. And when it gets hairy, I've seen that in you."

"You're probably right." Pharaoh leaned forward, and his phone rang. He answered, "What's up?" He listened a moment, then his mouth began to fall open. "You're kidding me. No, go in. Check it out. See if they've seen Rock. Right now. Call me back."

"What?" asked Zulu.

"Figueroa and Grimm just IDed one of our targets walking to the cement factory. He and another guy came out of the hotel down the street. We need to get everyone back there—including Walrus." Pharaoh turned to Nasser. "Let's move!"

Nasser fired up the engine.

Walrus took down the last drop of water from his plastic canteen, then glanced over his shoulder at Gator, whose face was glowing and bathed in sweat as he closed the gap between them.

"My old granny can climb better than you," said Walrus.

"Your granny has a mustache."

"Come on, you turd. SERE and Robin Sage were harder than this little hike."

"I'm out of water."

"So am I. Don't matter. I think I feel a breeze coming in."

"You're so full of—" Gator cut himself off as Walrus answered his ringing satellite phone.

"Where are you now?" asked Pharaoh.

"Pretty far out. You want GPS?"

"Negative. Need you back now. We just IDed one of our targets at the cement factory. There's a good chance the other one and Hassan are there."

"Roger that."

"What's your ETA?"

"Five, six hours."

"What?"

"Captain, I'm sorry but like I said, we're pretty far out, and we're moving in on foot now."

"No, you're not that far out."

"Sir, like I said, we're on foot."

"Is Gator there?"

"He is."

"Let me talk to him."

"Roger that, sir." Walrus chuckled under his breath and lifted the phone. "Captain wants to talk to you."

Gator reached the small ridge, took a deep breath, back-handed the sweat from his brow, then accepted the phone. "Hey, Captain."

"I can't get a straight answer out of him," said Pharaoh, his voice easily loud enough for Walrus to hear. "Where the hell are you?"

"You don't know? He told me he called you. He lied."

"He didn't call."

"What the hell are you doing?" cried Gator.

"Nothing."

"Captain, we're more than halfway up a goddamned mountain, about an hour away from the top. Walrus thinks we'll have a view into the valley on the other side. He thinks the Iranians got something going on there, military, maybe nuclear."

"No kidding."

"Give me the phone." Gator handed it over. "Captain," Walrus began, his tone growing more emphatic, "you don't need us on the primary target. Give me an hour to get to the top. You won't regret it."

"I already do. Stand by."

Walrus cupped the receiver. "He's a fool if he denies us."

"I can't believe you didn't call him. You stood there and faked the damned call right in front of me."

"That was the practice call. I forgot to make the real one. I must be getting senile."

"You're not funny, you asshole."

"Walrus, we're moving on the cement factory. You got one hour to get up there and make a report."

"Excellent, sir. You can count on us."

"And, Walrus, when you get back to Cobra, you're going to be looking at forty-five days extra duty and a half a month's pay for two months. That's just to start."

"I understand, sir."

"Good. Report to me within one hour."

Walrus breathed a heavy sigh and glanced over at Gator, who was shaking his head. "You're the assistant detachment commander. You talk about duty, honor, and respect, talk about how Zulu pissed on Bull's grave, but you don't have any respect for our captain, do you?"

"Son, they come and go. Maybe I'm just getting too tired of it. I don't know."

"Well, it's not professional. In fact, in a lot of ways, you're a disgrace to this team. Some of us have been shocked over how you've acted, stuff you've said. Couple guys think you may have lost it."

"Wow, I admire your bravery. That's a lot to say to my face."

"Call 'em like I see 'em."

"Well, Gator, you just kicked yourself up a notch in my book. If I die next to you, I won't be as disappointed as I thought."

"Threats, backhanded compliments, you're a role model."

Walrus grinned to himself. This kid he liked.

Figueroa led Grimm into the hotel, and they slowly approached the concierge, a young man with an odd look on his face as he aggressively finger-combed his wiry beard. "We have no more rooms available," he snapped.

"We don't want a room," said Figueroa. "We're looking for one of our friends. A tall man, long hair, smoked a cigar." Figueroa motioned with his hand.

The concierge shook his head.

"You're sure you haven't seen him?"

The man shook his head even more emphatically.

"Come on, let's go," said Grimm.

Figueroa narrowed his gaze on the concierge. "You're sure?"

"Yes."

Figueroa sighed in disgust, then nodded at Grimm. They turned for the door as the desk phone rang.

The concierge reached to answer, and his sleeve slid up, revealing a Breitling Chrono Avenger watch, titanium-brushed and glare-proofed.

The watch caught Figueroa's eye because Rock himself was the proud owner of one exactly like it and had shown it to the entire team.

This watch, however, did not fit the concierge very well and dangled slightly from his wrist. Anyone who had purchased a watch that expensive would have had links removed to ensure a perfect fit—unless, of course, one had received that watch in a hasty trade or worse . . .

Consequently, Figueroa listened to his gut and reached across the counter. He grabbed the concierge by the throat with his left hand while hanging up the phone with his right. Figueroa's blood ran cold. "That's a nice watch," he hissed.

"Let me go!"

"Jon?" cried Grimm.

"He's got Rock's watch."

Figueroa literally dragged the guy over the top of the counter and down onto the other side, where he pinned him on the floor. He drew his sidearm and shoved it against the man's head. "Tell us where our friend is right now!"

"Don't shoot me."

"Tell us where our friend is!"

"Let me get up. Just don't shoot."

Figueroa released the man but kept his pistol trained on his head. "Where is he?"

"Come with me." The concierge stood, rubbed his throat, then opened a door behind the counter.

Figueroa and Grimm followed him down a narrow hall toward a small, grimy door at the end. The concierge opened the door and stepped aside.

On the floor of a crowded and dusty utility room lay a mummy in bloodstained sheets.

"Is that him?" Figueroa demanded.

The concierge nodded gravely.

"Grimm?"

The medic moved past them, hunkered down, and unwrapped as much as he could to expose the face. He recoiled and turned back. "Jesus, it's him."

"What happened?" Figueroa demanded.

The concierge shrugged. "I found him upstairs in the hallway."

"I don't believe you."

"Then I am ready to die."

"Why didn't you call the police?"

"Because I don't want people to know a murder happened here. That's bad for my uncle's business. But I was scared, too. I took him down here, bundled him up, got him ready to be taken away. I don't want to be involved in murder."

"But you took his watch."

"Why not? I don't know him."

"Hand it over. And you'd better not be lying."

"I have no reason. I just want to protect our business." The concierge unclasped the watch and gave it to Figueroa, who quickly pocketed it.

Figueroa's thoughts began racing too fast for him to catch up, and sweat dripped from his brow. "Uh, Grimm? Go get the car, bring it around back in the alley. Wait there."

"Roger that. I'll be right back."

Figueroa lifted his chin at the concierge. "You help me carry him out." Then he tugged out his phone, thumbed Pharaoh's number. "Sir, we found Rock in the hotel."

"Tell that asshole I want to talk to him right now."

"Sorry, sir, I can't. He's dead."

27. REVELATIONS

Inspired by Walrus's unrelenting harassment, Gator had climbed ahead, and Walrus actually had difficulty keeping up with the younger man. He dropped back a dozen meters or so and was forced to pick a path slightly east of Gator's to avoid the dust and the rocks being dislodged by his partner.

The sun beat heavily on their backs now, and Walrus suspected that if they didn't reach the summit soon, he was going to need a long break before hiking any more. He'd never tell Gator that, but the water was gone and his desire for glory was now lying abandoned on a ridge thirty meters below.

"I think we're almost there," the weapons sergeant called back. "Come on, old man."

That jibe set Walrus's feet in motion. He dug deeper, the tips of his boots plunging into loose earth as he leaned forward to keep balance and seized a clump of dry roots to pull himself up. His breathing grew more labored, the sweat running heavily down his neck now.

He was just closing the gap when he heard the young man gasp and cry, "Oh my God!"

"What is it?"

"Dude, get up here! Fast!"

Walrus took a deep breath and dragged himself toward Gator, the adrenaline finally kicking back in, the excitement now barely containable. What was up there?

Gator was on his hands and knees, peering over the summit, as Walrus arrived at his side.

What lay below took Walrus's breath away.

As Pharaoh and Zulu raced back to the airport to pick up Hojo and Weathers, Nasser was muttering something through his teeth and twice banged his fist on the steering wheel.

"Rock was a good friend, huh?" Pharaoh asked.

"Yes, James, he was. We have always been honest with each other, and when he told me what he was doing here, I said, go home. If you stay, you will not live long."

"Maybe you jinxed him," said Zulu.

"Maybe *you* did," Nasser spat back. "All of you."

A shudder of panic ripped across Pharaoh's shoulders. They were in Iran, and now their best source of intel was gone. "Nasser, you're all we have now. If Rock told you anything, I mean if you know anything . . ."

"Rock was a very smart man. Always careful with a plan—when he could be. I do have a message from him. He told me that if he didn't make it I should tell you that Hassan is meeting two members of parliament tonight at the concrete factory. The meeting is scheduled for about six P.M. If you want to get all of them at the same time, you should wait till then."

"And he had us running wild-goose chases all over the city: the airport, the railroad—"

"He didn't know where Hassan and the two agents were until this morning."

"Then that phone call you got earlier, after we lost Rock. That wasn't from your cousin. It was him."

"Yes. I'm sorry I lied. He wanted to get to his friends first."

"His friends? He told us they were just acquaintances."

Nasser shook his head. "No, we have all known them for a very long time. Rock didn't come here to kill them. He came here to save them. And they killed him for his efforts."

"You know that for a fact?"

Nasser gave him a look.

Pharaoh pursed his lips and nodded. "Yeah, I see." He took a deep breath. "Nasser, we can't get this done without your help. Are you still with us?"

"You don't know this, but I owe Rock my life. You were, in a way, his enemies here. He did not want you to interfere with his plans, but now I wish you had. I will call Yousef and Kourosh. We have some time. We will meet at my house and make our plan."

"Thank you, Nasser." Pharaoh glanced back at Zulu, whose eyes were already burning with the desire for payback. He had known Rock longer than anyone, and although they'd had their differences, Pharaoh knew that Zulu and Rock were, in fact, blood brothers. Zulu was, no doubt, already grieving the loss.

Yes, the entire team loved and hated Rock, but in the end, they all had the best interests of the United States in mind. And now they would, in the name of democracy, get the bastards who had killed Rock and take out the leader of al-Qaeda in Afghanistan.

The mission objectives had always been clear, but now those objectives were further motivated by the loss of one of their own. And of all the operators present, Pharaoh knew that Zulu would push the limits of mortal men to exact his revenge. For once that didn't bother Pharaoh. He'd cut the pit bull's leash and let him run.

"Audacity," Pharaoh told Zulu, referring back to one of their first missions together up in the mountains near the Pakistani border.

"Audacity," Zulu repeated. "And no mercy." He opened his Jani-Song, the knife's inner handle flashing out to reveal the shimmering blade. "No mercy."

Figueroa and Grimm, per the captain's orders, were headed back to Nasser's place, with Rock's body in the trunk of their car. Ondejko and Kourosh were moving to a more secure location to maintain surveillance of the cement factory.

"I tell you, when this is over, I'm going on a date with a twelve pack," said Figueroa.

"And I'm dating her sister," said Grimm. "My brain is on overload. Back in the 'Stan at least we got some control over the situation. But not here. I feel like one wrong turn, and it's all over. All this sneaking around is wearing me down."

"Me, too. And remember that shot that hit my helmet? I thought I was the luckiest man in the world. Dude, I should be dead right now. But I needed to survive." Figueroa sighed and his tone turned somber. "Somebody had to find Rock, I guess."

"I think you're alive for more important reasons than that. I don't want to sound cold, but I never liked the bastard."

"You sound cold. But I wasn't a fan either. And now I'm thinking we need to get the hell out of here. The Agency's got stuff going on that's way above our pay grades. They're setting us up. And who knows? Maybe they whacked Rock."

"Don't get too paranoid yet. The captain didn't sound too worried. He's got more intel than us."

"He doesn't know everything."

"Oh, yeah? What do you mean?"

"I'm just saying, don't put too much faith in him."

"He's a good guy. Best captain we've had. Zulu's working him like a dog, too."

Figueroa glanced over at Grimm, who looked like he had the dry heaves. "You all right?"

"Yeah."

"Hey, man, don't let it get to you."

"You mean seeing Rock?"

"Yeah. I gagged a little, too."

"That ain't it. Jon, can you keep a secret?"

"What?"

"I can't take it anymore. I just can't. Rock bought it. And I'm thinking, what if I do and no one knows, then what? Steve won't talk, the bastard."

"What are you saying?"

"I'm saying that Steve and I know what happened to Church, but we made a pact."

Figueroa cursed in surprise, then glanced over at Grimm, who was shaking his head, clearly guilt-stricken. "Dude, are you kidding me?"

"Look out!"

As Figueroa returned his gaze to the road, he realized that a man on a bicycle had been crossing in front of the car. Because Figueroa had not slowed, he clipped the man's rear tire and knocked him to the pavement.

Figueroa swore again and began to slow. "Should you get out? Make sure he's okay?"

"Are you nuts? Don't stop!" hollered Grimm.

"He's down. What if—"

"Just floor it! Get the hell out of here!"

Figueroa checked the rearview mirror. Several pedestrians were pointing at their car as he hit the accelerator and raced toward the next intersection.

"I'm calling the captain," said Grimm. "We could get pulled over before we get back to Nasser's. Damn it!"

Ondejko and Kourosh had parked their car in the employee lot of an old warehouse across the street from the cement factory. Kourosh had a friend who loaded trucks, and this friend helped them gain access to the warehouse's rooftop, where they could maintain surveillance of the factory with better cover. News of Rock's death had all of them even more paranoid, and Ondejko had temporarily abandoned his plan to hijack one of the cement block trucks. It was just as well. The truck hadn't moved, even after they'd finished loading it.

The factory, actually three large, rectangular blue buildings beside a large dome and a half dozen smaller structures, had several large preheater towers along with a massive kiln jutting up into the sky, past the satellite dishes and other large aluminum vents and apparatus. According to Kourosh, whose brother-in-law worked at a similar factory on the other side of the city, the dome-shaped structure was where the "clinker" was cooled and where many of the backup generators and fuel tanks were positioned.

Ondejko kept close to the small stone ledge and scanned those towers with his binoculars, expecting to find at least a guard or two in each. No surprise. He spotted a man posted along the catwalk of each tower; however, both were seated on the rails, leaning back, hands folded over their chests, and fast asleep.

"Looks like the guys up top won't be a problem for now."

"They're still sleeping off their lunch. But they'll be called," said Kourosh.

"Yeah, they will. If Gator gets back here in time, he and I will be in position to take out a lot of these guards."

"You are snipers?"

Ondejko lowered his binoculars and glanced over at Kourosh. "You'll see."

"Always such bravado, you Americans."

"Not bravado. I just hope we get the targets and get out before nightfall."

"I agree. You make me very nervous."

Ondejko fished out a small notebook from his hip pocket and began making a rough sketch of the factory, noting where each guard was posted. In a few moments he would forward that intel to Captain Pharaoh.

"There they are, right there," came a voice in Baluchi from behind them.

Ondejko whirled to find two gray-haired men coming toward them, perhaps the warehouse foremen, and Kourosh was immediately speaking to them as his friend, the loader, rushed up behind.

"Great." Ondejko moaned.

Pharaoh, Zulu, and Nasser were waiting in the back alley behind the market as Figueroa and Grimm came roaring up. The moment the car stopped, the two men leaped out, and the others got to work like an Indianapolis 500 pit crew, removing the body, weapons, and other gear from the trunk, then Nasser climbed into the car and sped off to turn it over to another of his cousins. To say he had a large family was barely scratching the surface.

Inside the storeroom, Pharaoh and Zulu unwrapped Rock's body as Figueroa came over. "Here's his watch. The concierge at the hotel tried to steal it, but I got it back."

"I'll hang on to it," said Zulu, taking the watch and immediately slipping it onto his wrist.

Pharaoh didn't have a problem with that. Zulu wasn't being greedy, and that watch would burn on the team sergeant's flesh.

"All right, gentlemen, we've only got a few hours, and we've got a lot of work to do." Pharaoh motioned them over.

"Sir?" called McDaniel, who was holding a satellite phone to his ear. "I have Cobra leader for you, sir."

Pharaoh braced himself and accepted the phone. He

had already updated Major Nurenfeld just fifteen minutes prior. "Hello, sir. This is Captain Pharaoh."

"Pharaoh, I got bad news. CENTCOM's just pulled the plug. They want you to exfiltrate immediately."

"Excuse me, sir?"

"You heard me, Captain. You will abort the mission and get back across the border A-SAP."

"Major, like I said before, we have a shot at the targets and Hassan. I still have Walrus on a possible secondary target. We can't pull out now."

"Captain, I didn't call for a debate."

"But, sir, what if the Agency's behind this? What if they got CENTCOM to pull the plug to cover their own asses?"

"You have your orders. You will follow them. And you'll keep me updated along the way."

Pharaoh hesitated. "Yes, sir."

"Captain, you know the consequences."

"Yes, sir. Good-bye, sir."

Pharaoh, utterly stunned, handed the phone back to McDaniel and stood there, staring blankly at all of them.

"We're going," said Zulu. "We're taking out the targets. Then we leave. We deny it all when we get back. It's not like they'd arranged the exfil anyway. Who's to say we didn't get delayed and had to kill a few people on the way out?"

"I'm in," said Figueroa.

"Me, too," Grimm said.

The others began to nod their ascent, and Pharaoh raised his voice. "We just got an order to abort. That's what we're doing."

"It's politics," cried Zulu. "We ain't playing politics! If we don't take out those guys, how many more good soldiers will die because of Hassan?"

"Zu, I agree with you, man, but we got the order. There's no more discussion."

"But, Captain—"

Pharaoh shifted up to the man, got in his face. "The mission is terminated. End of story."

"You said it yourself. We can't pull out now."

"What can I tell you, Zu? We got the order. That's it."

"And if the orders are unconscionable?"

"Look at me. We . . . have . . . orders."

Zulu widened his eyes. "This ain't right. You know it's not. You know what we have to do."

"Yeah, leave."

Zulu spun around, and began to loose his breath, then turned back. "You're not going to change your mind?"

Pharaoh shook his head.

Zulu threw his hands into the air. "Jesus Christ, we got a man lying dead there! What the hell's wrong with you?"

The outburst shocked the entire room, leaving every man motionless.

Pharaoh clenched his teeth. "Stand down, Sergeant."

"I will not. Fuck those orders!"

Pharaoh seized Zulu by the neck and drew back his fist as the others moved in, ready to break it up. Zulu just held his ground but made no move to defend himself. "We have orders! We're not breaking them!"

Zulu struggled to speak but managed, "Why not?"

Team Sergeant Robert "Zulu" Burrows had no idea that he had just cut the wrong wire on the ticking bomb inside Pharaoh's heart. "You want me to break orders, but I won't! I won't be my goddamned father! I won't do it! *Now shut your hole!*"

Pharaoh was trembling violently, his eyes burning with tears. He could barely breathe as he released Zulu with a shove and once again stood there before his men, their gazes probing him for answers.

Lowering his head, Pharaoh rubbed the corners of his eyes. "Saddle up. We're out of here. We're going home."

Several of his men swore under their breath as Pharaoh's satellite phone began to ring with a call from Walrus.

"This is Pharaoh. What do you got?"

"Captain? You're not going to believe this."

"Oh, yeah? Try me—'cause I have a little news for you."

28. SHORT FUSE

When Walrus and Gator reached the mountaintop, they had stood there for a few seconds until the enormity of the moment—and what they were looking at—hit home, and both of them dropped to dirt.

"You were right," Gator had said. "They got something huge going on down there."

Walrus chuckled under his breath and was thrilled by the prospect that they had hit the jackpot of all reconnaissance mission jackpots. "You have no idea what you're looking at."

"Uh, no. Not exactly."

They crawled forward on their elbows and began surveying the valley through their digital camera binoculars.

Satellite imagery would reveal nothing, because the entire site lay below a complex patchwork of camouflage netting. However, from their vantage point, Walrus and Gator had an unobstructed and chilling view.

The black sedans were parked beside a pair of Quonset huts that Walrus assumed were part of the support and/or power complex. Two dirt access roads led out past the camouflage netting, one ending at side-by-side helicopter pads where an attack helicopter and a transport chopper were parked. The other road ran back around the mountains. A large instrumentation bunker was positioned on the south side, near a motor pool with three heavy earthmovers and several dump trucks parked in a row. A second motor pool on the west side was comprised of smaller military vehicles: a pair of troop carriers and a few jeeps with .50-cals mounted on their backs. The troops themselves had established a simple but effective perimeter, with a man posted every twenty meters or so.

And smack dab in the middle of the valley, like the main pole of a circus tent, rose a thirty-meter-tall tower supported by a half dozen support cables spanned by even more netting. Walrus had zoomed in through that netting to observe a three-by-two-meter reentry vehicle shaped like a nose cone. The vehicle was suspended from the tower by fire control and other cables. Directly below lay a wide hole fenced off by concertina wire lest anyone fall to his death.

At least three Iranian technicians were up in the tower, and Walrus had assumed they were making their inspections to ensure that the vehicle containing the warhead was ready to be lowered into the hole. Walrus observed the hills of dirt nearby, hoping the Iranians had dug at least three hundred meters deep.

In point of fact, Walrus was no stranger to nuclear test facilities. Just last year during a reconnaissance mission he had seen almost an exact replica of the site at Chagai Hills, Baluchistan, Pakistan. The Paki site had a huge earthen berm and a tunnel to bury the device into a mountainside. As many had suspected, Pakistan and Iran had been talking to each other, and all those stories about that Pakistani scientist Kahn were probably true. With some help from the North Koreans, Kahn had been spreading Islam with a twenty-first-century twist. The elaborate operation below was proof positive to Walrus that these guys weren't just playing with conventional weapons. He'd bet his life that there was a nuke up in that tower.

So there it was. The Iranians had nuclear weapons, and they would detonate a warhead to ensure that they didn't have duds perched atop their missiles. However, if those clowns hadn't dug a deep enough hole, a cavity would form upon detonation. The open cavity would allow the pressure to vent radioactive debris and dust upward into the surrounding atmosphere. At adequate depth, once the pressure in the pit fell below the level needed to support the overburden, the rock above would fall back into the pit, sealing the bulk of the debris and dust, and ultimately capping it with a telltale chimney of rubble. Walrus wouldn't put it past the Iranians to screw up this one.

If only Walrus could obtain the exact time of the test—because the best way to take out the warhead was to do so while it was still above ground. Once the Iranians lowered it into that pit, all bets were off. Even after Walrus called in a strike, they could never be sure they had destroyed the weapon. They needed to destroy the thing now.

As he finished sharing the news with Pharaoh, he got dead silence on the other end. He glanced over to Gator, who'd been taking pictures and video of the site. His digital camera binoculars were communicating via Bluetooth with the pocket-sized Explorer 110 mobile satellite device. It was uplinked to one of the four Ka-band transponders of the military's Global Broadcast Service (GBS) in the Middle East. Higher was already viewing their data.

"Hey, Walrus, man, I just finished the last upload. They got everything they need. Let's go," said Gator.

"Hang on one sec. I'm waiting for the captain."

Pharaoh finally answered, "Walrus, I need you guys back at the safe house. We're pulling out the second you get back. We're done here."

"What do you mean 'we're done'? What's going on?"

"We got orders to abort."

"Orders from who?"

"The major called me. Orders come down from CENT-COM."

"Then the orders are bullshit."

"What are you talking about?"

"Captain, think about it. We were sent here by orders of the President of the United States. You're obligated to carry out the last order given by the highest authority. You call the major and ask him if he's got a presidential order rescinding the finding, otherwise we still got the green light."

"Are you kidding me?"

"Captain, the way I see it, the spooks are all over this one. They got to someone in CENTCOM, who sent down the order to Nurenfeld. Like I said, it's all bullshit. You tell the major unless he comes up with a no-go from the president himself, we will continue the mission. Period."

"You're right. I didn't think of that."

"It's okay, Captain. That's why I'm here. I'm more than just a pretty face. And if it all goes south, well, you know why they created commissioned officers, right?"

"Yeah, so they got someone to hang when the shit hits the fan."

"You got it. So we're heading back down now. They need to take out this warhead A-SAP, hopefully before they put it in the ground. Sorry, but we ain't sticking around to paint this target. Not this one."

"Roger that."

As they rose to head back down, Gator cried, "Check it out! The two cars are leaving. They might spot our ride. Dude, we have to move!"

But as the words escaped Gator's mouth, Walrus already knew they would not reach the vehicle in time. "Over here!" he cried, then started sidestepping across the ridge, toward a long row of boulders about thirty meters north. Gator followed, and they hustled toward the cover as the sedans began coming around the mountain, the dust rising behind them.

They had parked the car at the base of the mountain, behind a small berm of talus and scree that had fallen and collected there. It'd been the best cover they could find. If the drivers of those sedans kept their eyes on the road, there wouldn't be a problem, but if they casually glanced right, they might catch the car's roof, jutting up behind the rock, or a flash of reflected light.

Walrus and Gator reached the boulders and tucked in tight, fighting for breath. Walrus peered out from behind his rock and lifted his binoculars.

The sedans were just now coming out around the mountain, gaining speed.

"Might be okay," whispered Gator.

"Why you whispering?" asked Walrus. "They can't hear us."

Walrus glanced back through his binoculars, and a curse rushed to his lips. The sedans had stopped dead, directly across from their car.

Kourosh turned away from the gray-haired men on the warehouse's rooftop and returned to Ondejko. The fat man wore a broad grin and had a dangerous twinkle in his eye. "They want money. Otherwise, they are going to kill us."

"How much?"

"At least five hundred. They're being paid off by a man named Hanjour to keep an eye on the factory."

Ondejko nodded. "Tell them we'll give them eight hundred. The money will be here in less than an hour. Now wait a minute. Do you think we can use these guys?"

"How?"

Ondejko wriggled his brows. "Here's what I'm thinking . . ."

Pharaoh was on the Shadowfire radio with Major Nurenfeld, who was, to put it politely, not pleased.

"I say again, sir, unless you can produce a presidential order rescinding the finding, the mission here will continue, sir."

"Captain, do you understand the position you're putting me in? Do you?"

"Sir, I do, sir. But we were sent here by orders of the president. Not you. Not CENTCOM. With all due respect, sir, if you can get me those orders, or have the president himself give me a call, I'll stand down and exfiltrate. Until then, the mission goes on." Pharaoh consulted his watch. "We have just ninety minutes until we hit the cement factory. The clock's ticking, sir."

"All right, Captain, I'll get back to you."

Pharaoh faced the rest of the team and sighed. "It was nice working with all you guys. I'll be greeting customers at Walmart after this is over."

"You did the right thing," said Zulu, then he lifted his voice to address the others. "Okay, gentlemen. Everybody knows his team, knows what he's got to do. Ondejko just called me, and he's setting up a fallback position inside the warehouse across the street. Snipers will use radios. The rest of us talk over the cells. Nobody's getting caught with a radio on him, we clear?"

The group murmured their ascent.

"This is it, boys. No mistakes."

As the team filed out of the room, Figueroa tipped his head toward Grimm, and they both moved behind a long shelf of canned goods. "Last chance if you want to tell me what happened to Church," Figueroa told the medic.

"Bad luck."

"What do you mean?"

"I mean I changed my mind."

"Steve got to you?"

"No, but if I tell you now, I won't be coming back."

"How do you know?"

Grimm sighed. "I need to make it through this, and when we get back, I'll talk to Steve, and we'll sit down with everyone."

"It's your decision. Just tell me—you guys didn't kill him, did you?"

Grimm's expression turned emphatic. "No."

President James Gallagher glanced up from his desk as Secretary of Defense Dennis MacIntyre entered the oval office. It was just eight A.M., and Gallagher had been expecting MacIntyre at any minute.

"Good morning, Jim. I'll cut right to the chase. Our ODA team in Iran has located a test site. The Iranians have a nuke. They'll detonate underground."

Gallagher smiled bitterly. The Iranians' timing was not accidental. In exactly two days, a top U.S. negotiating team was meeting in Geneva with their Iranian counterparts. The Iranians had already let it slip that if the U.S. lifted sanctions and one day accepted them into the nuclear family, they were willing to convince Iraqi insurgent groups to negotiate a political solution for a lasting peace in Iraq.

"They picked Zahedan because it's close to its neighbors' borders and our ongoing operations," MacIntyre continued. "They're putting us on notice. And they're on a short fuse because they want a successful test before the Geneva conference. They want equal footing at the bargaining table. I guess everyone knew this was coming. It was just a question of when."

"Let's get the Joint Chiefs in the situation room right now."

"They're already on their way. And, sir, we've got another problem. It seems CENTCOM tried to pull out our Special Forces."

"What?"

"They're not sure what happened, but someone sent orders to the team, piped 'em right down to their company commander. The ploy almost worked, but Pharaoh didn't take the bait. He said he's on task unless he hears otherwise from you. That's a soldier who understands the chain of command."

"You're not kidding. I think we need to call our friends at the CIA to see if they know anything about this." MacIntyre nodded knowingly as Gallagher rose from his chair. "All right, Dennis. Looks like we're in for one hell of a morning. And do me a favor, put me in touch with Captain Pharaoh. I want that young man to know he's exactly where he belongs."

"We'll make that happen, sir."

29. THIRTY-THREE MINUTES

One of the drivers had stepped out of his black Mercedes and, with pistol drawn, tentatively approached Walrus and Gator's car. Walrus would have taken him out, but the bastard was well out of range, and the wind had picked up, making the shot even more difficult. Worse, he and Gator were toting pistols and AK-47s, not long-range sniper rifles.

The driver, wearing a dark suit, had glanced up into the mountains, shielding his eyes from the sun, then immediately lifted his cell phone, while the other driver jogged over from his car.

Walrus got Pharaoh on the line. "We got a little problem. Those two sedans we followed? Well, the drivers spotted our car, and we're stuck up here in the mountains. We need higher to take out this site now."

"What about you guys?"

"Don't worry about us. I'll follow up." Walrus thumbed off the phone. No need to get the young captain all bent out of shape. Better to keep his mind focused on the factory and taking out the targets.

Meanwhile, Gator had smashed the memory cards and was burying the cameras, which had done their job and were better left in the dirt than in the hands of the Iranians.

When Gator was finished, Walrus glanced at him and said, "We need to get down there before they get one of their birds in the air. That's what he's doing now—calling for help."

"Well he's not calling the wife for the grocery list."

Walrus muttered a string of curses and ended with, "We need to get the hell out of here."

Gator snickered. "Why'd I let you talk me into this?"

"Don't blame yourself. I'll take full responsibility for your misery. Ready?"

Gator nodded, and they emerged from cover and began picking their way down the hill, mindful of every step across the piles of loose rocks.

"Start waving," said Walrus. "They might hold fire."

One-handing his AK, Gator waved, as did Walrus, who smiled and spoke through his teeth, "Hey, Uncle Bobby, come here so I can shoot you in the head."

The two drivers once more shielded their eyes and spotted them. Both raised their pistols while one guy continued talking on his phone.

"Do you hear a helicopter?" asked Gator.

"Just your imagination." Walrus lifted his voice and, in Arabic, cried out, "Hello! Hello! Can you help us with our car?"

Gator rolled his eyes. "Yeah, we accidentally broke down near your nuclear test site."

"You got something better?" Walrus retorted.

One of the drivers shouted back up, "Put down your weapons."

"Just a little closer," said Walrus as they began losing their footing on the softer earth. "At least going down's a lot easier."

"Oh, yeah, right, as we're about to be captured."

"Gator, I don't get captured."

"Yeah, I know. Dude, we're not going home. Are we . . ."

"Sure we are. Just a little closer, then we'll hose down these bastards. I got the guy on the right. Get ready."

Walrus had a good eye for distances. Maximum effective range for their AKs was about four hundred meters, but Walrus wanted to get them in a little closer than that. He led them toward the next ridge and decided they would hit the deck there.

"See it?" he asked Gator.

"Yeah."

"You hit and drop. On three . . ."

Pharaoh and his men arrived at the warehouse across the street from the cement factory, and Pharaoh exhausted his supply of greenbacks to pay off the managers for their help. Ondejko and Kourosh had done very well for them, and Pharaoh was eager to get the ball rolling.

Weathers, McDaniel, Borokovsky, and Grimm were the truck team, tasked with searching and rigging up the two flatbeds loaded with concrete blocks parked at the loading dock. Initially, Pharaoh had thought they'd use the trucks for the ride home, but now he had other plans for them.

Because Gator was out with Walrus, Hojo assumed the job of sniper, along with Ondejko, and they were already en route to the rooftop to set up.

Zulu would lead the engineering team of Figueroa and Sullivan to the dome-shaped building, to rig the generators and fuel tanks with a modest amount of C-4.

Meanwhile, Pharaoh, Nasser, and Kourosh were the diversion team, positioned near a bank of windows facing the factory and armed with rocket-propelled grenades to draw off as many of the security guards as possible, while the warehouse guys lived up to their well-paid end of the bargain.

Pharaoh checked his watch. The members of parliament

were scheduled to arrive in exactly thirty-three minutes. His mouth was already going dry. He glanced over at Kourosh and Nasser and nodded. "Thank you."

"Thank us when it's over," said Nasser. "We are glad to rid al-Qaeda from our city. Not all Iranians are terrorists, Captain Pharaoh, as your liberal news media seems to suggest."

Pharaoh pursed his lips and glanced away. A beep came from his satellite phone, and he didn't recognize the number. "This is Pharaoh."

"Captain Pharaoh, this is Jim Gallagher. How you doing out there, son?"

Pharaoh lost his breath. On the other end of the line was the leader of the free world.

"Captain, are you there?"

"This is the way it goes down," Zulu told Figueroa and Grimm as they huddled inside a car parked alongside the rear of the factory. "All you care about is setting the charges. The two guys near that gate are mine."

"Just be careful, Zu," said Figueroa.

"Don't worry about that. And now we wait."

Zulu pushed his head farther back into the seat, closed his eyes, and remembered the intelligence photos he'd seen of Jersey and Libra, and the others taken of Hassan. He wanted to burn those images into his thoughts so when the time came, he would recognize them immediately.

Yes, he would make sure that the engineers got their charges set. But after that, he wasn't falling back.

Grimm, Borokovsky, Weathers, and McDaniel were seated inside a small delivery truck that had just been unloaded. Bags of rice were stacked on a pallet below. The engine was idling, and the driver, a kid barely twenty, had received his instructions.

After a deep breath, Grimm leaned over to Borokovsky and said, "Steve, when it's over, it all comes out. I already told Figueroa we know. No details, but I gave him enough. It's the right thing."

Borokovsky closed his eyes. "I don't want to think about it right now."

"I'm just saying."

"Just shut up."

Ondejko and Hojo were communicating via radio, their earpiece/mikes hidden beneath their *shemaghs*. This was a luxury afforded to the snipers since they were in standoff positions at opposite corners on the warehouse's rooftop. They wanted to be in close contact as they removed guards with their specially modified 7.62mm subsonic ammunition designed to dampen their rifles' reports. Their Russian-made Dragunov SVDs with detachable ten-round box magazines would do the job. Ondejko wasn't a huge fan of the rifle, but he also wasn't a huge fan of being caught and IDed as an American, based in part upon the rifle he carried. Their scopes were PSO-1s with infrared detection capability and range-finding reticles calibrated to a man-sized target of 1.7 meters. As Hojo would say, "It's all good, man."

And for the time being, it was. Ondejko had his guy in the tower sighted, Hojo had his.

"If we'd go right now, I'd have a perfect shot," Ondejko said.

"Roger that. My guy smoked a cigarette, then fell back asleep."

Ondejko was sitting cross-legged, the rifle balanced on its bipod seated along an inner ledge that allowed him full cover and exposed only his muzzle. When the time came, just a slight part of his head would appear before a click echoed down from the roof, and a man slumped with part of his head splattered on the wall behind him.

* * *

President Gallagher ended the call with Captain Pharaoh and returned to the head of the situation room, framed by a wall of flat panel displays all showing various satellite images of Iran and Zahedan.

Gallagher raised his brows at the men seated around the long table. "Pharaoh's man on the ground called. We need to take out that site right now."

Admiral Gundlach, chief of naval operations (CNO), a leonine, charismatic man with a glistening white crew cut, glanced up from the laptop on the table before him. "Mr. President, I've got a Virginia class sub, *Seatiger*, in the Arabian Sea. She's within five hundred miles of the target with a full complement of Tomahawks on board. She's already closed the gap to within four hundred miles and launched a Predator."

"Flight time on those Tomahawks?" asked Gallagher.

The admiral worked his keyboard. "At that range . . . about forty-eight minutes, sir."

"Very well." Gallagher regarded General David Voorhis, chairman of the Joint Chiefs of Staff, whose expression had soured. "What is it, General?"

"Sir, after we take out that site, the Islamists will point their fingers at Israel. Are the Israelis ready to skin that cat?"

"It's our 140,000 troops in Iraq and the 32,000 in Afghanistan that concern me, General. What do you think the Taliban and al-Qaeda reaction will be when their primary backer announces they have nuclear capability?"

Voorhis nodded. "I understand, sir."

The president studied each of his military advisors, then spoke softly, deliberately: "Transmit the E-A-M to *Seatiger* ordering the immediate destruction of the device and the test site. Emphasize that collateral damage is not, repeat, *not* a primary concern. Copy the Israeli Mossad director. Make sure she gets everything we've got and will get. I'll call the Israeli prime minister and tell him to hunker down."

General Rahim stood inside the bunker at the nuclear test site and, through the North Korean translator, explained to the Korean contingency exactly how the warhead had been constructed.

Fissionable material for the bomb had been extracted and refined at Iran's Natanz Nuclear Facility near the town of Deh-Zireh. The material had next been transported by rail to a secret assembly facility at Tabas, a city of 30,000 adjacent to the Afghan border. Tabas specialized in the production of ballistic missiles and high explosive devices, and its engineers had shaped the uranium into a football-like spheroid with a perfect cavity or pit at its center. Next had come the HE and meticulously spaced firing squibs, each terminating inside solid state circuitry capable of delivering an exquisitely timed firing sequence. This sequence crushed the sphere down to its critical mass, generating the explosive energy of a miniature sun.

When completed, Tabas engineers calculated their bomb had a nominal yield of five kilotons—maximum. While this was a minuscule explosion by WMD standards, it was an eruption of Krakatauan proportion to western governments. The final assembly had next been trucked to the test firing range south of Zahedan.

The North Koreans were pleased, very pleased. Rahim sighed with relief. The speech had gone well, and he'd repeat it to the Pakistani contingent when they arrived. They were running late, and the drivers were off to fetch them at the airport.

As Rahim was about to offer the men some drinks, one of his aides stormed into the bunker, shouting, "General, two men were spotted on the mountain!"

*   *   *

Admittedly, Walrus had been a little too cocky about their range. He and Gator had hit the deck, firing at the drivers below. Walrus felt certain he had hit one man, but both managed to drop and find cover behind Walrus and Gator's small car.

Walrus sprang back up and charged down toward the pair, reaching into the web gear beneath his baggy shirt and tugging out one of six grenades he'd packed.

Gator fell in behind him, and as the first man leaned out in an attempt to fire at Walrus, Gator let him have it with another salvo, the rounds punching hard into the car's rear window and trunk. Glass shattered. The guy leaned out once more, and fired a round that struck the dirt a meter from Walrus's boot.

With a deep breath, Walrus wound up and let his grenade fly. Hell, hc didn't care if they blew up the piece-of-crap car Nasser had loaned them; they'd drive back to Zahedan in a Mercedes, in style.

The grenade hit the ground a few meters in front of the car, then began rolling forward.

Boom! The vehicle lifted up on two wheels, the rest of its windows shattering as one man, a hand to his ear, made a last-ditch run for his Mercedes. Walrus cut him down with a trio of shots.

Just as Walrus turned to his right to look for Gator, Gator issued a gasp and went rolling past Walrus. Damn it, he'd slipped.

Nasser's loaner had caught fire now, the fuel tank soon to explode, in Walrus's expert opinion. Gator stopped his roll and turned onto his back.

"I give you a ten for that fall. I'll pin the medal on your ass. Get up." Walrus proffered his hand.

Gator rose, but he winced. "Shit, I hurt something. My ankle's on fire."

"Left one?"

"Yeah."

"Good. You can still drive."

Walrus draped Gator's arm over his shoulder and helped him farther down the mountainside.

At the bottom, they noted that the other driver had died in the grenade blast. Walrus hustled forward and put Gator into one of the sedans. He fetched the keys from the first driver and tossed them to Gator. "Go."

"What?"

"Go. I'll be right behind you!"

Walrus jogged off to the second driver and found the other set of keys as Gator tore out, leaving fountains of dirt. Walrus hopped into the other Mercedes, jammed his boot on the accelerator, and wheeled around, heading back for the test site.

His phone began to ring. It was Gator. Walrus shook his head. Now that the Iranians knew they were there, they'd drop the warhead into the ground as a safety precaution—and Walrus hadn't come this far to let that happen.

The phone kept ringing. *Sorry, kid.*

30. LAST HURRAH

The 377-foot USS *Seatiger* SSN-804 was a nuclear attack submarine with a bow bundle featuring two large-diameter payload tubes. The multiple all-up-around canister inserted into each tube contained cells for six Tomahawk missiles and an additional center access cell.

The two payload tubes retained the twelve-missile capacity while providing a unique ability to deploy new payloads. One of *Seatiger*'s tubes housed a modified Predator unmanned aerial vehicle. *Seatiger*'s skipper, Commander Frank Redmin, had been ordered to launch that Predator immediately after the test site in southeastern Iran had been detected.

Moments after the Predator arrived over the test site, six Tomahawks programmed to take out the device, tower, chopper pad, and outbuildings would deliver an unmistakable message from Washington. Hitting the outbuildings meant dead civilians, an aborted nuclear detonation, and breathing room for a second strike in the unlikely event the first strike left the warhead intact. War *was* hell.

Now, as the six Tomahawks erupted sequentially out of a calm Arabian Sea, Redmin marveled at what his crew and ship had done—ramping up from a submarine's classic covert posture to delivering a deadly inferno. *Seatiger* was now the hottest node in the military network centric warfare chain as its steerable sixteen-inch HDR dish antenna captured the TV show streaming from the lone Predator. Redmin briefly shuddered, pondering who might be with him on the world's most expensive party line.

The Predator video would tell the initial story but the litmus test would be the "eye in the sky" with a sniffer to pick up increased site radiation—evidence that the warhead had been breached and rendered useless. Nothing could hide that.

"There they are," said Pharaoh, as a shimmering white Lexus sedan, the flagship model, rolled up toward the cement factory and turned into the employee parking lot on the south side. A car like that in Iran was an uncommon sight. So much for those parliament members keeping a low profile.

"They're early," Nasser added. "Unusual for politicians."

The car stopped before a pair of side doors, and a tall, well-dressed man exited the driver's seat and opened the rear door. Two gray-haired men left the car, one lean with a closely cropped beard, the other stout, his beard much longer.

"Well they're not here to buy concrete," said Pharaoh as he made the first call to Zulu. "We're good to go! Move out!"

Inside the cement factory, near the entrance to the main loading area, Saeed Hanjour wrung his hands. The engineers in the back were ready to show the members of parliament all of their work, and the sheikh seemed anxious, although all preparations had been made. Hanjour had finally managed to secure "entertainment" for the parliament members, despite the disaster of his last transaction with the old woman, who had wound up killing the girl Hanjour had been with and getting shot herself. If recent events were any indication, then the world of prostitution was more dangerous than arms smuggling.

The two shipments of explosively formed projectiles hidden within the blocks awaited inspection out on the loading docks, and the sheikh would demonstrate to the members how cleverly the engineers concealed the devices. The trucks would drive away before the members' eyes, bound for Afghanistan. They would see firsthand the work the sheikh was doing to gain the upper hand against the infidels.

Still, all did not feel right to Hanjour. The sheikh's arms dealers were at his side, but Hanjour noted something in Libra's eyes, a sense of guilt perhaps, he wasn't sure, and an unevenness in the man's tone. Hanjour shifted over to Libra and muttered in his ear, "Are you feeling dizzy again?"

"No, I'm all right," snapped Libra. "Thank you."

"You seem nervous. These are the sheikh's friends. There's no need to worry."

"From what the sheikh has told me, I'm not the one who should be concerned. If those shipments don't reach Afghanistan, he'll have your head. And you've had some difficulties at the border, I'm told."

Hanjour was about to answer when the members of parliament appeared from behind an open door. The sheikh smiled and greeted them with outstretched arms.

The small delivery truck's driver took Grimm, Borokovsky, Weathers, and McDaniel to the north side intersection then turned left, running alongside a six-foot-tall chain-link fence until they neared a row of Dumpsters. The driver promptly stopped in the middle of the more narrow road, got out, and lifted the hood on the truck. He banged twice on the side panel: the team's signal to go. Grimm opened the back door, and he and the others hopped out and ran around the truck.

The fence stood between them and the loading docks. Weathers got to work with his big cutters, clipping wire with a steady *clink* while McDaniel helped peel back the fence. The Dumpsters concealed them from view of the two guards posted one at each end of the docks, and the jog across the road to the docks themselves would take no more than ten seconds. At the moment, the docks themselves were devoid of workers, the large rolling doors cracked open about a meter for ventilation.

Once the team began slipping through the fence, the driver shut down the hood, wheeled around, and headed back for the intersection, where his truck would "stall" once again.

Even as Grimm hunkered down near the Dumpsters with the others, drivers behind them began to honk their horns as not one but two trucks now broke down in the middle of the road between the old warehouse and the factory. The street had been effectively cordoned off by the trucks, drawing the attention of the two guards. A temporary traffic jam was exactly what they wanted to kick off the big show—a natural diversion, one that would call some but not too much attention to itself, until the guards began to realize that the odds of two trucks breaking down at the same time were pretty steep.

Weathers called up to Ondejko, told the sniper they were in position and waiting for him to clear the path.

Grimm tensed, looked over at Borokovsky, who repeatedly rubbed his eyes. "You all right, Steve?"

"Just a little dust."

As the car horns began to grow in number, Ondejko's pulse mounted. His boy had moved to the tower railing to have a look down in the street, and Ondejko had his crosshairs floating perfectly over the guy's head.

"I got mine," he whispered into the radio.

"Me, too," answered Hojo.

With that Ondejko took a deep breath, held it, then tensed and squeezed the trigger.

A cloud of blood sprayed the wall behind the guard, who dropped so quickly that Ondejko had to blink several times, then squint to find the man lying on the deck. He panned down with his scope toward the second tower, where Hojo's guard was slumped over the railing, missing a sizable portion of his head.

"Loading dock next. You're going right," said Ondejko. "I got left."

"Roger that. Got mine sighted. Time to get to work, baby."

Ondejko locked onto his next target, a guard positioned on the left side of the loading docks. *"Allah Hafiz,"* he whispered as the man's chest exploded.

Two seconds later, Hojo's guard fell. No need to call back to Weathers; Ondejko watched as the truck team advanced the moment that second guard dropped.

Gator checked his rearview mirror once more, but he could barely see through all the dust he was kicking up. For a moment, though, he did catch a glimpse of Walrus's car, the other Mercedes, heading in the wrong direction—back toward the mountains.

He tried to call Walrus again, but the crazy bastard wasn't answering. So he called Pharaoh, gave him the SITREP, asked if he wanted Gator to go back after the man.

"No, buddy, you get back here now," said the captain.

"Roger that, sir."

Gator suddenly removed his boot from the accelerator. What the hell was he doing? Running away like a coward, when Walrus had gone back there alone? Was the old man just a fool? Or was he buying Gator more time to escape, and if Gator didn't accept the offer, then they'd both just die.

Walrus had made his decision.

But it was killing Gator to make his. He thought of the helicopters, of his family and friends back home, and thought Walrus was doing him a favor, and he'd take it. He slammed down the accelerator once more, kicking up more dust, as his eyes grew sore.

That old bastard. Gator still hated him, maybe even more now, for making him feel like this.

But what a warrior. No one could take that from him, not even Zulu.

All the car horns did a decent job of blanketing the click from Zulu's pistol. Yes, the long silencer suppressed most of the noise, but a little help was always welcome. He had slipped up behind the guard and fired into the man's back at point-blank range.

Now, as Figueroa and Sullivan waited, Zulu jogged around to the other side of the dome, an arc of some ten-to-fifteen meters, until he nearly ran over the next guard, who looked up as Zulu drove his Jani-Song into the man's heart while seizing the man's neck to stifle any scream.

They hit the ground hard, and Zulu punched the knife home once more, his breath coming loudly, his mouth filling with saliva, his eyes bulging.

Once he was certain the guy was dead, he pocketed the knife, dragged the man along the wall, and lay him beneath a stairwell and service ladder, out of sight. He charged back around the dome and gave Figueroa and Sullivan the hand signal to move forward and begin planting their charges.

Then he took off, heading toward a long bank of windows that looked in on the main loading area.

A slight pang of guilt took hold. He was supposed to be

covering the engineers, not heading off on his own hunting expedition.

Figueroa and Sullivan were very capable operators. They would be perfectly fine without him.

In fact, the entire team would be better off without him.

Walrus had no desire to die, but the moment he'd spotted that driver on the phone, he figured only one of them would make it away from the site. He would be the diversion because the kid, Gator, still had a lot more living to do.

Then again, so did he. But if his number was up, he could look back and say, *Hey, I had a good life.* He only had one last regret: that he'd taken the moral high ground with Zulu, so as he drove around the mountain, the sound of a helicopter growing even louder, he dialed up Zulu's cell phone, and lo and behold, the team sergeant answered.

"Hey, Zu, how you doing?"

"Jesus Christ, you asshole, what're you doing? You get out of there yet?"

"Not yet. Just want to tell you something. I still think what you did was wrong, sleeping with another operator's wife, but I just want you to know that I understand."

"What the hell are you calling me for? I can't talk now."

"Just listen to me for one second. Way back when, Melissa came on to me, too. I didn't take the bait, but ever since then I dreamed of having an affair with her. You got to have that. Maybe in my own screwed-up way I was jealous. Maybe that's why I really came after you. I never admitted it to myself, tried never to think about it. Two wrongs don't make a right, but I wanted you to know that."

"You bastard. I can't believe you're telling me this shit now."

"We all have to pay for our sins. Just do the right thing, Zu. From now on, do the right thing."

Walrus thumbed off the phone. He took a deep breath, rounded the corner, and came head-on toward two jeeps with those .50-calibers mounted on the back.

He rolled down the window, stuck out his hand, and began waving to them, as the jeeps kept coming. He slowed down, just a little, then suddenly floored it, veering off the path slightly and roaring past them. He checked his rearview mirror, as one jeep began turning around, the gunner bringing his weapon to bear on him, just as that smaller military helicopter thundered overhead.

All Walrus needed to do was get close enough to the test site to spook the engineers. Get them out of the tower and delay their operations. That's all he needed to do.

He jammed his boot all the way down on the accelerator, the needle whipping to the right, heading toward 200 kph on the dial or 125 miles per hour. The Mercedes bounced as though cutting across a ship's heavy wake, and Walrus clung hard to the steering wheel, as in the distance, the tower suddenly appeared from behind the mountain.

The helicopter's *whomp*ing grew even louder, and he knew that if that bitch was equipped with rockets, the pilot would be taking his shot any minute now. He didn't have long to wait.

An explosion sounded so loudly behind him that Walrus thought his eardrums had burst.

The road was gone, replaced by the sky, then the road once more, as the car began hurtling through the air, tumbling end over end until it came to a stop, remarkably back on its wheels. Flames roared behind him as he tried the door: jammed. He broke out the window with the butt of his rifle, his air nearly gone, the black smoke choking him.

He crawled through the window and fell onto the ground as the jeep came roaring over and the soldiers hopped out and raced toward him. Shrapnel from the blast had penetrated his arms and legs, the blood oozing through his clothes.

Walrus lifted his rifle, already losing consciousness, but he never got off a shot.

Six brilliant flashes appeared in succession at the test site, the tower suddenly engulfed in a mushroom cloud. He glanced back at the soldiers, smiled, then turned around and faced doomsday. He raised his hands as the ground rumbled and the heat and light finally reached him.

31. NO SURRENDER

In the span of four minutes, Figueroa and Sullivan planted their charges and double-checked their remote detonators. They used a small amount of C-4 intended to rupture the two backup generator fuel tanks and begin a flood of fuel. The muffled pops would not be detected by those inside the main buildings—if they did their job right.

Figueroa was about to signal to Sullivan to head back off toward the fence line, but Sullivan, who was crouched down at the opposite side of the long, submarine-like tank, shook his head vigorously. Then he pointed his finger toward the main building on the other side.

Frowning, Figueroa darted over to him. "What the hell?"

"Zulu took out the guard, then he ran off."

"Where?"

Sullivan cocked a thumb over his shoulder toward the main buildings.

"Aw, man." Figueroa groaned. "What the hell's he doing now?"

Sullivan frowned. "I don't think he wants to come. We can't let him do this."

"We got orders to set charges and fall back."

"We can't leave him."

"He knows what he's doing."

Sullivan snorted. "You really believe that?"

Figueroa took in a long breath, then sighed in disgust. No, he wouldn't leave Zulu, either, but he didn't have to like going after the man. "This is bullshit. Come on." He led Sullivan back toward the main building, his gaze flicking left and right, ever wary of the next guard. They'd find out what Zulu was doing, all right, and probably get shot in the interim.

"What the hell is that?" asked Sullivan as the ground began to rumble.

Gator could pry no more speed from the sedan's engine, and he could barely keep his grip on the wheel as the car literally went airborne several times and the ground turned to mush. Thick mushroom clouds flickering with fire rose from behind the mountains.

Yes! He thrust a fist in the air and hollered. Higher had come through—and with good timing to boot.

But his celebration ended before he lowered his fist. All the rattling and engine roar hardly dampened the terrible drumming of that helicopter, now somewhere on his tail.

He checked his mirror: nothing.

Then he stole a glance in the side-view mirror and saw it. The helo resembled one of the U.S.'s attack helicopters, the Cobra, and its three-barrel 20mm gun panned toward Gator's car like the eye of a flying Cyclops.

The first rounds punched into the trunk, then another salvo shattered the rear window as those slugs hissed near his ear. He rolled the wheel to the right, out of the gunner's bead, then rolled left, weaving a serpentine path.

But he took the second turn too hard, and the car suddenly went up on two wheels.

"No, no, no," he cried as the Mercedes rolled over onto

its side, the momentum forcing it over now, belly up, with Gator hanging from the seat belt as a cloud of dust rose around him. He immediately grabbed the belt, unbuckled, then swung himself down, onto the roof liner, the engine still running, shattered safety glass still clinking all around him.

Panting, he fumbled for his phone, speed-dialed Captain Pharaoh, and waited as the phone rang.

The captain answered tersely, "Gator, where are you?"

"Still near the site. Walrus went back. Sorry, sir, but I need to finish something here. Don't come back for us. It's all right." Gator let the phone fall from his grip.

The clouds of dust were already clearing around the car, and now the chopper had landed, but the pilots remained in the cockpit, the rotors whirring, the 20mm gun pointed at Gator.

Standoff. They were waiting for him to get out, so they could either gun him down or hold him there until reinforcements arrived. But what reinforcements? Didn't these idiots know their precious test site was gone, along with all of their buddies?

Staff Sergeant Gregory "Gator" Gatterson, ODA-555's assistant weapons sergeant, call sign *Tombstone*, a man whose passion for the Florida Gators football team had earned him that nickname, removed the safety clips on a pair of M67 fragmentation grenades.

He shoved open the door, burst from the inverted car, and hurled both frags at the chopper as the pilot cut loose with his cannon.

Gator lasted but another few seconds before the 20mm rounds tore into him, but he got the satisfaction of watching as his grenades exploded beneath the chopper, setting off a flurry of sparks and smoke. He wasn't sure how much damage he had inflicted, but he had fought to the bitter end. They could ask no more. He could give no more. He had done his job.

And then, before the world went dark, a light struck

him, brilliant and roiling, along with enveloping heat, and he knew that the car's gas tank had exploded under the gunfire. He was the flames now, Hell itself, reaching out toward the chopper to consume the machine and the pilots within.

Libra and Jersey followed the group as they headed back toward the engineers' work area, where Hassan would give the parliament members a tour of how the EFPs were produced.

A rising rattle accompanied by a wobbly feeling in Libra's legs made him pause.

"Do you feel that?" asked Hassan, glancing up as the entire building began to shake, shelves creaking, walls groaning under pressure. "A tremor?"

"Perhaps a small one," said Saeed Hanjour matter-of-factly. "We have them all the time." Hanjour turned to one of the guards at the far door and ordered him to find out what had happened.

As the building began to grow quiet, Libra noted that Hanjour kept eyeing him, along with the pair of guards keeping close to the group.

Just a minute prior, Libra had received a call from back home. Bad news. Their little ploy to ward off the ODA team had failed, damn it. And their contact in CENTCOM was now running scared. Part of Libra wanted to abort the job right now. The other part wanted the money.

And so he followed the group, with Jersey giving him wary expressions and the heat of Hanjour's gaze intensifying to the point that Libra pulled him toward the back and said, "If you need to tell me something . . ."

"No."

Libra nodded and stepped back, glowering at Hanjour, even as the tiny camera built into Libra's collar snapped photo after photo of the parliament members joking with the leader of al-Qaeda in Afghanistan. Meanwhile, Jersey's camera recorded audio and video of the meeting. Within a few hours, their clients in Washington would have all the proof they needed that the Iranian government was supporting terrorism in Afghanistan.

"Now this, look at this," Hassan was saying to his bestest buddies, gesturing to a long table loaded with electronics parts. "This is, as the Americans say, where the magic happens. And this is, as we say, how we kill them."

The politicians chuckled heartily.

Libra and Jersey feigned their own laughter. Out of the corner of his eye, Libra caught movement from behind one of the windows across the room, but when he turned his head, there was nothing.

He glanced sidelong at Hanjour. "I'm going to use the bathroom." Then he started off.

Zulu checked his knife, his pistol, then brought around his AK-47 and loaded a fresh magazine, just to be sure. He had spotted Hassan, Jersey, and Libra. They were all there, and within the next few moments, they would be his.

He shook his head as he took in a deep breath, then reached for the entry door that had been guarded by a man once alive, a man now lying in a blood pool at Zulu's feet. Zulu inserted the key, turned the handle, and slowly pushed in the door to find a small office and another closed door leading out to the main loading area.

The idea was to get near the group and lob in a couple of grenades, inflicting as many casualties as possible while firing like a madman before the farm was his.

Or maybe he'd get lucky and get to go back home with the team, only to be disgraced when he got there. No one would ever look at him the same way. Yeah, they might, like Pharaoh, forgive and understand, but they would never forget.

Walrus had been right. They all needed to pay for their sins. And they all needed to do the right thing.

"Zu?" came a whisper from behind him.

His shoulders shrank. He whirled into Figueroa's gaze. "Fall back."

"You, too."

"I got 'em IDed."

"Then we do this together. ODA *Team*, remember?"

"Jesus Christ."

Figueroa spaced his words for effect, his teeth flashing. "With all due respect, Sergeant, shut the fuck up. You're not going to throw it away here. Let's go."

Zulu grinned to himself. He'd trained them too well.

But as they went to open the next door, it opened, and the mercenary Zulu recognized immediately as Libra, froze, his jaw falling open in shock.

Zulu grabbed him by the neck and dragged him back into the office, while Sullivan closed the door after them. Zulu already had his pistol in his free hand, and he shoved it into Libra's temple as he drove the man up against the wall. "Why'd you have to kill Rock?" Zulu asked.

"We didn't. He got too close. They did," the man said in near-perfect English.

"Bullshit."

"You can't get in the way. You have no idea how big this is. We're on the same side. War must come to this country. It's inevitable."

Zulu was about to respond when Libra's head jerked back and blood splattered all over Zulu's face.

Figueroa had come up and shot him point-blank with his silenced pistol. "Too much talk, Sergeant. Sully, call the captain. Tell him we're inside. Tell him we got the first target. Tell them to hold off on the charges for another minute. I'll get some pictures of this bastard."

Zulu let Libra's corpse slide to the floor, then he glanced bug-eyed at the engineer. "I wasn't done with him."

"Keep your head clear, Zu."

The engineer was right. There shouldn't have been any

discussion. It didn't matter whether or not they had killed Rock. Killing them was the mission. Two more to go.

"Zu, the captain wants to talk to you," said Sullivan, proffering his cell phone.

Zulu stiffened, took the phone. "Yeah?"

"Fall back."

"We're inside. We need to make sure they're dead. Then we blow this place."

"Zulu, listen to me. We lost Walrus and Gator. If you guys aren't out of there in two minutes, I'm giving the order."

"That's all I need, Captain. Two minutes."

"That's all you got. Go."

Zulu turned to Figueroa and Sullivan. "Detonate the charges. Start the leak. We got a minute and thirty now." Zulu opened the door, peered out, then ran toward a wall of pallets stacked two meters high with concrete blocks.

"What's the story on the ground?" President Gallagher asked.

General Voorhis raised his chin toward one of the flat screens. "Tomahawks have just hit the target. We have the playback from the Predator coming in now."

The president watched as huge balls of flames swelled all over the test site. The absence of sound made the explosions seem less severe, but the more he watched, the more Gallagher realized the utter devastation those Tomahawks had produced. The tower went the way of one of the helicopters, and the explosion of the instrumentation bunker momentarily blurred as the first shock wave jostled the tiny Predator five miles away.

"Jesus," muttered the president.

"Mr. President, there's a very good chance the warhead was still above ground when we hit them," said the general.

"Excellent. Extend my congratulations to all involved."

By now the test site was obscured by smoke and dust. It would be several hours before the Predator could disclose a meaningful damage assessment.

Gallagher turned to his chief of staff. "When they plant me in the ground, I want that footage running on continuous loop in my presidential library, Vern. You hear me? I want the taxpayers to *see* how I spent some of their money." He then contacted his personal secretary to get the CEO of Raytheon on the horn.

Responding to the quizzical look from his chief of staff, he explained, "I don't tell him what I used it for, but I made a deal with Martin years ago that whenever I fly one of his birds I call him up and say, 'Thanks.' Now, let's see what Captain Pharaoh is doing about Hassan and those two mercs."

"Satellite shows a major traffic jam around the concrete factory," said the general. "Have a look."

"T-Rex and Thunder, this is Titan 06," Pharaoh called into the radio to the snipers up on the roof. "SITREP?"

"We've taken out all the guards outside," said Hojo.

"Roger that," added Ondejko. "Zulu got the rest. Truck team has their charges set and have fallen back to the stalled trucks with an EFP they found in the blocks. They said there are dozens of them inside. Just waiting on Zu and the engineers, over."

"Okay. Just stay sharp. One minute now. Get the Javelin ready."

"I'm on it," said Ondejko.

Pharaoh took a deep breath and lowered his binoculars. His arms were getting tired of keeping them in position, and Nasser and Kourosh were doing a good job of observing the factory from their positions along the windows.

When Bull died, Pharaoh had been forced to confront the worst part of commanding troops: losing them. Writing a letter to Bull's family was one of the hardest things he had ever done in his life.

And now he would do it all over again. Walrus's letter might even be harder than Gator's. How could he say nice things about a man he truly despised? Well, he would focus on the warrior, not the attitude. And he hoped now that Zulu hadn't just led himself and the engineers into a trap. That the team sergeant had the courage to go inside to ensure they took out the targets was remarkable; that he'd come back alive seemed unlikely, and Pharaoh was, God help him, prepared to order Ondejko to launch that Javelin:

In one minute.

32. CONCRETE LANGUAGE

At the far end of the building, past a section cordoned off by wire fencing and a gate with a chain and lock, Zulu spotted the group.

Figueroa and Sullivan rushed up behind him, and Zulu gave them the hand signal to move in. They were, of course, the demo team. He had instructed them to set off grenades and shred the entire group. Meanwhile, he would shift around the warehouse, taking out the remaining guards posted at the doors. He wouldn't let his ego—or his desire for payback—get in the way of who did what. He was the most skilled close-quarters guy, and they were experts in blowing stuff up.

And somehow or other, they'd do it all in one minute.

No, they wouldn't. No way.

He called Pharaoh and whispered, "Give me five minutes now."

"Shit, Zu, come on, man."

"Five minutes."

"Three."

"Done. Pleasure doing business with you." Zulu took off running, as did the engineers.

The warehouse area was about ten thousand square feet, and Zulu had his work cut out for him.

He charged along the perimeter wall, toward the rolling doors leading out to the docks. One guard was posted there, his AK pointed downward, his eyelids heavy. He did, however, perk up and turn his head as Zulu lunged at him. He might have seen the blade flash, he might not. Zulu had a hand over his mouth and was already performing brutal surgery before he realized what was happening.

With blood still dripping from his blade, Zulu ran on toward another door at the far end, where a guard had just left, moving toward the fenced off corner. He might've spotted the engineers.

Figueroa realized with a start that the group of men had turned back for the gate, getting ready to leave that area. They were talking and laughing, and as Figueroa peered out from behind a pallet of blocks, he spied Sheikh Abu Hassan himself.

"So as you can see," said the sheikh, "we can build a wall along the side of the road, and the bombs will already be there. We just wait for the right time."

Figueroa looked to Sullivan, who nodded and had already removed the safety clips and pins on his pair of grenades and was clutching them in both hands.

But in that instant, a guard rushed up behind him, shouting for him not to move, his rifle pointed at the back of Sullivan's head.

Sullivan whirled, knocked the rifle up and away, but as he continued to turn, shouts echoed from behind him.

Figueroa could not see the shooter, but a salvo of bullets from the group ahead ripped into Sullivan's back.

And in that heartbeat, Sullivan dropped his grenades

and raised his hands, screaming, "Jon, get out of here!" His eyes rolled back and he hit the floor.

Figueroa stepped out from behind the blocks and tossed his grenades at the feet of the group then threw himself behind the pallet of blocks as, nearly in succession, all four grenades went off.

With the debris still raining down and the smoke billowing, gunfire erupted from above, and Figueroa, unsure if he'd been hit or not, blinked hard and looked up, as a figure appeared from atop one of the pallets:

Zulu. He stood there, the Grim Reaper himself, hosing down what was left of the parliament members, the remaining mercenary, and Hassan. He was screaming at the top of his lungs, something about Rock and about the United States Army and about God and America, but it was all twisted and distorted—and Figueroa wasn't sure if he was actually hearing that or hallucinating it, since the explosions now sent a wave a dizziness crashing down and the hearing in his left ear felt all but gone.

Zulu, though, leaped down from the blocks and ran forward, digging into his pocket for his digital camera. He squatted over the remains of the men and turned their heads toward him. "Say cheese, you bastards."

Figueroa dragged himself up, felt the sharp stings in his legs and arm—shrapnel wounds—then went around the wall of bricks and shuddered. Sullivan lay on the ground, legs gone and one arm gone, half his face torn apart. "Aw, Jesus, Larry . . ." He lost his balance and fell onto the floor.

Zulu hustled over, eyeing his watch. He glanced at Sullivan and pursed his lips. "We have to go. You can smell the diesel. Come on." He reached down and dragged Figueroa to his feet, draped an arm over his shoulder.

"What about Sully?" Figueroa asked.

"No time to come back for him."

They started for the doors as with one hand Zulu dialed up Pharaoh and cried, "We're coming out! We lost Sully. Tell 'em to wait till they see us!"

* * *

Ondejko now had the Javelin antitank missile launcher balanced on his shoulder and was just waiting for the signal from Hojo. From his vantage point, Ondejko couldn't see the street below. The team had toted the Javelin for any close encounters with armor (you never knew), but with a little fuel thrown in the mix, the missile could create a decent explosion. It was, at the very least, a most effective way to light the match on their powder keg.

"They out?" he asked Hojo.

"Not yet."

He took a breath. "Anything?"

"No. Yes. There they are. Only two. Jon looks hurt. Wait. Wait."

"Fire the Javelin," Pharaoh ordered over the radio.

"Sully's not with them."

"I know. Fire!"

Blocking the news from his mind, Ondejko stiffened and sent off the missile, its thrust kicking him back, the projectile screaming away and heading straight up into a sky tinted pink by the setting sun.

He lowered the launcher and watched in awe as the missile arced and came straight down toward the domed building and leaking fuel tanks. Some fifteen hundred gallons of diesel fuel had already spilled throughout the facility.

After a flash of reflected metal, like a needle tumbling past him, a brilliant white-orange fireball rose above the dome, just as Pharaoh, Nasser, and Kourosh fired their RPGs from below. Secondary explosions rocked through all three buildings as the fuel tanks went up and fires whipped across and rose throughout the facility. ODA-555 had just spoken the universal language of destruction, and al-Qaeda would surely get the message.

Now the RPGs penetrated windows and exploded unseen within the buildings, the muffled explosions like corn popping, and then smoke poured from shattered windows, the stench growing as people began gathering at the street corners.

"Captain, we're coming down," Ondejko reported over the radio. "Hojo, give me a hand!"

Zulu's ears were ringing from all the explosions as he guided Figueroa directly across the street, toward the alley between warehouses. The two trucks sitting at the loading docks, loaded with concrete blocks and EFPs, exploded behind him, with secondary booms resounding as the EFPs themselves cooked off. Figueroa winced and moaned as they ducked into the alley, where the delivery trucks, not unlike those aluminum step vans used by UPS, were already waiting for them.

The second truck parked ahead had just moved out of the street to clear the traffic, and now Nasser took the wheel of that one while Kourosh opened the driver's side door of Zulu's ride.

Zulu helped Figueroa into the back, where Pharaoh and medic Grimm were already waiting.

"What happened to Sully?" asked the captain.

Zulu averted his gaze as the others climbed aboard.

Pharaoh turned to Figueroa, who was already being treated by Grimm. "Jon?"

"Captain, can we talk about it later?" asked Figueroa.

"Sure, but you know, we have to. The fire will take care of his body."

Figueroa closed his eyes and choked up. "Yeah."

Zulu tapped his breast pocket. "Jon and I got some pictures higher will want to see. Nice close-ups."

"Beautiful."

"Yeah, but it ain't over yet. Not till we get out of this godforsaken country."

"Roger that. All right, let's go!" Pharaoh ordered Kourosh.

Five delivery trucks in all would be leaving the warehouse, all at the same time. Each one would take a different route, two of them eventually heading north, back toward the border.

As they pulled out of the alley, police and fire sirens wailed throughout the city, and a thick carpet of gray-and-black smoke continued to unfurl overhead. Zulu peered out the rear door window, rifle at the ready. They turned onto another street, the van rattling.

Kourosh answered a call on his cell phone, then glanced back from the road and cried, "They've already stopped one of the trucks. Hang on. We'll have to move faster."

With that, the old Iranian put the pedal to the proverbial metal, and Zulu found himself tossed to the driver's side wall, where he found an overhead strap used for tying down loads. He gripped it hard and glanced over at Pharaoh, who was clutching a metal rung built into the wall, as were Ondejko and Hojo.

"Well, maybe I cheated with Bull's wife, but I just killed the leader of al-Qaeda in Afghanistan," Zulu said, his tone awkward, the remark made even more awkward by his strained laughter.

There—he had finally admitted it, as if the latter would make the former go away.

No one responded.

Pharaoh's satellite phone began to ring. He answered quickly. "Pharaoh here. Hello, Mr. President. Yes, we did, sir. We have pictures we'll upload now. Thank you, sir. We're on our way to the border now. Yes, sir, that'd be great, sir. Thank you." The captain glanced up at Zulu and said, "They're sending two Black Hawks to pick us up. We just need to get past Rock's buddies at the border. Start that upload."

"Roger that."

"Captain Pharaoh," cried Kourosh, lowering his cell phone. "Nasser just called. They're heading toward a roadblock, and he says he will not stop."

Zulu's pulse hesitated, or at least it felt so. Ondejko,

Hojo, Borokovsky, Weathers, and McDaniel were in that other van, and they were about to paint a bull's-eye on their backs.

"Where are they? Get us over there!" cried Pharaoh.

Hojo was clutching the back of Nasser's seat as they headed northwest on a heavily cracked and uneven road that would take them toward Iran's A78/13 Highway leading up toward the tri-border zone.

Between the explosion down south in the mountains and now the concrete factory detonation, the word had gone out to cordon off the city, and that word had traveled a little faster than the team had anticipated.

Hojo cursed. Nasser floored it.

The roadblock was created by a pair of military jeeps and two police sedans, all lined up across the lanes. Theirs was the only vehicle now approaching, and two soldiers began waving their arms for them to slow down.

"Open the back doors," Hojo hollered. "I want heavy fire directed on them. Rudy? Jerry? Drop frags as we crash through."

They shouted their assent.

"Keep low," hollered Nasser. "They're getting ready to fire! Here we go!"

The pitch of the van's engine grew even higher as McDaniel opened the pair of back doors and let them swing freely.

"Ready on the grenades," shouted Weathers.

"Here comes the fire!" cried Hojo as rounds began pinging all over the van.

He stole a glance through the windshield, just as they roared up to the gap between two police cars. He held his breath and braced himself.

33. THE EXFIL

Hojo winced. Three, two, one. The sound of the collision was like an explosion, low and hard, shoving him back, his knuckles going white on the back of Nasser's seat. Then came a *whoosh* of air and shattering glass as the step van plowed through the roadblock. The commo guys lobbed frags like beads at Mardi Gras as the van itself shed pieces of headlights and bumper, as though it'd just hit the wall at Daytona.

The eight or so cops and soldiers at the roadblock whirled and continued firing before the grenades went off, taking down four of five of them in clouds of blood and smoke as Nasser cut the wheel hard left, believing they were still firing.

At the same time, Borokovsky released a long groan, dropped his rifle, then fell back, clutching his chest.

The others were still laying down fire while Hojo screamed the medic's name, dropped to him, and forced away the man's hand to examine the wound.

"Oh, man." Hojo gasped. The shot was near the medic's heart, to be sure.

"Get the big trauma bandages out of my pack," the medic said through his agony. "Get an IV going. Get some fluids in me. Come on."

"All right, all right," said Hojo, frantically digging through the medic's supplies but knowing that a chest wound like that was bad, very, very bad.

"Hey, Hojo?" called McDaniel. "They're sending two cars after us."

"Take them out. Now!"

"Roger that, Sergeant. Let's reload, boys!"

While Hojo continued to tug out what he needed from the pack, the two commo guys slapped home fresh magazines and directed their next volleys at the windshields of both vehicles. Hojo stole a glance up, just as one vehicle veered wildly off the road, its driver no doubt killed, while Weathers held his bead on the one behind it. A few seconds later, that one, too, drifted off the highway, rumbling across the dirt under Weathers's unrelenting salvos.

Pharaoh had slid open the step van's side door and had balanced his AK-47 on the metal bar supporting the large side-view mirror.

"There it is," said Kourosh, gesturing ahead toward the pair of shattered police cars and bodies lying in the road under a veil of dissipating smoke.

"Yeah, that looks like Hojo's work," cried Zulu.

Two soldiers rose from behind one of the mangled cars and began firing at them as Kourosh veered into the other lane. Pharaoh returned fire, keeping the men pinned down as they raced past the cars.

Zulu took over from there, firing from the open back doors, brass *clink*ing all over the floor as his rounds found the soldiers, who doubled over like boxers about to hit the mat. They toppled in succession, still clutching their wounds.

"Should be a straight run to the border now," hollered Zulu. "No problems!"

"Don't be so sure," said Kourosh.

Pharaoh pushed himself back inside the van and slid shut the door. He mounted the steps and stood there, beside Kourosh, who was shaking his head as he listened to someone speaking frantically in Arabic on his cell phone. Then he looked at Pharaoh and said, "Nasser has a friend at the border who says they are closing down the main checkpoint."

"But I told you guys we weren't using that one. There's a little way around it."

"Yes, but when they close down the main one, the Pakistanis double their security."

"We bribed 'em once, we'll bribe them again, although I'm out of greenbacks right now."

"You don't seem to understand, Captain Pharaoh. Even the Pakistanis have been paid off by al-Qaeda—more than you could ever afford."

"Had do you know this?"

"Because my brother-in-law is the one who just called. He works up there. And he's told me that if we come, the Pakistanis will not talk."

"So we blast through."

"Not this time, Captain. They have rockets. They will blow us up before we even get close."

"Just keep driving." Pharaoh cursed under his breath and reached for his satellite phone.

"I know what happened to Church," said Borokovsky, his throat filling with blood. He coughed, and more blood flowed down his chin like winding red veins.

"Don't talk," said Hojo, as McDaniel helped him start the IV. "It's okay, Steve."

Hojo glanced away to make sure McDaniel was almost

finished with the bag. When he looked back, Borokovsky's gaze was vacant. Hojo released a string of curses and looked away toward the front of the van, battling off the emotions. No one else said a word. Nasser glanced back and pursed his lips.

Hojo's phone rang. Pharaoh shared the bad news. Hojo shared his own. There was a second of hesitation between them, but the captain got back to business, his even tone no doubt forced, but they were professionals. He wanted them to meet up at the mountains, just before the turnoff to the checkpoint bypass. Hojo knew the spot and told Nasser, who got on his own phone and began talking rapidly with someone.

During the next twenty minutes, Kourosh kept the step van racing north up the highway, narrowing Nasser's lead to the point that they saw the truck far ahead, a small box set against the hazy wallpaper of jagged mountains and the dregs of blue sky.

McDaniel called from the other truck to say that he was in contact with the Black Hawk pilots on the other side of the border. They had strict orders not to engage the Iranian checkpoint forces or the Pakistanis at the alternate point, which had been reinforced by two troop transports and about twenty soldiers, along with Rock's buddies.

As predicted, the Pakistanis had been tipped off and paid by al-Qaeda, and they figured they'd capture the group and sell them back to the terrorists.

Pharaoh thought about calling Major Nurenfeld, but then he thought, *What the hell, I've already gone to the top.* He had the president's personal satellite phone number, given to him by the man himself. He dialed, waited.

"Hello, is that you, Captain Pharaoh?" asked President Gallagher.

"Yes, it is, Mr. President. We're nearing the border, but we've got a problem."

"We already know, Captain. We've been watching you. The problem is, I can't order those Black Hawks into Iran or Pakistan right now. Not officially anyway. An incursion like that would undermine everything you've done so far."

"Yes, sir, but quite frankly, sir, I don't think we have the firepower to breach that new checkpoint in Pakistan. We certainly don't have the money. Terrain's too tough for these trucks, and I don't think we'd make it on foot before their air support picked us up."

"We're on the phone with the Pakistanis right now, but you and I both know their forces on scene have been bought."

"Sir, I just need some fire support on that checkpoint. Just to keep their heads down."

"I'll see what I can do for you, son."

"Thank you, sir."

Pharaoh hung up, once again chilled over the fact that he, a lowly captain, had a direct line to President Gallagher. He shouldn't get too excited, though. He might be dead before the sun went down.

"Captain, trouble ahead," said Kourosh, pointing toward a pair of jeeps heading directly toward them, about a kilometer out past Nasser's van. "They were sent from the border."

"We got a bird," hollered Zulu as the thumping of rotors from the back grew distinct. "Pull over, I'll jump out. You still have two more RPGs. Maybe I'll get lucky."

"No, no, no," hollered Kourosh. "That is a police helicopter. The pilot is a friend. Yousef is the copilot. They are just in time."

The chopper roared overhead, past them and Nasser's van, then swooped down on the jeeps. Armed with a small cannon, the chopper pitched its nose, and the cannon began belching fire, with subsequent sparks lighting across the jeeps' hoods and bumpers.

"Look at that!" cried Zulu. "We got us a little air support!"

"And free commentary," Figueroa added, still grimacing at Zulu.

As the chopper roared over the jeeps, then wheeled around to set up for another strafe, the drivers pulled off the road, the four troops in each jeep pouring out, with at least two of them hoisting RPGs onto their shoulders.

Nasser's truck thundered on by, taking fire from only a couple of soldiers, while Kourosh approached and Pharaoh hung back outside the door and drilled them with several more volleys, even as they set up to fire at the chopper.

Just as their van moved on by, the helo came around again, firing, while Zulu targeted the pair of soldiers with the RPGs. He shot one, but the second got off his missile before he took a round.

The rocket sped upward, hissing and casting a harsh glow over the desert before striking the chopper's canopy dead-on and exploding in a white-hot shower haloed in orange.

With the engine sputtering and plumes of smoke coiling from beneath the rotor, the chopper banked right into a corkscrewing dive, then immediately plummeted nose-down toward the highway.

Pharaoh's mouth hung open as the bird struck the asphalt with an echoing concussion, the fuselage folding up as it was swallowed in a fireball. The impact was so powerful that they could still feel it while driving away. Kourosh hollered in Arabic, a lament it seemed for Yousef, his lost cousin.

A black column of smoke rose from the crash site.

And then utter silence. Only the drone of the step van's engine for several minutes until Pharaoh spotted Nasser's van turning off the road.

"We're here," he said.

"Yes, but unless we have some help, we will not make it across the border," said Kourosh. "We will not."

"You guys don't have any other tricks up your sleeves, huh?" asked Zulu.

"Sergeant, this is all we can do now."

* * *

Hojo backhanded the sweat from his eyes and glanced around at the others. "Locked and loaded?"

"Hooah," grunted Weathers and McDaniel.

Ondejko was sitting up, his rifle lying across his lap. "I'll be your stationary gun, Hojo."

"Feed 'em lead."

"Absolutely."

The van trundled hard over the rocks and ruts, each of them grabbing onto the wall rungs for support. "Everybody, listen up," said Grimm. "Steve's dead. And if I go, I want you guys to know that nobody killed Church. He said it was an accident, but we think he did it to himself. We didn't want him to go out like that. We covered it up. We had no idea it'd turn into this. I'm sorry."

Given their exhaustion and the moment, the news came as no tremendous shock to the others; at least that's the way Hojo interpreted it. In fact, they looked more relieved than anything else.

Hojo slapped a palm on the medic's shoulder. "Forget about it. Let's just get home."

"Hey," said Weathers, lowering the mike on the team's Shadowfire radio and gaining their attention. "Just talked to the Black Hawk guys. They're five clicks out now, right on the border."

"Tell them we'll be right there," said Hojo. "Soon as we take out those twenty Pakistanis and their rockets." He reached for his ringing phone. "Hey, Captain."

"Pull over near the same place where we came in. We'll link up there."

"Roger that. You got a plan, sir?"

"I thought you did."

Hojo grinned to himself. "We'll work it out, sir. See you there."

"Hey, Hojo," called Weathers. "Pilots are telling me we might have a real problem now."

Hojo snorted. "Oh, yeah?"

"The Pakistanis got two Cobras in the air, ETA five minutes. Of course we sold them those helos. Isn't that special? Could be a real showdown on our hands."

"I'll call back the captain. I'm sure he'll be thrilled."

34. THE BLADE'S EDGE

Pharaoh gathered the men between the two step vans, while Weathers and McDaniel kept in close contact with the Black Hawk pilots. Pharaoh ordered Hojo and Ondejko to recon the defile. They jogged into the hills and estimated they'd be in position in less than ten minutes.

Pharaoh had not heard back from the president, but Major Nurenfeld had called to say that a pair of Apache attack helicopters was now within striking distance of the defile. They could fire their Hellfire missiles from Afghanistan and strike the target; however, the Pakistanis would, as the major had put it, "be incensed to the point of counterstrike." Zulu translated that as "go ape shit." Yes, they would.

So the team had two Black Hawks waiting to pick them up. There were two Apaches coming in, ready to fire. And the Pakistanis had sent in two of their Cobras.

Things were about to go boom in the night.

"Nasser? Kourosh? If you want, you can take one of the trucks and go back. I don't expect you to drive through that," said Pharaoh.

Nasser smirked and looked at the heavier man. "You really don't understand, do you, Captain?"

"I guess I don't."

"We will be with you all the way."

"Are you sure? I mean, you got a family."

"I would not if Rock had not helped me. This is what we do. This is, for many of you Americans, hard to imagine."

"Not anymore. At least not for me. Thank you." Pharaoh's phone rang. "I have to take this." He answered, "Yes, Mr. President?"

"Okay, Captain, we've twisted a few arms, and here's the way this'll go down . . ."

Ondejko crawled up to the top of the hill and peered into the defile.

Two olive-drab army trucks were parked in a V-shape in the middle of the road, .50-caliber machine guns mounted on their backs, both guns manned.

The rest of the men were divided into two eight-man teams positioned north and south of the trucks, up along the ridges, having established good firing and covering positions behind the larger rocks. Each team had at least one RPG, but they could have more. Ondejko figured the pair of officers were probably holding back with Rock's buddies, on the east side, behind the army trucks.

Indeed, if the team didn't get any help, they'd be riding into a hornet's nest, with incoming from the front and flanking fire from the hills. They wouldn't last more than a minute. He got on the phone and reported their findings to the captain.

Hojo crawled over to his position and said, "I thought the hard part was back in the city."

"I'm wondering if they leave us behind. We take out the two guys on the fifties, then go for the rocket guys. All they'll have to deal with is the small arms."

"And then what do we do?"

Ondejko smiled. "Run . . ."

"Your plan sucks."

"It's a good plan."

Hojo shook his head. "You'll never be an officer."

"Thank God," muttered Ondejko.

The two Cobras were already roaring toward Pharaoh and his men as they rushed into the step vans and took off toward the defile, with Pharaoh's truck in the lead.

"All right," he began. "We have to trust these guys."

"But we don't have to like it," said Zulu, squatting down in the back of the truck.

In fact, all of them were keeping low, anticipating the *clank* and *pop* of incoming fire. Pharaoh could already hear the din in his head.

The Cobras were fitted with 70mm Hydra rockets, with nineteen in each of four pods. They were armed for bear and began unleashing those rockets on both sides of the defile, but their shots were deliberately wide, not striking the trucks or either of the dismounted troop positions.

As the president had put it, the attack was a delicate matter of getting help from the Pakistanis against their own corrupt forces without actually killing those men, who would be dealt with later. The attack needed to look as though the Cobras were after the step vans so that any collateral damage to the Pakistanis could be confirmed as such.

So the pilots had been hired to create an elaborate fireworks show to distract the border force. That was exactly what Pharaoh had ordered from the menu.

Meanwhile, Ondejko and Hojo, who'd mentioned running a sniper mission, were given the honors of hanging out the sides of both step vans and directing fire on the .50mm gunners, whose gazes were in the air, about to turn their guns on the choppers. They slumped.

However, the men in the hills, while still distracted by

the explosions raging around them like mushrooms of smoke and fire sprouting through the magic of high-speed camera work, held their positions long enough to realize the trucks were moving by them. Pharaoh estimated that at least half of them turned their fire back on the trucks.

Kourosh floored it, and they bounced like Baja racers over the ruts, the rounds still pinging off the van or punching holes overhead. Kourosh turned left, around the two army trucks, and that's when Zulu swung open the back doors and began returning fire on the men along the south ridge.

Pharaoh dove forward toward the back of the van, pushed up on his elbows, and joined Zulu. With the rifles rattling and growing hot, and the brass scattering and falling from the back of the truck, they kept the men pinned down until the ground heaved as though a subterranean bomb had detonated.

In fact, an RPG had struck between both trucks, and Nasser's van hit the fiery ditch created by the explosion. His tires dropped hard amid the rippling flames, his front bumper colliding with the rock.

"He's stuck! He's stuck!" cried Zulu.

"Stop the van!" Pharaoh ordered.

It only took Hojo a couple of seconds to realize that not only were they in a ditch but that there was no way in hell Nasser could get them out before some clown in the hills leveled his RPG on them.

So as the Cobras wailed overhead and fired another round of rockets, he cried, "Everybody out! Get to the captain's van! Now! Now!"

He and Nasser seized Borokovsky's corpse and dragged it from the back of the van as the others ran forward to where Pharaoh's ride had stopped.

Zulu was on the ground, his face a mask of fury as he

rattled off rounds. The captain and Ondejko were at his sides, doing likewise. The captain was shouting for them to move out, but it was slow going with the heavy medic's body strung between them.

As they neared the truck, Nasser's right leg seemed to give out, and he went down. He hadn't tripped. Hojo saw the blood from the gunshot wound.

A few breaths later, as Hojo was coming forward to grab Borokovsky's corpse by the shoulder straps, he felt a sharp sting in his right thigh and threw himself to the dirt, clutching at the pain. He'd been shot before, but this one was a bitch, the pain like a poison-tipped icicle repeatedly jabbed into his leg.

He wasn't sure if the round had hit his femoral artery, but he figured if it had, he was going to bleed out before they got help. He willed himself to remain calm, lied to himself about the wound not being that bad—so he could muster the will to get back to the van. There was no giving up. Pain was, indeed, weakness leaving the body.

More rockets sent firelit debris arcing over the hills, and in the flickering glare, silhouettes appeared over him: Zulu, Pharaoh, the commo guys. He was suddenly on his feet and being helped back to the van by Pharaoh, gunfire ripping lines in the dirt near their boots, the reports echoing near and far, distances growing indistinguishable.

The others were screaming and swearing, but the back of the van was right there, and the captain dragged him inside. Hojo sat up, drew his pistol, and began firing toward the hills, unable to see any targets but determined to help.

Zulu alone got Nasser's arm around his back and helped the man into the van. Then he ran to help Pharaoh, whose shoulder was covered in blood.

"Captain!" he said, gaping at the wound.

"Come on!" screamed Pharaoh, and with only one good

arm, the captain helped him drag the medic's corpse forward.

There was so much incoming gunfire that Zulu couldn't help but wince and grimace as they moved. There were too many sounds to discern any one, all of them cracking and resounding over one another like wood in a gigantic bonfire. He would be shot, he told himself. It was only a matter of when.

With the van's exhaust now whipping in their faces, they loaded Borokovsky, then Pharaoh hollered for the commo guys to get back inside, along with Ondejko.

The two Cobra pilots, seeing what was happening, had descended to screen the van from at least some of the fire.

For a moment, Zulu glanced up and actually saw one pilot flash him a thumbs-up before banking away.

As Pharaoh ordered Kourosh to hit the gas, Zulu leaped into the back of the van, spun around, and, with Hojo now clutching his back so he wouldn't fall out, he emptied his magazine into the hills. Then he reached out and slammed shut the back doors, muffling the helicopters' chaotic drumming.

"Zu! Zu!" groaned Pharaoh. "If I pass out, you know what to do."

Zulu cocked his head, saw Pharaoh slumped against the side wall, his eyes growing vague.

"Captain needs help!" he cried to Grimm, who was already treating Weathers's gunshot wound to the calf.

As he looked around, Zulu realized that every operator had been shot, some multiple times. Even Grimm had a blood-soaked shirtsleeve.

But Zulu had walked away without a scratch.

He called to Grimm, told him he'd help, and accepted a couple of big trauma bandages. He got to work cutting open the captain's shirt with hands beginning to tremble.

"We made it," said the captain, now slurring his words.

"Was there any doubt?"

Pharaoh grinned weakly. "No. I think maybe, when this is all over, I should go see my father."

"That's good, but don't worry about that now." When the captain's shirt fell away, Zulu took a deep breath over the purpling hole in the man's shoulder. "You got a little scratch."

Pharaoh didn't answer. His head lobbed to one side, and he closed his eyes.

Panicking, Zulu checked for a carotid pulse and got one—weak and thready, but it was there.

As Zulu applied the big bandage, the gasps and groans of his teammates grew more evident, rising now above the dull *thump*ing of the van.

And somewhere out there, hope rose in the sound of more rotors.

Pharaoh's satellite phone began to ring. Zulu checked it and froze. Aw, what the hell. He thumbed on the phone. "Mr. President, this is Sergeant Robert Burrows, sir. I'm the team sergeant. Captain Pharaoh's been shot, unconscious, but it might be all right. We're all shot up pretty bad. Well, at least most of us. We should be at the border in a few minutes, if the Pakistanis don't give us any more trouble."

"Okay, Sergeant. The Cobra pilots came through for you, though?"

"Yes, sir, they did."

"Excellent. You tell Captain Pharaoh when he comes around that I said excellent work. You tell all your men, Sergeant. God's speed. Safe trip home."

"Thank you, sir."

He hung up and looked around once more, at all the blood and suffering. How does one walk the blade's edge and not get cut? Only by the grace of God?

Zulu closed his eyes against the burn and the pit in his stomach. He didn't know what he was feeling. Good to be alive? Guilty that he hadn't been hurt? Angry that he hadn't thrown himself into the fray and died in a blaze of glory? It was all too much, and his heart ached in a way it had never before.

A hand fell on his wrist. He opened his eyes and found Nasser staring at him. The Iranian slowly nodded.

35. THE FORGOTTEN WAY HOME

Pharaoh learned that they'd linked up with the two Black Hawks and that Zulu had single-handedly assisted the air crews in loading every operator on board the choppers. Medics stabilized the more seriously wounded like Hojo, and after a brief landing at FOB Cobra to refuel, they had transferred everyone northeast to the army field hospital at Bagram Airbase. Zulu had issued a quick after action report to Major Nurenfeld, then he had been given permission to travel with the rest of the team to the hospital.

"What time is it?" Pharaoh asked, sitting up in his bed and glancing over at the team sergeant, who was sitting in a chair, arms folded over his chest.

"About eight. You want coffee? Breakfast? I'll go get it."

"Nah. The anesthesia's still making me nauseous."

"Okay. Hey, I said good-bye to Nasser and Kourosh for you. The major says they'll be smuggled back into Iran by the end of the week."

"Good."

"He also says he's going to tear you a new one for breaking the chain of command and calling the president."

"I think he'll get over it."

"Shoulder still aching?"

"Yeah, but the meds help a little."

Zulu winced. "I didn't even see you get shot."

"So what? You go see Hojo this morning?"

"Just before I came here. He's okay. There was a delay getting him blood, but he's doing a lot better now. Everybody else is in good shape, considering."

Pharaoh nodded. "Grimm was here just before you."

Zulu sighed. "He tell you?"

"Yeah."

"Why didn't they just come to us? We would've done the right thing."

"Maybe you would've kept their secret, but they know me. I would've gone to Nurenfeld, dumped it on him. That would've been the right thing—not lying, making everyone paranoid. The point is moot now. Church was dying. He just went out the way he wanted to."

"And I guess Steve paid for his sins, too, huh?"

"Don't say that."

"He had a lot on his mind for a long time. I think he knew he was going to die."

Pharaoh tensed. "I don't want to talk about it. All I know is, I got four letters to write, and those alone are going to kill me."

After a long, awkward moment, Zulu blurted out, "I'm sorry."

"Forget it."

"No, I'm sorry. Really."

"For what?"

Zulu sat there, his eyes glassing up as he stroked his graying beard. "I don't know. For not getting shot?"

"We're good at making war, but making peace with each other . . . and ourselves . . . that's a bitch."

"Where'd you hear that?"

"I don't remember."

"Fucking Kowalski." Zulu sighed. "Goddamned Walrus. The bastard goes out a hero. He was a better soldier than I'll ever be. He lived it to the bone."

"But you're not done yet. Walrus was a great operator, but I'd hardly call him a great man."

"I don't know. I'm taking a long leave. I've got a lot of time coming."

"What're you going to do?"

"Go hunting, fishing. Go tell Melissa that what we did was wrong and that it's over."

"You think that'll help?"

"I hope so."

"Then good."

"What about you?"

Pharaoh leaned back and closed his eyes. "I'm going to Disneyland."

Six weeks later Pharaoh was seated in the waiting room inside the United States Disciplinary Barracks (USDB) at Fort Leavenworth, Kansas, the only maximum security correctional facility in the Department of Defense. The army encouraged visits from family members and in their documentation noted that they provided a "friendly, cheerful, and informal atmosphere."

The forced smile on the watch commander's face was certainly a testament to that.

They called his name. He rose and, in full dress uniform, shifted restlessly into the small visitation room, where he took a seat in front of a table with edges worn down by hundreds of forearms. His leg was shaking. A door opened, and a lean, gray-haired man he barely recognized entered and began to lose his breath.

"Jimmy." He gasped. "Look at you. You're a man."

Pharaoh took a long breath as his father came around the table and gave him a brief, awkward hug. "Hey."

"I, uh, I can't believe you wanted to do this, after all these years. I figured you'd forgotten about the old man, and in a way, I guess, that was all right. Sit down."

Pharaoh complied. It was hard to face the man, but when he did, he realized his father's eyes were much bluer than he remembered.

"So you're a captain. Wow."

"Yeah. I wasn't sure how you'd, uh—"

"No, it's good. At least you're an officer. Special Forces, huh?"

"Yeah."

"You like it?"

"Good days and bad, right?"

His father's gaze turned distant. "Good days and bad." Then he blinked and smiled. "You here to break me out? Going to pass me a nail file under the table?"

Pharaoh's grin made him feel guilty. "Yeah."

"I'm glad you came."

"I'm sorry."

"Me, too. I know how it is. The longer you stay away, the more scared you get. Time makes it worse. But now we're here."

"Yeah. I don't know what to say."

"Then don't say anything. Just sit there, and I'll tell you my story. Not the one your mother told you, or the one you heard from everyone else, including the army. Let me tell you my story, so you know. Maybe that's what you really want. Maybe that's all you need."

"Okay."

Pharaoh listened to his father's cool, even voice, the rhythm and cadences of a well-educated man who'd had nearly two decades of incarceration to reflect upon his life. He conveyed the tale slowly, carefully, incorporating even the smallest details, revealing that he'd gone over it a thousand times, perhaps ten thousand times, and nothing escaped him, not the sights, the smells, the faintest cries of his dying men, not the moment when he believed he'd gone over the edge, filled with utter anger and frustration, and given the order.

When he was finished, he leaned back in his chair and backhanded the tears from his eyes and said, "That's my story. I didn't mean for it to happen that way. But it is what it is, and I'm not going to sit here and feel sorry for myself. I've never done that. But I am sorry about us. I never wanted you to be embarrassed. Sons want to be proud of their fathers. I've always been proud of mine."

Pharaoh nodded.

"Now tell me what you've been up to."

Pharaoh took a deep breath. He'd been afraid to open up, afraid of getting hurt, but his father's honesty had touched something deep inside. So he began sharing his life with the man. It was the moment he had dreamed of, the moment he had thought would never come. As he spoke, the prison walls fell away, and they were just two men, soldiers and scholars, home at last with each other. Home at last.

ABOUT THE AUTHOR

Peter Telep is the author of more than thirty novels. With the help of dozens of technical advisors from all branches of the service, he has documented the exploits of Force Recon marines in Pakistan, U.S. Army tank platoon commanders in Korea, and mercenary fighters in Angola, Uzbekistan, and Vladivostok. Mr. Telep has written under the pen names P. W. Storm, Pete Callahan, Ben Weaver, and others. More recently, his heavily researched work reached the *New York Times* bestseller list. In addition to his writing career, Mr. Telep is also an English instructor at the University of Central Florida, where he teaches creative writing courses. He invites readers to visit his website at http://web.mac.com/ptelep.